BLIND FAITH

EMMA NICHOLS

First published in 2019 by:

Britain's Next Bestseller
An imprint of Live It Publishing
27 Old Gloucester Road
London, United Kingdom, WC1N 3AX

www.bnbsbooks.co.uk

Song lyrics: Show Me Heaven, by Maria McKee (1990)

ISBN: 9781081091781
Also available in digital format.

Other books by Emma Nichols

To keep in touch with the latest news from Emma Nichols and her writing please visit:

www.emmanicholsauthor.com
www.facebook.com/EmmaNicholsAuthor
www.twitter.com/ENichols_Author

Thanks

Without the assistance, advice, support and love of the following people, this book would not have been possible.

Bev. Thank you for your insight, wit, and considered thought throughout. You know your shit, chicky.

Valden. Thank you for your instructive feedback. It's always fun and I learn every time. I'm glad you loved it.

Mu. Thank you for your on-going support, creative ideas and nailing yet another brilliant cover. We should hire your services out.

To my wonderful readers and avid followers. Thank you for continuing to read the stories I write. I have really enjoyed writing the second romcom in this series – Drew's story – and I hope you enjoy another spin with the quirky villagers – and of course – slightly edgy, hot, summer romance. Did somebody mention buns?

With love, Emma x

Dedication

To Mum. Still laughing.
x

1.

Drew sprayed the surface of the café table and wiped it down with lazy movements. Market day always felt longer, bustling with visitors eager to take advantage of the locally sourced artisan produce, handmade crafts, and the recent addition of Delia's potions and predictions stall. She ambled back to the counter, unhooked the coffee filter, knocked out the grains and rinsed the equipment under the tap. The roaring noise from the road outside attracted her attention and she looked up to see a bright red Ducati motorbike easing to a stop at the curb. The rider switched off the engine, climbed off, and leaned the bike onto its stand. Drew watched the stranger; the slim figure in black leathers and black helmet. The rider seemed to assess the surroundings, looking across the square and down the street in both directions as if taking in the village – as most visitors did. Then the rider turned to look at the sign above the café and peered through the window as they undid and removed the helmet. Drew's mouth became suddenly dry as she watched the woman shake out shoulder length jet-black hair in a funky cut.

'Who the fuck is that?' she mumbled to the empty café.

The woman stepped confidently toward the door and Drew's heart skipped rapidly as she watched her approach. Shit, she'd locked the damn door already. She dove out from behind the counter and ran to unlock it. This was one sale she didn't want to miss.

She fumbled to open the door with a racing pulse, and her cheeks flushed as she stared wide-eyed at the attractive biker. 'Hi,' she said, stumbling over the short word, the air compressed in her chest, her heart pounding to escape.

'Sorry, are you closed?' The woman held Drew's gaze.

The voice had a slightly husky tone to it that resonated through Drew in a flow of warmth that settled in her core and it took a moment for the question to register.

'No, it's okay, come in,' Drew croaked. She held the door open with a welcoming smile, her gaze lingering on the dark green eyes that had touched her with respectful interest.

The woman's smile was warm, inviting, and she seemed to respond openly and without reservation to the eye contact. She followed Drew to the counter, resting the helmet on a table as she passed.

Drew felt the woman staring at her back, causing the hairs on her neck to rise in a wave of pins and needles that tingled down her spine. This was crazy! She moved behind the counter, faced the coffee machine and tried to breathe. She watched her hands shaking, confused, as she plucked up the courage to turn and face the attractive biker. What the fuck was going on with her?

The woman waited, pondering the few remaining cakes in the cabinet.

As Drew turned and held the woman's gaze again, she struggled to ask her what she wanted to drink and instead blurted, 'What's a gorgeous woman like you doing in a place like this?' She felt the cringe sweep through her body. What the fuck? What possessed her to say that? It was like a bloody line out of Casablanca! Heat flushed her cheeks and she tried to smile away her embarrassment, turning her attention to the two iced buns with cherries on top in the food cabinet. That didn't help. She felt her throat constrict and the desire to bury herself beneath the counter overpowered her and then her cheeks darkened further with the carnal images that lingered as the buns transformed in her mind's eye.

The woman smiled at Drew.

Drew stood, transfixed by the sparkle in the dark-green, almond-shaped eyes, the fine lines that graced her engaging

2

smile. Her throat was desert dry and all rational thought evaded her. Who the fuck was this woman? She cleared her throat and managed to speak. 'Sorry, I didn't mean to offend.' Drew worked hard to maintain eye contact and continued with a more appropriate line of conversation. 'Welcome to Duckton-by-Dale. I'm Drew,' she stuttered. That was more like it. 'What can I get you?' Excellent, well done, Drew. And breathe.

'None taken,' the woman said in an easy-going tone. She seemed to assess Drew with a quizzical gaze for a moment before responding to the question. 'Cappuccino, please,' she said and considered the cakes again then looked up. 'I'm Faith,' she said.

Drew swallowed as the woman looked directly at her and smiled softly.

'Are you on holiday?' Drew said and turned towards the coffee machine. The grinding noise was a welcome distraction and she took her time to prepare the coffee, imagining Faith's eyes assessing her from behind, a shiver teasing down her back.

'No,' Faith said.

Shit! Drew felt the disappointment sink in her stomach and said, 'Just passing through.' It was a statement rather than a question since she couldn't think of any other reason the woman would be in the middle of nowhere at 6 pm on a Friday evening. Surely, someone this hot had better places to be?

She drifted in thought, wondering how old Faith was. She looked young, vibrant, with beautifully clear eyes and a fresh, slightly tanned complexion. She pitched her at twenty-nine, secretly hoped she was closer to thirty-five then wondered what the hell she was doing imagining anything to do with this stranger. Sexy stranger. Worse still, a sexy stranger who was just passing by. The machine hissed and coffee trickled into the waiting cup and she poured milk into the jug and held it under the steamer. She hadn't been aware of the woman removing her jacket, and when she turned to face her across the counter she literally stopped breathing.

It wasn't the beautifully crafted tattoos running the length of the fine, muscular arms exposed by the black short-sleeved well-pressed shirt that caught her attention. It wasn't the way the firm breasts carried that shirt and revealed the delicious woman that she clearly was. It wasn't even the attractive smile that graced her finely shaped lips that stopped Drew's breath.

It was the narrow white strip that passed just under Faith's chin that had Drew staring with a wide-eyed, open-mouthed, look of sheer horror. Faith was wearing a dog collar. Holy fucking shit! Faith was the new Vicar.

'Fuck!' Drew blurted and the flames of Satan engulfed her and she felt utterly lost for words. 'Shit, I'm so sorry.'

Faith chuckled at the outburst. 'It's okay. It probably wasn't what you were expecting.'

Fuck, fuck, fuck! Drew felt her insides groaning in torment as she turned from the new Vicar, closed her eyes, tried to rewind the past five minutes, and released a long slow breath. She picked up the silver jug with trembling hands and poured the milk unable to concentrate on the frothing liquid, the only white in her mind's eye – the dog collar! Fuckety, fuck. She had just made a pass at the Vicar. 'I'm so sorry, Vicar,' she said again.

'I'm the replacement for Elvis,' Faith said to Drew's tense back.

Drew looked over her shoulder, strained a smile and nodded. She was still struggling for words as she handed over the drink. 'Can I interest you in my buns?' she said then closed her eyes until the cringing sensation had passed.

Faith smiled, studied the cakes. 'Yes, thank you.'

Drew picked up the tongs with trembling hands and juggled a bun onto a plate.

'I'm sorry for your loss,' Faith said, taking the plate.

Drew looked at Faith vacantly, then the words registered and she nodded. Elvis's sudden death had come as a shock to the village, and so soon after the glorious summer fete they had all enjoyed together, but right now the bigger issue was the woman standing in front of her, with those stunning green eyes and that gorgeous smile, and that fucking white dog collar. 'Thank you,' she croaked.

'How much do I owe you?'

Drew smiled and shook her head. 'It's on me.'

'That's very kind, thank you.' Faith took the cup and plate to the table.

Drew inhaled a deep breath, released it slowly and poured herself a double Espresso, hoping the effect of the coffee would overpower the visceral response that had taken control of her mind and body in the presence of Faith.

*

Grace groaned at the loud banging on the front door.

'Ignore it,' Harriet mumbled and continued kissing her, more firmly, and encouraging another guttural moan of pleasure from her lover.

The banging came again, louder and more urgent this time. Grace eased Harriet from her lap and held her dark, tempting gaze. 'We need to get to the meeting, anyway,' she said, her voice hoarse. Harriet helped her to her feet and she placed a kiss to Harriet's nose and swept the hair around her ear.' You're so irresistible.'

'Hmm,' Harriet said and smiled.

Grace smiled at the ever so slightly wonky front teeth. So, adorable! She leaned closer, placed another kiss to Harriet's lips, breathing her in and released another moan.

The banging came again and she pulled away. 'Coming,' she shouted. She bolted to the door and opened it to Drew's pale, wide-eyed look of alarm. 'What happened? You look like you've seen old Hilda Spencer alive.' She chuckled. 'Come in, come in.'

Drew paced into the kitchen and Harriet studied her. 'Hey, what's up?' she said with a look of confused concern.

Drew looked from one woman to the other and clasped her head in her hands. 'I just made a bloody pass at the new Vicar.'

Grace frowned and then tried to hold back a chuckle and failed.

Harriet assessed Drew with enquiring eyes. 'What?' The only thing that sprang to mind was the fact that Elvis had been well into his eighties and she'd not known any vicar to be under the age of fifty-five. The thought wasn't appealing!

'The new Vicar just showed up at the café and I made a fucking pass at her.'

Harriet frowned. 'Her?' She'd never seen Drew flustered, let alone close to hysterical and grinned at her rattled state. She watched her friend pace frantically around the kitchen, amused by the fact that, one: Drew had actually made a pass at a woman, at last, and: two, of all the potential contenders who had frequented the café over the years, she had chosen to make that approach to the new Vicar.

Harriet smiled as she continued to observe Drew grappling with her emotions. She'd always suspected a woman would come along at some point and turn Drew's eye, but never had Drew openly made a play for anyone. The irony of the situation bubbled inside Harriet and she stifled a laugh. Yes, Drew had joked with her about having decent eye-candy to look at when Grace arrived. She had even said that if things didn't work out with Grace to let her know, but Harriet had known she had been teasing about Grace. Drew looked positively shocked, distressed, and completely taken aback. Harriet couldn't work out whether those things were down to what Drew had said to the new Vicar or the fact that Drew had experienced genuine feelings of intense lust for another woman.

'And now, I've got to go and sit in a bloody meeting with the hottest woman in the village.' She stopped talking, suddenly aware of the two-pairs of attentive eyes on her and said, 'I said that out loud, didn't I?' Grace and Harriet nodded with amused smiles and Drew continued pacing around the kitchen, head in hands and pulling at her hair. Then she stopped and looked from Grace to Harriet and slumped into the kitchen chair. And then a grin slowly appeared. 'Yes, alright, I think she's hot.' She started to chuckle.

'Well, I never,' Grace said, grinning. 'A hot Vicar, eh?'

Harriet started to laugh. 'What did you say to her?'

'I asked her what a gorgeous woman like her was doing in a place like this,' Drew said, and cringed.

'Corny,' Grace said with a tilt of her head.

Harriet elbowed her in the arm. 'Doesn't sound too bad.'

Drew tilted her head and screwed up her face. 'Thanks. I feel so much better for that,' Her tone was dripping with sarcasm, then she grimaced. 'I couldn't stop staring at her, and when I asked her if she'd like one of my buns she looked at me oddly.'

Grace couldn't hold back the laughter anymore and burst into a fit of hysterics and then Harriet joined her.

'Much fucking help, you two are, not!' Drew said and then started laughing. 'I know. What am I going to do? I can't face her at the meeting.'

'You have to go,' Harriet said. 'It's about Elvis's funeral arrangements.'

Drew started to pace the room again and Grace looked at Harriet, a furtive grin spreading across her face. Drew had got it bad, that much was clear. Who was this sexy Vicar? Grace was intrigued.

'Fuck!' Drew said, scratching her head.

She was looking decidedly hot under the collar, eyes searching the room and then shifting between the two women who were staring at her.

'I'm sure she'll just be flattered,' Grace said. 'Who doesn't love having a pass made at them?' Then she blushed. Harriet nudged her in the arm, flashed a mock-stern look, and Grace smiled sheepishly. 'I mean,' she started to explain.

Harriet tilted her head and with raised eyebrows, said, 'Don't dig any deeper missy,' then she smiled and pressed a thumb to Grace's lips.

Drew released a long slow breath and gazed out the kitchen window. 'I feel weak in her presence,' she said, oblivious to the seductive glances passing between Harriet and Grace.

Harriet looked at Drew. 'What?'

Shit, she must have voiced her thoughts aloud again. 'Err, nothing,' Drew said and turned towards the door. She watched another look pass from Grace to Harriet and said, 'Are you two coming, or what?'

Grace cleared her throat in what sounded like a groan of pleasure.

Drew tutted and hurried out the door.

'You're a dreadful tease, Grace Pinkerton,' Harriet said, and planted a languid kiss that elicited another groan, this time from her own lips. Easing out of the kiss, 'Come on, we'd better get going,' she said.

They caught up with Drew, linked arms with her, and strode in silence towards the village hall next to the church.

As they turned up the lane towards the hall, Grace spoke. 'What are the rules on Vicars being lesbian?'

'Grace!' Harriet said.

'Well, I think it would be good to know,' Grace said and shrugged. 'You know, before Drew gets too invested.'

Too late for that, Harriet thought, shaking her head at her girlfriend.

Drew was shaking her head too. She couldn't identify with her own thoughts and feelings on the matter. At some level, it felt wrong to have lustful thoughts about a woman of the church, other than in the world of fantasy maybe. But that level of integrity had failed to register with her body, which was still reeling from the after-effects of setting eyes on Faith. Christ, even thinking her name brought a shudder of pure desire to parts of Drew that she hadn't realised existed.

'I think it's legal for a Church of England Vicar,' Grace continued, nodding her head.

'Grace!' Harriet said.

Drew was still shaking her head. It wasn't a legal matter; it was something more ingrained. Something that ran far deeper. Bugger it! Faith was so hot. Faith had charismatic beauty and then, there were the tattoos. So, fucking hot. Drew shuddered at the image of them and the arms, hands, and Faith's fingers. She had noticed a lot about Faith. Faith was unconventional, intriguing, and so fucking damn sexy. Drew's heart was racing with the vivid impression of Faith stood at the counter in black leathers and then... the dog collar appeared and the vision shifted and the impulse dropped through her like a lead brick. She held back the frustration that had her wanting to scream.

'It is legal,' Grace said, nodding in affirmation.

2.

Drew had zoned out to Grace's voice before they reached the entrance to the hall, consumed by her concerned thoughts as to how she could possibly face the new Vicar. She opened the door and peered inside.

Doris looked up. 'Good evening Drew.' She continued setting up for the meeting as the women filed into the room; placing the sheet of paper with one agenda item on it on the table in front of her, and the gavel that Elvis had recently decided to buy for the meetings in the centre of the table. He had only ever used it once to get the attention of the committee back on track. Most often, the conversation would be allowed to wander and Doris as Chair was able to keep control with a little gentle coaxing, or Elvis had interjected with a deep clearing of his throat.

Drew felt the relief in a sudden rush of sound that assaulted her ears. She looked around the room and with no sign of the Vicar, breathed in. 'Good evening, Mrs Akeman, Sheila.'

'Harriet, Grace, good evening.' Doris looked at the dainty gold watch hanging loosely from her bony wrist then assessed the two women and smiled. 'How lovely to see you all, and so early.'

'Shall I minute that, Mrs Akeman?' Sheila Goldsworth said looking up from the pad and ruler she had just laid out in front of her. The Secretary looked to Doris with reverence, the pen hovering in her arthritic hands over the paper. The seat Elvis would have sat in remained empty between the two women at the top of the table, as did the other seats around the sides and bottom end of the table.

'No, Sheila, I don't think we need to minute that the girls are first to the meeting today,' Doris said and smiled with uncharacteristic warmth.

Drew took the seat furthest from the top of the table knowing full well that the Faith would take Elvis's old seat. She needed to be as far away from eye contact as she could get. She leaned her elbows on the table, rested her head in her hands, and gazed at a scratch mark on the wooden surface.

Harriet sat next to Drew and Grace took the seat next to her, putting her closest to Doris. They waited.

'I hadn't realised we were this early,' Grace mumbled, just as the door opened and Drew's parents, Doug and Esther, entered the hall.

'Evening, ladies,' Doug said. 'Scorcher of a day.' He smiled as he took the seat opposite Grace, Esther at his side.

Drew lifted her head and gazed at the familiar faces, but it didn't stop her feeling sick.

Mumbles of 'Good evening, Doug,' and, 'Hi Esther,' filtered around the room and then the greeting extended to Vera, Jenny and Delia who joined the meeting and sat along the bottom of the table.

Drew studied the empty seat between Doris and Sheila and a ray of hope relaxed her with the thought that Faith might not be in attendance after all.

And then the door opened, and a silent hush filled the small space. All eyes were on Faith, except Drew's.

Drew's heart leapt into her throat and she wasn't sure whether she had moaned or it was Grace who had groaned in approval. Judging by the swift elbow to Grace's ribs, Harriet at least must have thought Grace had uttered the expression of admiration. Even Drew's father had straightened in his seat as the vision in black stood and smiled warmly at everyone.

'Ladies and gentlemen,' Doris started, but all eyes were still on the new Vicar. 'I would like to introduce you to our new, temporary Vicar, Faith Divine,' she said.

Drew didn't quite understand why Doris had felt the need to emphasise the temporary bit of the sentence and felt irrationally irritated by the fact. Then she became mindful that the other villagers had already introduced themselves, welcomed Faith, and she found herself staring at the Vicar, open-mouthed; the Vicar staring at her, smiling, hand outstretched.

'Hello again, Drew,' Faith said.

Drew couldn't breathe, her heart pounded and her legs abandoned her as she stood. She took the outstretched hand, and that didn't help as a shock of electricity pulsed through her. 'Hello, Fai.' She stopped, panicked at how easily the informality had slipped from her lips and said in a loud voice, 'Vicar.' An inferno burned her cheeks. And in that moment, all eyes around the room were directed at her.

Grace sniggered and she became aware of the pressure of Harriet's hand tightening on her thigh.

Faith smiled warmly and then took Elvis's old seat at the head of the table.

Doris cleared her throat in a vain attempt to draw the ogling eyes and distracted minds back to the meeting.

Esther nudged Doug in the ribs and he closed his mouth and turned to look at Doris. That dulled his senses!

Harriet squeezed Grace's leg harder and she let out an audible groan.

Vera looked at Jenny with a frown and whispered, 'We need a plan.'

'Ooh,' Delia said, overhearing the comment and diving into her handbag for the Tarot cards.

'Later,' Vera said.

Delia nodded and slipped the cards back into her bag.

'If I could have your attention, please?' Doris said, in her most authoritative voice.

The room quieted.

'As you are all aware, we are here tonight to discuss the funeral arrangements for our dearly passed Vicar, Elvis.' She plucked a white cotton handkerchief from her handbag and pressed it lightly to the edges of her eyes.

'That we are,' Doug said, shaking his head and lowering his gaze to the table. He and Elvis had been friends for as many years as they had lived in the village together, and that had felt like a lifetime. Not only had Doug been a regular churchgoer, but he had also been a regular at the Crooked Billet where Elvis had been the landlord. Elvis didn't have any next of kin; the community he served had become his family.

'So, on that note, I'll hand over to our new temporary Vicar, to apprise us of the arrangements,' Doris said.

Faith smiled and was just about to speak when Doug fidgeted in his seat and cleared his throat. 'I'm sorry Doris, but could we conduct this in a more informal tone? I don't think Elvis would appreciate everyone being so serious and you're making it sound like a bloody death has just happened,' he said.

'Agreed. Elvis has left the building,' Vera said and chuckled. 'We should be celebrating his life, not being morose about the fact that he's gone. He had a good innings.'

'That he did,' Doug said and chuckled with a memory that came to him. 'Do you remember the year he got out for a duck? He wasn't happy about that.' Doug was shaking his head and smiling at his memory of Elvis marching off the cricket pitch in a strop having declared before the match that he was going for a personal best before he retired from the game and Kev betting him he wouldn't get close even if he bowled underarm to him.

'He settled down when Kev admitted to doctoring the ball,' Vera said. 'Little bugger!'

Faith's lips curled a fraction and Drew was acutely aware of how her green eyes seemed to sparkle, as if she were enjoying their fond reminiscing.

And then Doug was staring at Faith aware that he had gone off track. 'Sorry, Vicar,' he said.

'Thank you, all,' Faith said. 'It is never easy to lose our close family and we all deal with grief in different ways, but I'm sure Elvis would have wanted us to remember him in celebration of his life. He sounds like quite the cricketer.'

Drew felt the Vicar's words tingle down her spine, though she couldn't recall what Faith had actually said.

'He was,' Doug said. 'Regularly knocked out a fifty.'

'Shall we go through the arrangements?' Faith said and observed the nodding heads around the room.

Drew felt the dark eyes rest on her, and then heat bolted south and pulsated in her core. She wriggled in her seat, tried to admonish herself for her body's response given the sobering topic of conversation, but she simply reacted with another rush of heat to her cheeks.

'The cremation will take place next Saturday at 10.30 am at the Ferndale crematorium. Then there will be a short service at the church where we will scatter the ashes under the old oak tree in the churchyard, and then there's the wake in the pub after the service. I understand Doug has provided a list of music that Elvis wanted.' Faith looked to Doug for confirmation and then continued. 'Vera and Jenny have elected to give a short reading at the crematorium and.' She paused, cleared her throat. 'And, Drew has agreed to help with the catering arrangements.'

Drew watched Faith hold her attention and smiled.

'Yes, that is correct,' Doris said. She hadn't missed anything from her earlier briefing to the Vicar.

'So, for the music,' Faith continued, looking at the piece of paper in front of her. She seemed to hesitate. 'As the coffin is taken into the Chapel we have.' She hesitated again, locating the words on the page. '*Leaving Here* by *The Birds*.' She looked up to Doug who smiled enthusiastically. Jenny and Vera were also nodding in approval from the bottom of the table. Faith smiled, looked at the notes again. 'And then during the service, *It's Alright* by *The Impressions*.'

'That's right, Vicar.' Doug nodded. 'He was a big mod fan.'

'Right,' Faith said, her tone shifting slightly. The next song definitely wasn't from the mod era. 'And then, *Ring of Fire*, by *Johnny Cash*?' she questioned.

'Yep!' Doug chuckled. 'Had a sense of humour, did Elvis.'

'He did that,' Vera said.

Faith smiled. 'Yes, I'm beginning to see that. And then the title for leaving the Chapel is, *Dancing in the Street* by *Martha Reeves and the Vandellas*,' she said.

'I've got a longer list for the wake if you need it?' Doug said, reaching into his pocket.

Faith smiled. 'Um, no, that's fine thank you, Doug. Maybe later, although I'm happy for that to remain as a surprise,' she said, secretly dreading the list that might appear.

'Well done, Doug,' Vera and Jenny said in unison.

'Yes, well done, Doug,' Doris said.

'Shall I minute that, Mrs Akeman?' Sheila said.

Doris nodded.

Drew watched Faith and a wave of sympathy flooded her. And then Faith spotted her staring and smiled. Then heat flushed her cheeks and she looked towards her father.

'Catering arrangements?' Faith said.

The words sent a shudder through Drew that caused her hands to tremble and her stomach to twist. All eyes were on her, but it was Faith's gaze that impacted her with an intensity that seemed to drive her insanely wild with desire. It was ridiculous.

'Yes, um, catering is covered. We can do tea and coffee at the church if anyone thinks it's needed? Otherwise, I have planned sandwiches and buffet for the wake,' she said, avoiding eye contact with the Vicar, concentrating her focus on her parents at the other side of the table who were nodding encouragingly.

'Will you have those delicious buns?' Faith said, smiling warmly.

Grace nearly choked and stifled the noise with a clearing of her throat, enhanced by Harriet's swift elbow to the ribs.

The blush on Drew's face lit up the room, though she hoped no one had noticed. 'Um, yes, of course, Vicar,' she stuttered.

'Are you alright, dear?' Jenny said. 'You look as if you've got a fever.'

Fuck! 'I think I might be coming down with something,' Drew said and patted at her forehead.

Grace withheld a snigger and whispered into Harriet's ear, 'She's got the luuuvvv buuuggg,' only to receive another slap on the arm from her girlfriend.

'Delia, maybe Drew needs some of your potion?' Jenny said, waving her hand to get Delia's attention even though she was sitting next to Drew.

'I'm sure I'll be fine, thanks,' Drew said.

'You look fine to me,' Doug said. 'A healthy glow I would say. It's this country air.'

Drew groaned as further embarrassment scolded her cheeks.

'If we could bring our attention to the meeting, please?' Doris interjected.

'Thank God,' Drew mumbled and hoped no one had heard.

Sheila raised her hand.

'Yes, Sheila?' Doris said.

16

'Sorry, Mrs Akeman, I wasn't sure if I should minute the point about Drew not feeling well?'

'Bloody hell, woman,' Doug said raising his hand to his forehead.

'No!' Drew shouted, her voice projecting around the room and bringing the group to silence.

Sheila looked momentarily flustered then picked up the ruler next to her pad and drew a line through the last note. 'Right, sorry,' she said.

'If we might continue,' Doris said in a stern voice, glancing at the gavel.

Drew noticed Faith reach across the table and put a comforting hand on Sheila's arm. She smiled at her warmly and the tenderness of the touch resonated through her as if the Vicar had caressed her own arm. She wished.

Faith turned and addressed the group. 'The scattering of the ashes will be a short service, so I don't think there's any call for drinks unless anyone else would like them?' Faith said.

'Drinks?' Doug said.

'Yes, I think that's where we got to. Drew offered to provide tea and coffee at the church,' Faith said.

'I think Elvis would rather we all got to the pub,' Doug said and chuckled.

'Wouldn't want his profits down,' Vera said, with a broad grin. She was teasing.

'I've got my reading done already,' Jenny said.

'Me too,' Vera said and squeezed Jenny's hand under the table.

'Thank you.' Faith said and paused.

'Is there anything else we need to discuss?' Doris said.

Faith nodded and continued to speak. 'I am happy to meet with anyone to go through the finer details of the arrangements, or if you have any personal needs at this time.'

Doug was nodding his head. 'Thank you, Vicar.'

Drew was nodding too, but her personal needs were well outside the remit of any discussion she proposed to have with the Vicar.

Faith smiled and looked around the assembled group.

Doug looked around the room then addressed Faith. 'Talking of drinks, do we know who's taking over the pub?' he said.

Grace sat up and gave her attention to Faith. The church and solicitors had taken on the administration of Elvis's estate so there had been limited communication with the villagers to date; just rumours. Maybe Faith would be able to provide clarity.

'My understanding is that the pub is to be sold,' Faith said.

A unified gasp filled the room, and then there was considered silence.

Doug mumbled.

'Can we get any details?' Grace said. She had heard the rumour that the Crooked Billet would most likely be sold and there were concerns that the pub would end up becoming part of a commercial chain and losing its charm in the process. Let alone the late-night lock-ins that would be stopped, and the chances were that some of their pub events would be affected by a change in ownership, too. And there was no way a new manager was going to let Jenny drink her hooch inside the premises. Prices were likely to go up, and even the menu would probably need to change since the chef had decided to bugger off with the boyfriend he had met on his summer holiday in Greece the previous month. Yes, the loss of the pub would have a significant impact on village life and she vowed to do everything possible to keep it as it had always been.

'I don't think an estate agent has been appointed yet, but I can give you the solicitor's details,' Faith said.

Grace smiled. 'Thanks, that would be great.'

Silence filled the space. The pub was the hub of the community, and it was also Elvis's legacy. Losing it would be as devasting to the village as Elvis's death had been. Doug nodded to Grace and she gave him a look that said she would sort it out.

Faith looked around the room, sensing the shift in mood despite Doug's earlier plea for levity. 'I'm really sorry for your loss,' she said.

'Thanks, Vicar,' Doug said and rubbed at his eyes.

Esther nodded wrapping her arm around Doug's.

Harriet squeezed Grace's leg and Grace reached down and took the hand in hers.

Drew was still nodding at the Vicar's offer of having someone to talk to, and then reflected with sadness on the fact that there was no way she could sit in front of those green eyes and that dark funky hair, and those tattoos, and the fine muscular arms and... she shook her head. Even if the wanted to talk, she wouldn't be able to speak coherently. She sighed.

3.

'Right, what's the plan?' Jenny said to Vera, sipping at her second glass of hooch. 'Tea's on the table,' she said to Esther as she sat, 'Unless you'd prefer raspberry gin?' she added and chuckled.

Delia waited for Vera's idea with an enthusiastic gaze and sipped at her drink.

'A cup of tea will be perfect, thank you, Jenny,' Esther said, with an upturned nose. She would never live down the fact that she had fallen asleep on the grass at the end of the summer fete, hugging a bottle of the liqueur drink. She had woken to Vera teasing her mercilessly about how loudly she snored. It seemed strange to think that the fete was only a few weeks ago, and of all that had happened in such a short time since.

'Here's to Elvis,' Delia said, as if reading her thoughts, and lifted her glass in the air.

'Elvis,' the other three women chorused and sipped at their drinks.

'So, what's this plan?' Jenny said to Vera.

Vera looked across the table at Esther. 'You noticed our Drew seemed a bit out of sorts at the meeting?' she said.

Esther looked at her vacantly.

'Yes, she didn't look herself at all,' Delia said.

Jenny nodded. 'She seemed irrationally distressed with what the Vicar was saying. Do you think Elvis's death has affected her?'

'I don't know,' Vera said. 'I was thinking, perhaps she needs a bit of cheering up.'

'What do you mean?' Esther said.

'You know. A bit of company?' Vera said.

Jenny pondered. 'You're right. She hasn't been on a date for as long as I can remember. Do you think she's lonely?'

'Could be.' Vera nodded.

'Wasn't the last chap she went out with that librarian from Ferndale?' Jenny said. 'Seemed a bit quiet to me.'

'That was never going to work,' Vera said with certainty. 'Drew's a strong independent woman and needs someone who can support that.'

Esther gazed from Jenny to Vera open-mouthed. 'Have you finished talking about my daughter?' she said, sitting stiffly in the chair.

'We're just saying,' Vera defended. 'Don't you think we should help her find love?'

Esther huffed, sipped at her tea. In truth, she had been concerned for Drew longer than she dared think. Drew seemed to struggle to find the right man; one she could settle down with. She'd been on the occasional date but nothing that had lasted, even though a good number of eligible bachelors had passed her way over the years. 'I really liked that handsome surgeon from Broadermere,' she said. 'Not sure why that didn't work out.'

'He was too up his own arse,' Vera said.

'V,' Jenny admonished.

'He was. I was in the pub and he talked about nothing other than himself and his work. Poor Drew came over quite pale during their meal as he started describing in great detail the prolapsed bowel surgery he had performed just before their date. She couldn't stop looking at his hands after that and I'm sure she wasn't wondering about what they would do to her!' Vera said.

'You're exaggerating,' Esther said and huffed again then crossed her arms in a defiant gesture.

'She couldn't even shake hands with him when they parted, and I know she's never seen him again,' Vera continued. She sipped at the hooch and drifted in thought, silence settling between them for a time. 'Perhaps we should be looking in another direction.'

Jenny and Esther looked to Vera who seemed to have a glint in her eye.

'I don't think there's anyone out Ferndale way,' Esther said, completely missing the point Vera was about to make.

Jenny smiled knowingly at Vera.

Delia watched the sparring she sensed was about to kick off.

'No,' Vera said. 'I don't mean that kind of direction. I mean, what if we should be looking for eligible women?'

'WHAT!' Esther exploded and slammed a hand to the table, and the china teacup rattled in the saucer. 'What are you talking about? My Drew's not like that.'

Vera's eyes widened and then her posture straightened in the chair. Her jaw tensed and she zeroed in on Esther and then with a calm tone that didn't match her features, said, 'What exactly do you mean by that, Esther?'

Esther continued, oblivious to the offence she had caused. 'My Drew is not a lesbian,' she asserted and crossed her arms again.

Oh, dear, Delia thought.

Jenny was shaking her head, studying their friend across the table. She sensed Vera's anger knowing exactly where it came from and felt sorry for Esther with her blind insensitivity. She was sure Esther didn't mean what she said. Did she? Esther had been a little out of sorts recently, too, Jenny had noticed. Elvis's death seemed to have affected them all in one way or another. She tried to hold Esther's shifting gaze and spoke to her in a soft tone. 'And if she were?' she said.

'She's not, and that's final,' Esther said, avoiding eye contact with the two women who were now staring at her.

'And how is it a problem if she is?' Vera said, stiffly, leaning across the table. She needed to press the point.

Esther couldn't face Vera and her eyes searched the room. 'She's just not like you and Harriet,' she said to Vera, her tone quieter.

Oh, dear, Delia thought, shaking her head.

Jenny watched the standoff building, sat up in her chair and sipped at her drink. This needed calming before Vera lost her rag completely. She placed a comforting hand on Vera's arm and squeezed. 'Well, how about we explore both options?' she said in a gentle tone, gazing from one woman to the other, hoping for a compromise.

Delia looked at Vera with compassion and settled on Esther with desolation.

Esther was shaking her head. She couldn't possibly conceive that her daughter might be a lesbian. Definitely not. That might be okay for others, like Harriet and Grace and even Jenny who was fluid and Vera who was just Vera. But it wasn't right for her baby girl. She studied the three women looking at her. She couldn't be a party to setting her daughter up on a date with another woman, but she would like to see Drew happily married to a man. And, she was convinced they, her friends, were wrong. She sat up in her chair, determined to prove the point, picked up her tea and sipped. 'I'm not setting her up with another woman,' she said. 'And I'll say no more on the subject,' Esther's nose lifted in the air and she looked away from the women at the table.

Vera smiled through tight lips, the glint of competitiveness in her eye shifting her from the indignation she had felt at Esther's bigoted response to her desire to prove that Drew was a lesbian. And prove it, she would.

Drew just hadn't found the right woman. There had been a point in time when Drew and Harriet were in their late teens that Vera had thought they might become lovers, but for whatever reason they never had. Jenny had hoped for that, too. When Harriet had been with Annabel, Drew had watched from a distance and always been there when Harriet needed support. Drew had been a constant in Harriet's life and whether Harriet had realised it or not, Vera had suspected that Drew loved her and cared for her deeply. With Grace coming into Harriet's life now, perhaps Drew was feeling the loneliness again. 'Right,' she said, deep in thought about how they might approach the dilemma.

Delia, sensing the tension wasn't shifting, reached into her handbag, pulled out a white cloth and laid it out on the table. Shaking the black satin-silk bag of stones, she closed her eyes. Vera, Jenny and Esther watched her expectantly. Delia moaned to herself, dipped her hand into the bag, pulled out a stone and placed it on the cloth. She repeated the process again, placing the next stone to the left of the first and then again until three stones with odd markings sat in front of the women.

'What are they?' Jenny said.

Delia took in a deep breath and released it slowly. 'Rune stones,' she said. 'I've just started working with them, so be patient with me.'

Esther rolled her eyes, and Vera glared at her.

'What do they mean?' Jenny said, moving to pick up the first stone.

Delia batted her hand away and said, 'Don't touch them.' She studied the pattern on the stone then looked through the guidebook. 'Right, so this is the stone that represents the problem,' she said.

'What problem?' Esther said.

'Drew's problem,' Delia said.

Esther stiffened in the seat. 'Drew doesn't have a problem.'

'Not a problem, problem,' Vera said, trying to pacify the defensive mother.

'The situation,' Delia said, smiling at Esther.

'Go on, what does the stone mean,' Jenny said, studying the diamond shape perched on top of another diamond shape, eager to discover the message that might help them.

Delia flicked through the pages of the book. 'OTHALA,' she said.

'Ooh!' Jenny said and sipped from her drink.

'It means freedom and independence.'

'We all know Drew's independent,' Esther interrupted, waving a hand dismissively at the three other women.

'Yes, but this is about releasing ideas that will keep you stuck,' Delia said.

'What does that mean?' Jenny said, enthusiastically.

'I'm not entirely sure, but it's likely that Drew has old beliefs and stuff that are stopping her from falling in love,' Delia said. She smiled warmly and with a hint of sadness.

'Harrumph!' Esther grumped.

'That's interesting,' Jenny said. She wasn't going to be put off by Esther's ranting. 'What about the next one?'

'So, this stone represents the challenge. It's called.' She paused, leafing through the pages again. 'PERTHRO. Gosh, that's a powerful stone. It's about something hidden, secrets and being free from entanglement, keeping your faith firm and letting go of everything.' She looked up; three pairs of wide-eyes staring back at her.

Esther frowned then curled up her nose. 'Utter poppycock!' she said.

'What does that mean?'

'The challenge is related to something hidden. Maybe something Drew doesn't even know about,' Delia said, though she didn't sound too certain.

'That's why she needs our help,' Vera said confidently and sat upright in the seat. She sipped at her drink, head nodding in affirmation.

'What's the third stone?' Jenny said, looking at the zigzag, lightning-like pattern.

'SOWILO. It means the path to self-awareness and self-knowledge. Seeing that which makes you destructive to yourself and others.'

'I've heard enough of this.' Esther stood from the table. 'My Drew does not lack awareness. She's kind, considerate and loving. She's not destructive. A load of bollocks!' she said and stormed out the door.

'Oh dear,' Delia said and looked quite upset.

'Don't worry about her, the old fart,' Vera said. 'She doesn't get it, but she'll come around in her own time.' She shrugged and sipped at her drink. She wasn't going to give credence to Esther's punishing words, she was just going to prove Esther wrong. She smiled, confident in her ability to win this particular battle. She turned her attention to Delia.

'This is about seeking change to heal and being complete with herself,' Delia continued.

'I think Esther could do with a bit of that there healing,' Vera said and refilled her glass.

'So, what do we think?' Jenny said, looking to the two other women.

'Drew's a lesbian,' Vera said with certainty.

'Esther's not buying that,' Jenny said shaking her head.

'Esther's delusional,' Vera said. 'And menopausal. It's not a good combination.'

Jenny nodded. Vera could be right on the latter point.

'What about setting up a speed dating event in the pub?' Delia said.

Vera and Jenny turned, studied her, and frowned.

'How does that work?' Jenny said.

'You invite people along who are looking for love and they all move around the seats when the whistle goes and speak to each other for ten-minutes or maybe less, I can't remember,

26

and see if they connect. I saw it on the L-Word,' Delia said and looked pleased with herself as she pulled another stone from the pouch.

'I understand that much,' Jenny said and raised her eyebrows. 'I mean, it would need to be for a target audience; lesbian, bi, straight, etc?'

'Speed dating won't work with a mixed group,' Vera said shaking her head in agreement. 'I'll have a look at one of the lesbian dating websites.'

'She could be bi?' Delia said.

Vera gazed at Delia and smiled. 'She might be, but if we're looking to find a woman for her, a lesbian is a good start point.'

'Good idea,' Jenny said.

'Is that the plan, then?' Delia said. She looked at the stone, studied the guide. 'JERA. Things will happen exactly as they should,' and snapped the book closed, with a satisfied grin.

Vera nodded. 'It's a start.'

The three women sipped at their drinks and then Delia reached for the Tarot cards. 'Now, what are we going to do about Esther?' she said, and started to shuffle the pack.

*

Drew slumped onto the sofa, laid her head back, and closed her eyes. An image of Faith appeared and she groaned. The dark-green eyes that seemed to lighten when she smiled, captivate her with the sparkle that held compassion and warmth, the beautifully smooth skin of her cheeks, the jawline that led to her tempting lips, the soft, sensual smile that reached in and tugged at her heart. Damn, she was busted. There was no denying this feeling. A Vicar, for Christ's sake! She chuckled at the irony. She rubbed at her forehead, but the image wouldn't leave her. The line of Faith's shoulders; the feminine strength,

27

and even the tattoos were striking on her naturally, lightly tanned skin. She was fit; athletic. Drew had noticed her firm breasts, slim waist, narrow hips and legs of perfect length. Jeez, the urge to touch Faith; have Faith touch her was driving her wild.

She groaned, rose from the seat and went to the fridge. It had been a long time since she had felt this strongly about anyone and those feelings she had learned to control; buried them, forgetting that they had ever existed and transferred them into a strong sense of loyalty and protection. Since realising her feelings for Harriet, she had felt nothing like it for anyone since.

Now this, Faith, had come out of the blue and quite literally blown her away. There was only one problem, well perhaps more than one, but the biggest issue at the forefront of her mind, the one that she didn't know how to get around, was that Faith was a Vicar, and that made her out-of-bounds! She pulled out a bottle of Sauvignon, poured a large glass and drank it in one hit. She refilled the glass and returned to the sofa, reclaiming the comforting warmth of the soft cushions.

She'd declined to go to the pub after the meeting. She couldn't talk to Harriet and Grace until she'd got to grips with her thoughts, and she certainly couldn't face the new Vicar until she'd worked out how to handle the emotional turmoil that had turned her world upside down in the last few hours.

She slugged the wine, emptied her glass swiftly, enjoying the dulling effect it was having on the continuous stream of competing thoughts. Was Faith a lesbian, or bi? What were the rules for a Vicar around same-sex relationships? Why was she even considering these questions? A Vicar was a no go, she repeated in thought.

Within a short time, she found herself relaxing and a loss of inhibition had her drifting into a fantasy about the dark-haired Vicar. Eyes closed, she undid her jeans and slid her hand down into the soft wet heat, locating the throbbing between her legs. She drew slow, delicate circles around the swollen bud, inflaming it and shifted to lie back on the sofa, spreading her knees wider, exploring more intimately. She groaned, writhed at the touch, and dipped her finger deeper into the folds, drawing the wetness over herself and then plunging deeper. Rhythmically, she repeated the pattern, toying with the pressure, jerking with the sensation. Faith's hands: Faith's fingers: Faith's tongue. Driving her up, filling her, and then overflowing, drowning in a sparkling shower of electric impulses, she screamed out. Her body in spasm, heat, lust infusing her she started to giggle and then tears slid down the sides of her eyes and she curled into a ball, hands clasped around her knees. What the fuck was she going to do? She needed to find another outlet for her desires. She would bake. That's what she needed to do. She eased herself off the sofa, did up her jeans and went to the sink. Buns came to mind and she couldn't shake the image of Faith smiling at her across the counter.

4.

'Thanks, mum,' Drew said. She walked past Esther at the café counter and dumped the carrier bag on the kitchen surface. 'Seems everyone wants tomato sauce today,' she said, still slightly bemused that she had managed to run out.

It had been an odd week though, and she had felt more than a little distracted. On a good note, she had managed to get to grips with her infatuation with Faith, having only had two lustful thought a day for the past two days. That was progress. With Faith coming to the café every day for coffee, it hadn't been easy, but, somehow, she had managed to see the stunning woman in a new light. A dog collar and religious kind of light, and that had served to dampen just about every amorous feeling in her body, if only for a short length of time. Sex with a vicar had never featured highly on her list of fantasies. There was just something wrong about it in her mind. Yes, the dog collar was a good deterrent.

'It's been a busy day,' Esther said. 'I don't know how you cope.'

'Market day usually is,' Drew said, unpacking the bag. 'Delia's potions and predictions seem popular.'

'Hello, Vicar, what can I get you?' Esther said, ignoring her daughter's comment.

Faith smiled. 'Hello, Esther, Cappuccino, please.'

'Right you are,' Esther said and turned to the machine.

Drew came through from the kitchen as a man in a trilby approached the counter.

'Hello, Drew,' Faith said and smiled.

'Hello, Vicar,' Drew said and smiled softly.

The man cleared his throat.

'Hi, what can I get you?' Drew said to him, feeling a tad irritated at the interruption.

'Latte, extra hot, please,' he said and held Drew in his lingering gaze.

Drew smiled at him, as she did all new customers, and he grinned.

'Latte, extra hot for the gentleman,' she said to Esther, who started to prepare a second coffee.

Drew took his money and she noticed the coins were very hot in her hand. The man was staring at her and smiling, his eyes dark and intense. His clean-shaven cheeks had a red complexion and he seemed a little on edge. 'Are you Drew?' he said.

Faith took a step back from the counter and observed the interaction between the man and Drew.

'Yes.' Drew said, dismissively.

Esther filled the cup with frothy milk and slipped it onto the counter for Faith and then returned to prepare the creamed milk for the man's coffee. She worked slowly, and a grin of satisfaction appeared.

'Thank you,' Faith said, taking the cup and sitting at the table closest to the counter.

Drew held the man's gaze. 'Sorry, do I know you?' she said. He didn't look familiar, and it wasn't uncommon for strangers to appear on market day or call her by her first name. Everyone in the village referred to each other by name.

'Err, no. I umm.'

Drew felt impatience tighten her jaw and she became acutely aware of Faith watching her closely. Heat seeped into her cheeks and the man smiled. He seemed to find confidence in her flushed state and cleared his throat. 'I've heard a lot about you,' he said.

Drew frowned. 'Oh!' she said.

Faith's dark gaze seemed to linger on the scene, though she wasn't smiling or smirking, just watching with curiosity and sipping the coffee.

'You are well known around these parts,' the man said and seemed to eye Drew's chest disconcertingly.

Drew's eyebrows shot up and Faith started spluttering.

'Sorry, I mean, everyone says good things about you,' the man corrected, and a rash formed instantly on his neck.

Where's the bloody coffee, mother. 'That's nice,' Drew said, bemused by the chatty guest. 'Can I get you a cake to go with the coffee?' She pointed to the cabinet.

Faith, choking, caught Drew's attention and she stepped out from the counter and approached her with a serviette. 'Are you okay, Vicar? Is there anything I can get you?'

'Thank you,' Faith said, taking the tissue and pressing it to her mouth. 'Liquid and breathing at the same time never works,' she said. 'Brings tears to the eyes.' She dabbed the tissue at her eyes, cleared her throat.

Drew watched Faith who seemed a fraction out of sorts and wondered what it would be like to be the one wiping the tears from her cheek with soft kisses. Fuck! She turned away from the thought and stepped back behind the counter.

'So, I was wondering if you'd like to go out with me one night?' the man said in a rush of enthusiasm. 'My name's Steven, by the way.' He held out his hand.

Fuck off! 'Err!' Drew mumbled. Where's the fucking coffee, mother? Drew looked to Esther's back. She seemed to be starting the process of frothing the milk again. What the fuck?

'We could just go to the pub or something?' Steven was saying, trying to get Drew's attention, withdrawing his hand and shoving it in his pocket.

Drew felt confused, and irritation flared inside her. The feeling was irrational, but the thought of entertaining this bloke riled her. She hadn't been ready for such a proposition. She glanced up, caught Faith staring in their direction and for some reason beyond any logical explanation, said, 'Okay.'

'Great!' Steven beamed a flushed smile and his eyes sparkled excitedly as he passed across a business card with his contact details embossed in a bright yellow font.

Purveyor of Things of Beauty was written in italics under the name, Steven Taylor. Drew squinted at the barely legible caption – yellow on white really was difficult to see – and wondered what the fuck one of those was. She looked up to watch Faith finish her coffee quickly and leave, just as Esther slid the man's drink across the counter with a beaming grin on her face.

'There you go, Steven,' Esther said. 'I can recommend the buns, they're the best you'll taste this side of Ferndale.' She smiled.

Drew felt her insides boiling, swallowed back the frustration, and smiled at Steven.

'Sure, thanks,' Steven said to Esther.

'That'll be another two-pounds-seventy-five, Steven,' Drew said with a hint of disdain that was directed at her mother. Not that Esther seemed to notice; she was too busy swooning over the man in his tweed jacket, brushed cotton checked shirt that seemed to clash with the tweed, and matching tweed trousers.

'Oh no, dear, this is on the house, Steven,' Esther said, and sought out the largest remaining bun on the counter and handed over to the highly delighted salesman.

'How about Wednesday, at the pub, seven-thirty?' Steven said as he moved away from the counter.

'Right,' Drew said and tried to smile. She was still asking herself why she had agreed to a date with him when Grace appeared at the counter.

'Hey Drew, Esther,' Grace said. Grace stared at Drew and frowned.

'Oh, hi,' Drew said, regaining her focus. 'Two coffees?'

'Yep, thanks.' Grace continued to observe Drew with a frown.

Esther, preparing the coffees looked over her shoulder at Grace. 'Drew's going on a date with a handsome young man from Ferndale,' she announced with more than a hint of superiority in her tone.

Fucking hell. Drew rolled her eyes. 'Mum!' she admonished. She tried to smile at Grace. Hang on, how did Esther know where the guy was from?

Grace frowned. 'Oh, right!' she said. Drew didn't look as enthused about the date as Esther, and Grace got the distinct impression Esther would have been better placed to go on this venture than her daughter. Grace sent Drew a questioning gaze and Drew turned away.

Esther, still with a satisfied grin plastered across her face placed the take away cups on the counter. 'Give my love to Harriet,' she said and Grace got the impression her tone lacked sincerity.

'Thanks,' she said. Grace looked towards Drew. 'If you fancy a drink later?' she said.

Drew looked at Grace with a pained expression. 'I'll be baking for the funeral tomorrow. Thanks, though.'

Grace nodded, picked up the cups, and headed back to the market stall.

Drew turned to Esther and was just about to speak when another customer approached the counter. Any conversation about Steven Taylor, Purveyor of Things of Beauty, would have to wait.

'Hi, what can I get you?' Drew said and smiled at the man who approached.

*

34

'What do you think about this one?' Vera said to Jenny.

Jenny looked at the picture on the profile, wavy fair hair, sky-blue eyes and a kind smile. 'She looks pretty; what does she do?'

Vera studied the woman's details. 'A reporter, I think.'

'Do you need to poke her?'

'Pardon!' Vera looked up, eyebrows raised.

'You know, poke her; make contact.' Jenny said.

'She's too young for me,' she said and chuckled. 'I'll send her a message.'

'Ooh, that's a good idea,' Jenny said. She finished the hooch in her glass and poured another. 'I'm knackered from working Delia's bloody stall all day. Non- stop! That new herb blend she's come up with was selling a storm again.'

'That's good,' Vera said, but she was tapping away on the keys. 'There.' she said. 'Sent. Fingers crossed.'

'Maybe she could do a lovely review for the café?' Jenny said. 'Did it say who she works for?'

'No.' Vera said. 'Could be great for publicity and visibility for the village. She might even report on our market, and create some interest in Hilda Spencer? Ooh, this could be really big.'

'I can see the headline. Duckton-by-Dale: Gays, Ghosts, and Great buns. The perfect holiday destination in The Lakes,' Jenny said and chuckled.

Vera leaned in and placed a brief kiss to Jenny's lips. 'Come on, bedtime. It'll be a long day tomorrow.'

'I thought you'd never ask,' Jenny said and pinched Vera's bottom as she passed.

*

'I still can't believe Drew's going on another date with a bloke?' Harriet said, deep in thought. She teased fingertips along the centre-line of Grace's toned abs, her breath hitching at the goose bumps rising under her touch. 'Mmm,' she moaned, pleasantly distracted and moving her hand lower.

Grace groaned, rocked under Harriet's movement. 'Seems very odd… to… me,' she said, struggling to form the sentence. She reached up, cupped Harriet's cheeks and pulled her into a long, tender kiss. Studying her deeply, 'I love you,' she said and then Harriet slipped into the warm wetness between her legs and silenced her.

'Feel this?' Harriet whispered.

Grace moaned lazily, biting down on her lip, her hips arching into the touch.

Harriet wore a provocative grin and a glint in her eyes that showed she had Grace quite literally at her fingertips. 'And this?' she said, her arousal mounting as she entered the hot wet silkiness. 'You feel so fucking good,' she said, her voice broken, her eyes closing, her concentration narrowing to the shifting sensation of Grace on her fingers.

'Fuck!' Grace moaned, and then suddenly levered Harriet onto her back, moved astride her and assessed her flushed cheeks, dark eyes and supple lips with hunger.

Harriet found Grace's sex again, the silky feel at her fingertips heightened by the penetrating gaze holding her with wild desire. Then Grace's hand was between her legs, exploring her with a gentle touch, the pressure light at first. Warmth flooded her then a burning sensation sent a bolt of lightning through her and she groaned. She reached up urgently and tugged Grace to her, claiming her mouth, writhing at the feel of the erect nipples grazing her skin, the increasing pressure on the sensitive spot that had her dancing with arousal.

Grace massaged the engorged silky bud at her fingertips with tenderness, her tongue dancing, tasting, pleading, and enticing Harriet to move with her. Drawing her up from the pillow, Harriet's mouth at her breast, the teasing and biting sent a tingling wave that surged through her, fuelling her throbbing sex. She pushed Harriet from her, shoved her back to the bed and kneeled over her. Studying her with intense longing, sliding her fingers between the hot, silky folds, she entered her. Observing intently, the guttural groan vibrating through her fingers, she took her deeper.

Harriet groaned, eyes closed flickering, lips separating quivering, her breathing coming in short gasps.

Slowly, Grace moved inside her, sensing every subtle shift, every unspoken desire, then she quickened the pace, thrusting deeper, bringing her to a rapturous peak. And when Harriet cried out, thrashed, and tensed in her arms, she held her in blissful orgasm until the shuddering eased.

Harriet blinked her eyes open and stared into the darkest gaze she had ever seen. Then she smiled, breaking the spell, softening the intensity between them. She placed a tender kiss to the enticing, lips hovering above her. 'I love you,' she whispered.

Grace smiled, snuggled against Harriet's chest and closed her eyes, delighted in the pounding heart at her cheek, the fingers toying with her hair, the intimate silence they shared. When Harriet's heart calmed Grace lifted her head, looked at her, and smiled. 'I put an offer on the pub,' she said.

Harriet grinned and tilted her head. 'You say the nicest things to a girl in a moment of post-coital bliss, Ms Pinkerton.'

Grace eased up the bed, rested on her side and studied the satisfied look on Harriet's face. 'Does it bother you?'

'That you're buying the pub? Of, course not. We discussed it.'

'Should I have said something more, romantic,' Grace said. Relationships were unfamiliar territory to her and she didn't want to get it wrong, but she was easily distracted by the thoughts that rushed into her mind and the sudden urge to share them.

Harriet chuckled, reached up and stroked the side of Grace's face. 'No,' she said. 'Are you still going to do the gin wagon?'

Grace smiled. 'Sure, the wagon's mobile and great for outdoor events.'

'You'll have to change the name. Pinkie's Gins is naff.'

Grace gave Harriet her best attempt at looking offended and failed. 'What's wrong with it?'

'You seriously need to ask?' Harriet said and chuckled.

'You sure you still want me to convert it?' Grace said, with a tilt of her head and raised eyebrows. 'Don't want another romantic weekend away, first?' Grace grinned. She had bought the camper van with the intention of them being able to spend time together and it had taken her best efforts to get Harriet to agree to their first long weekend break – and as it turned out, their last.

'Absolutely. And, you'd better make sure that bloody rat doesn't appear and start serving gin.'

'It was a field mouse,' Grace said and chuckled. 'Tiny, brown, cute eyes and little whiskers.'

'Bloody long tail and sharp teeth,' Harriet countered. 'Scared the shit out of me.'

'Well, yes.' Grace conceded and nodded. 'I guess if I'd woken to the little guy sat on my chest licking his whiskers, I'd probably have jumped through the roof too.'

'It wasn't that little,' Harriet said and shuddered at the memory.

'Ah, my poor little country bumpkin,' Grace teased. 'Anyway, I won't work at the pub. I was thinking I could ask Tilly if she wanted to come and work for us. She's good; got potential too.' Grace nodded her head. She had been impressed with the bar woman from Upper Duckton, and she was good looking. It would be a real coup for the village if she moved to The Crooked Billet.

'Us?'

'What's mine's yours,' Grace said, and leaned across and kissed Harriet with tenderness. Harriet's lips were still hot and so soft, and for a moment Grace felt distracted by the rush of energy passing through her. 'I've spoken to your dad about day-to-day management and he's happy to continue. He was pretty much doing the job before Elvis died.'

'The Duckton Arms aren't going to be happy with you stealing Tilly from them.' Harriet chuckled. 'Maybe it will stop Doug from heading up that way. I think he's got a thing for Tilly, too.'

'No chance there,' Grace said.

'I know, Esther would have him by the balls.'

'Tilly certainly wouldn't,' Grace said and laughed.

'What?'

'You didn't know?'

'What?' Harriet turned to Grace and pinned her to the bed.

'She bats for our team,' Grace said.

Harriet moved on top of Grace and looked down at her.

Grace felt the dominant gesture in the shuddering that had her insides burning with desire. She moaned when Harriet's lips met hers with fierce hunger, then instantly there was a space between them and Grace opened her eyes to Harriet gazing at her quizzically. 'And when did you find out this little nugget about Tilly, Ms Pinkerton?'

Grace pressed her index finger to her lips, feigning deep thought. 'That would be the point at which she made a pass at me.' She couldn't stop from laughing as Harriet's mouth sat agape and her eyes widened.

Harriet slapped Grace on the arm then tweaked her nipple as added punishment. 'Right, Ms Pinkerton, you asked for this,' she said and pinned Grace's hands to the bed.

Grace studied the wild-frenzied look and moaned. 'Bring it on,' she gasped.

5.

Drew took the last tray of sandwiches from the kitchen and squeezed her way through the crowded bar to the buffet table set out on the dance floor.

The pub was already buzzing with chatter and judging by the fact that people had been standing in the aisles of the chapel for the cremation service, the wake was likely to be a bigger affair then they had first thought.

Drew started to unwrap the plated food.

'Would you like a hand?'

The voice sent a shiver down her spine and she turned to face Faith smiling at her. 'I'm good, I think.' She scrunched the cling-film into a ball and squeezed it tightly. At least she could string a sentence together in the presence of the Vicar now. She found herself staring at Faith and broke eye contact.

'Is there anything else to bring out?' Faith said.

Drew assessed the table even though she knew the answer. 'No, I think we're all good. I'll bring dessert options out later.' She held Faith's gaze. It didn't help. 'Thank you for a lovely service.'

'You're very welcome. I'm glad I was here to help. Doug's song choices seemed to go down better than I anticipated,' Faith said and chuckled.

'Yes,' Drew said, but she'd already forgotten the songs that had been played at the service.

'Vera and Jenny's speeches went down well, too.'

She couldn't bring those to mind now either. She nodded blankly.

'Vicar, I just want to thank you for a wonderful service,' Doug said, interrupting the conversation.

Drew jolted out of the trance she had drifted into and noise filtered into her awareness. 'Right, I'd better crack on,' she said and headed back to the kitchen.

She stood with her back to the sink, her heart racing. Fuck it! Maybe she didn't have this thing under control after all. Maybe the date on Wednesday would be a positive distraction. She tried to think of Steven but found it hard to recall the colour of his eyes. Did he have much hair? She couldn't remember. Bugger!

'Drew, Drew?'

Drew jumped at the sudden interruption and looked towards her mother. 'Yes?'

'Come here, there's someone you should meet,' Esther said. 'Come on. He's from Broadermere way. Owns his own farm,' Esther was saying as she made her way through the kitchen door.

'Mum, I don't need another supplier for the café.'

'Well, just speak to him, dear. You know how we like to keep things local.'

Drew followed Esther's back and then stopped when she did.

'Drew, this is Mitchel; Mitchel this is Drew.' Esther announced.

'Hi,' they both said at the same time and smiled. 'Your mum tells me you own the café,' Mitchel said.

Drew smiled. 'That's right. You're a farmer?' she said. Mitchel laughed and Drew thought he had a sweet smile.

'Yes,' he said. 'It's been in the family for years. We're always happy to supply locally if there's anything we can help you with.'

Drew couldn't help but notice he had a kind voice. He didn't seem presumptuous at all. She liked that.

'Did you do the spread?' he said, indicating to the buffet.

'Yes, have you tried it?'

He looked at her and smiled. 'It's very good. Clean flavours and natural ingredients; perfect in my book. Our farm is about as organic as you can get. Did you make the bread?'

'Yes.' Drew liked this guy's ethics. 'Perhaps we should talk about supplying the café,' she said.

'Great.' Mitchel handed over his business card. 'I just need to catch up with.'

He pointed over his shoulder to Kev and Luke, excusing himself and Drew nodded. As he turned away, Drew saw Faith staring at her from across the room. There was intensity in the gaze that was interrupted as Grace approached the Vicar, and Drew felt the absence of it as soon as Faith looked away. She sighed, walked to the buffet table, stacked the empty serving plates and took them back to the kitchen.

'Huh-hum, Vicar,' Grace said, drawing Faith's eyes from the object of her attention.

'Hello, Grace. Seems to be going well?' Faith said, referring to the wake. 'Did you get in touch with the solicitors?'

'Yes, thanks, that's in hand. I wanted to ask your thoughts on another idea I've got.'

Faith smiled and nodded. She popped the last bite of sandwich into her mouth, put the plate on the table next to her, and picked up her glass of wine.

'I was wondering if we could do some fundraising activities to renovate the park?' Grace said.

Faith tilted her head and nodded. 'Did you have something in mind?'

'I was thinking about activities for the kids, you know, those wooden climbing frames and rope swings and stuff like that. It's pretty drab and could really do with an uplift. Hopefully we could attract more families to the area.'

Faith nodded and sipped from her drink. She'd seen the park and it certainly needed attention if it was going to appeal to a younger audience. She would be able to help them get the fundraising under way while she was here. 'Yes,' she said. 'What do you think about a skate park, too, providing there's the space?'

'Great! We can bring it up at the next committee meeting. I can't see anyone objecting. I'll get some plans knocked up so we've got something to present,' Grace said, excitedly.

'I suspect we will need a sub-committee.'

'Easy.' Grace said. 'I'm sure Drew, Doug and Bryan will want to be involved.' Faith smiled and Grace studied the way her focus shifted and the fine lines at the corner of her eyes lifted revealing hidden pleasure. She knew what that kind of look meant. Hell yes. The Vicar seemed very happy that a certain person would be associated with the sub-committee. 'I'll throw the idea past them,' she said.

Esther approached and Grace smiled. 'Hi Esther,' she said.

'Grace,' Esther said and Grace couldn't help but wonder at the way her nose seemed to lift when she spoke. 'Vicar, I wonder if I could have a word?' Esther said. 'Wonderful service,' she went on to say, dragging Faith away from Grace.

Grace wandered towards the bar. 'Nice buns,' she said to Drew as Drew walked past with a tray, heading for the buffet table.

'Fuck off,' Drew said, in a loud whisper.

Grace chased after her. 'Want a hand?'

Drew grinned at her. 'There are more cakes where those came from,' and Grace followed her back to the kitchen.

'Hey, do you want to work on a project to renovate the park?' Grace said.

'Sure, what's involved?' Drew said, pointing at a tray for Grace to collect. Grace picked it up and followed Drew out of the kitchen.

'Don't know all the details; we'll need to discuss it at committee. Planning, fundraising, that kind of thing?'

'Sure. Who else is involved?'

'Me, Harriet, though I haven't asked her yet, Doug, Bryan, I need to ask them too, oh and Faith said she'd like to get involved. She's thinking of a skate park as well, which would be amazing.'

Drew put her tray on the table and turned to take the tray from Grace. 'Count me in,' she said and smiled, aware that her hands were shaking and hoping it wasn't obvious to Grace.

'You okay?' Grace said.

Fuck! 'I'm fine, why?'

'You seem a bit distracted,' Grace said.

'There's just a lot going on today,' Drew said, hoping she had recovered the situation.

Grace nodded. 'Faith gave a beautiful service,' she said.

Drew cleared her throat. 'Yes, she did.'

'Vera and Jenny did well. Very funny,' Grace said.

'Yes, it was all very beautiful. I'm sure Elvis would have approved. I think he would be pleased you're buying the pub too,' Drew said.

Grace smiled, holding the sincerity of Drew's gaze with her own. 'Thanks.'

'Ah, Drew, there you are,' Esther said as she approached and Grace couldn't help but think the woman was hunting her daughter down.

'Mum.' Drew said, and rolled her eyes to Grace who grinned.

'There's someone I want you to meet,' Esther said, reaching for Drew's arm.

Drew shrugged off the hand. 'Not now, mum; I'm busy.' Drew headed back to the kitchen leaving Grace staring at Esther staring at her.

'Lovely service,' Grace said.

'Did you see that?' Jenny said to Vera. They were sat in the corner of the room and had been watching Esther the whole time. 'She's up to something with Drew.'

'Yes, I saw her. She's barking up the wrong fucking tree. Daft old bat,' Vera said and shook her head.

Esther was looking oddly at Grace. 'It was a lovely service,' she said then turned quickly towards the buffet and plucked a bun from the tray.

Grace winced as Esther went straight for the cherry and devoured it before heading hastily through the crowd to the other end of the bar.

'Hey, sexy,' Harriet slurred as she approached Grace.

'Are you a little tipsy, Ms Haversham?' Grace said and a wicked grin came over her, remembering the first time Harriet had got drunk and thrown herself at Grace and tumbled them both to the ground; the same night that Harriet kissed her. Grace felt the heat spread through her in a blanket of sensual warmth.

'Nice buns,' Harriet said, plucked one from the table and took a large bite.

'I think so too,' Grace said and shifted her gaze from Harriet's breasts to her eyes. She leaned closer and felt Harriet's breath hitch as their cheeks brushed. 'I'll be sampling yours later,' she whispered, and then moved back and raised her eyebrows.

Harriet seemed to find it difficult to swallow, her cheeks only a shade lighter than the red cherry on the cake in her hand.

'Come on,' Grace said, taking Harriet's hand and leading her through the bar. 'I need to have a quick word with Doug and your dad about a project.'

'What project?' Harriet said, taking another bite of the iced bun.

'To renovate the park, come on.'

'Sounds fun,' Harriet said.

46

*

'Thanks for helping,' Drew said to Faith as she piled the last stack of plates on the kitchen surface.

'My pleasure,' Faith said. 'Thank you for the buffet; it was scrumptious.'

Drew flushed. She broke eye contact, loaded more plates in the dishwasher, threw in the washing tablet, closed the door and set the programme to run. 'Nearly there,' she said.

'Everyone's so supportive here,' Faith said. 'It's a beautiful community.'

Drew nodded. She supposed it was.

'You're very lucky.'

'Would you like a drink?' Drew blurted then felt a rush of anxiety at the potential for rejection. Faith smiled at her and she couldn't tell if it was a look of compassion or something else.

'Would you like to get off your feet?' Faith said.

Drew hadn't been expecting that response. She nodded. 'They are killing me,' she said. 'The rest of this can wait until tomorrow.' Drew led them out of the kitchen and through to the empty bar.

Bryan looked up from the glass he was drying. 'You off?' he said.

Drew smiled wearily. 'Can we get a drink?'

'Of course, petal.'

Drew looked to Faith.

'I'll have a small white wine, please,' she said.

'I'll have the same, thanks Bry.'

'Grab a seat; I'll bring them over,' Bryan said, and plucked the chilled bottle of Sauvignon from the ice-filled bucket at the back of the bar.

Drew slumped into the soft-back chair and groaned. 'My feet ache,' she said, suddenly realising the strain on her body.

'You've been on them all day,' Faith said.

Bryan placed two drinks on the table in front of the women.

'Thanks,' they said in unison.

'Well, congratulations,' Faith said, and raised her glass in a toast. 'I'm sure Elvis would have approved.'

Drew nodded then sipped her drink.

Faith looked around the room. 'It's a quaint pub,' she said.

Drew gazed at her and with genuine intrigue said, 'Where are you from?'

Faith held her gaze. 'I was brought up in Manchester,' she said.

'Do you have family there?'

'My foster-mother lives there, yes.'

'I'm sorry.' Drew bit down on her lip, irritated that she might have asked something too personal. She hadn't intended to offend Faith.

'It's okay. I love her very much. I lost my family in a car accident.'

Drew felt the news as a thrust that threw her back in the seat. 'Christ, that must have been awful,' she said then realising the slip, said, 'Sorry.'

Faith smiled and held her with a look of tenderness and when she spoke her tone was silky-soft. 'I'm not precious, Drew, so no need to apologise, okay?

Drew nodded.

Faith's gaze was gentle, and she continued in the same soft tone. 'I've worked with children and young adult offenders over the years, and believe me they say a lot worse.' She chuckled, kept looking at Drew, eyes widening, encouraging a response.

Drew nodded. She was entranced.

'Losing my family was a long time ago.' Faith said. 'They were killed instantly. I was the one who survived and, believe me, I have questioned why me for a lot of years before coming to terms with reality.' Her smile held genuine acceptance and love.

'Devastating,' Drew said and she felt sorrow deep in her gut.

'It was,' Faith said, and the smile that seemed so confident suddenly had a sense of vulnerability about it.

They sat in silence for a moment, each sipping their drinks.

'How long is temporary?' Drew asked.

'Temporary?' Faith said.

'Your tenure here.'

'I said I would make a firm decision within three months,' Faith said and her smile was back to normal.

Drew felt a tingling wave shoot up her spine and the hairs on her neck rise. 'Oh!'

'I didn't know whether I would fit in here,' Faith continued to explain. 'I'm used to a larger and less remote community. But, I like it. The people seem very welcoming and we've already been talking about a community project. Community is important to me and it seems there's a strong one here.'

Drew nodded. She was still with the words 'fitting in' and the fact that Faith would decide whether she stayed on a permanent basis. Faith certainly fit into Drew's world. 'I'm glad we've made you feel welcome,' she said.

Faith sipped at her drink. 'So, Doug and Esther are your parents?'

Drew nodded and rolled her eyes.

'They seem nice,' Faith said.

'They are. Typical parents,' Drew said and then winced as it dawned on her that Faith hadn't been lucky enough to have her parents around. 'Sorry,' she said again.

Faith reached across and touched Drew's hand and Drew jolted as sparks shot up her arm. 'No sorry, remember?'

Oh God, there was that gorgeous smile again. 'Right,' Drew said, barely able to speak.

'Any brothers or sisters?' Faith said.

Drew shook her head.

'Your parents run the shop?'

'Yes.'

'How did you get into the café?' Faith said.

'Umm!' Drew paused. 'Honestly, I don't know,' she said and smiled. 'What about you; how did you get into the church?'

'I guess I fell into it,' Faith said and when she held Drew's gaze, Drew got the sense that she didn't want to say any more on the topic.

'Yes, I fell into the café too,' Drew said.

'Well, you're good at it,' Faith said and finished her wine.

'You are too,' Drew said and blushed.

Faith laughed. 'I'm better at skateboarding.'

Drew frowned. 'Really?'

Faith nodded. 'Yep. Skateboarding was my first love,' she said. The sparkle in her eyes revealed her true passion, she looked younger at that moment.

'Hence the.' Drew indicated to the tattoos, uncharacteristic of a minister of the church.

'Kind of, yes! Body art was a part of that era for me,' Faith said.

Drew cleared her throat and finished her wine. 'It's cool,' she said, thankful nothing more intimate had come out of her mouth, given the thoughts that had just passed through her mind.

Faith nodded and started to stand. 'Thanks for the drink,' she said. 'It was nice being able to chat. Usually, you're working.'

'Likewise.' Drew stood, picked up the glasses and took them to the bar.

'Thanks, petal,' Bryan said with a glint in his eye, his gaze moving from Drew to Faith and back again. 'You ladies have a good night,' he said.

'Thank you, Bryan,' Faith said.

'I'll sort out the kitchen first thing,' Drew said.

'I'll clean up the rest. You'll have enough on with the café,' Bryan said.

'It's Sunday, I get a lie-in,' Drew said and chuckled.

'Lucky for some, eh?' Faith said and winked at Bryan.

'I'll see you for the 6 am service, Vicar,' Bryan said.

'I'll be there,' Faith said. 'Good night.'

Drew watched Faith as she left the pub then turned to Bryan who smiled at her.

'She seems nice,' he said.

Drew smiled. Nice! That wouldn't be one of the adjectives she would use to describe Faith. Nice just didn't cut it. She sighed and smiled at Bryan. He looked tired. 'I'll give you a hand with the kitchen,' she said.

6.

Drew stood at the steamy window of the café, staring out at the pouring rain. Temperatures were still mild, the air muggy and oppressive. With the café enjoying a moment of much-needed tranquillity after the constant flow of customers, she watched the passers-by, umbrellas aloft, smiles on their faces. Holidaymakers and hikers didn't let the weather impact their enjoyment of the beautiful landscape, the quaint shops, pubs, and many eateries the area had to offer.

Drew jolted as the tattoos that had become familiar to her flashed into view and then came to a sudden stop outside the window of the shop. A white sleeveless t-shirt and black Lycra shorts clung to the athletic form, dark hair straddled the shoulders, and a warm smile reached straight into Drew and squeezed the breath from her. Fuck!

Drew dived towards the door to open it at the same moment the door flung open, leaving the palm of her hand just a centimetre away from Faith's right breast. 'Shit, sorry,' Drew blurted, lowering her hand quickly and turning sharply towards the counter, but not before eyeing the rain-soaked woman that stood before her. 'You look like a drowned rat,' she said, through a nervous chuckle, settling herself behind the counter. The physical barrier between them didn't stop the surge of lust that swept through her at the sight of Faith. No dog collar, she noted. That, really, doesn't help. How deliciously wet?

'I got caught in the rain,' Faith said with a damp smile. She wiped at the water trickling down her face.

No shit! Drew's eyes wandered. Faith's dark hair hung slightly longer when wet, and a little bedraggled with loose strands that stuck to her flushed cheeks, the beads of water trickling down the side of her cheek from her forehead. She watched Faith wipe her eyes and felt the urge to reach out and touch her soft smooth skin. The cheekbones that accentuated eyes that smiled deeply, the line of her jaw and the beautifully kissable, moist, inviting lips that had Drew's heart racing. And then her gaze lingered on Faith's delicious, athletic body. Oh my God! Drew forced her eyes to look directly into Faith's, though through her peripheral vision she could still see the erect nipples pressing against the thin vest. She found it difficult to swallow; difficult to breathe; difficult to speak.

'Can I grab a coffee, please?' Faith seemed to wince and smile at the same time. Drew turned to the machine and started to prepare the drink. 'I, umm, I don't have any money on me, but will pay you back later?'

Drew looked over her shoulder and smiled. 'That's what all the girls say,' she said, then flushed and turned her head sharply back to the coffee.

'I'm sure they do,' Faith whispered under her breath.

'How far did you run?' Drew said, pouring the milk into the jug.

'About eight miles,' Faith said.

'Fuck, they'll be calling you Forrest Gump if you're not careful,' Drew said. She looked up, assessed Faith, hoping she hadn't offended her. Green eyes held her gaze and Drew noticed the shade as lighter than it had been previously. God, she was gorgeous.

Faith smiled. 'I try and get between five and ten miles in a day.'

'Definitely, Forrest Gump,' Drew said, her voice softened by the piercing gaze that had her entranced. She smiled with tenderness.

Faith seemed unsettled by the moment and looked to the front window. 'Certainly, is wet out there,' she said.

All kinds of wet in here too! 'Yes. When it rains here; it really rains. Doesn't stop the visitors enjoying themselves though. Hardy lot. It's kind of expected that it rains in the Lakes,' she said with a tilt of her head, watching the glow develop in Faith's cheeks. She looked delicious and the thought of licking the rain from every part of her body caused Drew to shudder. She turned her attention to the milk and tried to let the sound of the machine distract her from her musings. It didn't.

'I love the weather,' Faith said. 'It always brings something different; something fresh, don't you think?'

Not the weather conversation! 'Yes, it does,' Drew smiled at Faith who seemed lost in thought. She placed the coffee on the counter. 'Would you like anything to eat?' she said, careful not to refer to the buns displayed proudly on the counter.

Faith turned to Drew and smiled. 'No, I'm fine thanks,' she said.

Drew caught a glint in the soft-green gaze and felt her throat constrict.

The café door opened and Esther virtually ran towards the counter. 'Right, dear, I'll take over from here so you can go and get dressed up for your date,' she said without giving a second glance in Faith's direction.

Drew watched Faith process Esther's statement and felt disappointed that she didn't see a reaction.

'Oh, hello, Vicar,' Esther said, eyeing Faith up and down with an odd expression. 'I didn't recognise you...' She stopped assessing Faith and smiled.

'No dog collar,' Faith said and indicated to her neckline.

Drew melted inside. It was a whole different feeling from the irritation that her mother's intrusion had stirred.

Esther studied Faith intently. 'Yes.' She paused. 'You look.' She paused again. 'Naked,' she said.

Drew started choking and excused herself. She wished!

Faith chuckled. 'Yes, I suppose so. I haven't found a running t-shirt yet that supports a dog collar,' and there was warmth in the smile she gave the older woman. She took a seat close to the counter.

'Yes, I can imagine.' Esther turned her attention back to Drew and glared at her.

'What?' Drew said, her cheeks crimson.

'Be off with you.' Esther said stabbing her watch with her index finger. She stepped around the counter, removed her coat and put it in the kitchen and then nudged Drew out of the way.

'It's an hour and a half before I need to be at the pub. The pub is one minute from here and it takes me no longer than half an hour to shower and put on a pair of jeans,' Drew said.

'Aren't you going to wear a nice dress?' Esther said.

Drew felt the hint of a smile coming from Faith in a warm glow that flooded her cheeks. 'When did you last see me in a dress?'

'That's not the point,' Esther said with a turned-up nose. 'I can cope with the café; it's not that busy.' She indicated the empty seats.

Drew sighed.

Faith finished her drink and stood. 'Right, I'll pop the money in for the coffee in the morning, if that's okay?' she said.

'That will be fine, thank you, Vicar,' Esther said distractedly.

'Definitely not; it's on me,' Drew countered and glared at her mother.

Faith smiled. 'Thank you,' she said and set off towards the door.

Drew watched her closely until the door shut and the vision in white had disappeared and only then did she realise Esther's beady eyes were on her. 'What?' she said, her tone reflecting her irritation.

'Steven's a nice man,' Esther said.

'Which reminds me,' Drew started. 'How do you know Steven?'

'I know his family from years back,' Esther said. 'They're a good family. They've got their own business.' She was nodding her head as if that was an important factor in the love equation.

Drew rolled her eyes. 'I'm going upstairs,' she said and walked out through the kitchen.

*

Drew entered the pub and looked around, and it occurred to her she couldn't remember clearly what Steven looked like; at least not well enough to spot him in a crowd unless he was the gawky one looking directly at her with an inane grin on his face and a trilby plonked on his head. That would be easy enough to spot.

'Ah-right petal,' Bryan said as she approached the bar.

'Hi Bryan, G&T, please.'

'Coming right up.' He looked Drew up and down. 'You got a date?' He was teasing but the grimace coming back at him answered his question. 'Oh, dear, like that is it? Who's the unsuspecting fellow?'

'Steven Taylor,' Drew said and sighed. She had thought about cancelling the date, which in her mind wasn't really a date at all, but decided against that. She needed to think about something other than Faith. A couple of hours respite from pondering her desires held some appeal, and at least it would shut her mother up for a bit.

'Oh, right!' Bryan shook his head. 'Don't know of him,' he said and squeezed lemon over the ice.

'I'll get that.'

Drew turned her head at the sound of Steven's voice, spotted the tweed jacket and matching trilby hat. He looked fifty years old if he was a day. Is this the same guy who came into the café? His smile looked familiar, and the glint in his eye seemed to strike a chord, though not an altogether pleasant one.

Drew cleared her throat. 'Hello, Steven.'

Bryan turned from the back of the counter and placed her drink on the bar. He eyed the middle-aged man and when he smiled he did so with politeness. 'What can I get you,' he said, addressing Steven.

'I'll have a half a mild shandy, please.'

'Coming up,' Bryan said and gave an apologetic smile to Drew.

Steven removed his hat and Drew stared at the bold, heavily receding, hairline. She could imagine he would look quite dapper with a much shorter cut around the back and sides, but the long thin strands that he had styled in a comb-over straddling the top of his head just didn't sit right and made him look closer to fifty-five. Where the fuck had she been when he had asked her out? She tried to smile but felt the strain of it in the tightness in her jaw and she didn't want to lead Steven on in any way. She needed this date to be over and done with as soon as possible.

'Have you seen a menu, my love?' he said.

Drew cringed and her insides formed a tight ball of resistance. She took a long slug of her gin. 'Um, no, I was waiting,' she said and then took another long slug. Bryan caught her eye and she indicated to him for another drink.

'Where would you like to sit?' Steven said. He scanned the dining options, pointed to a cosy corner away from the bar area which was already becoming occupied and smiled.

'How about here,' Drew said, picking a table in the centre of the room, exposed on all sides with no hint of intimacy.

'Yes, whatever you like, my love.'

Irritation flared. Stop calling me that!

'Shall I put these on the tab?' Bryan asked.

'Yes, of course,' Steven said and went to pick up the drinks.

Drew reached the gin before he did and the sense of his fingers grazing her hand sent a shiver of disgust through her.

'Oops, sorry!' he said, and giggled, which was almost more irritating than being called my love. Drew tried to smile and Steven headed for the table. 'I'll pay for my share,' she said to Bryan, who nodded.

Drew sat back in the chair and studied Steven, trying to find something she liked about the man. He had nice shaped eyes, but that look felt all shades of disconcerting. He was fit, which was a plus, but aside from that nothing came to her. 'What are you a purveyor of?' she said, reminded of his business card and short of something to talk about in the silence that sat heavily between them.

Steven seemed to grow taller in the chair. 'Antiques,' he said and grinned with pride. 'Our family started the business three generations ago. We have several shops now.'

'Oh, right. Are you a collector?' Drew didn't know the first thing about antiques, other than the fact that it was about old things that were of value today.

'Yes, I'm a big stamp collector.' His grin widened.

'I'm sure that's very exciting,' Drew said, totally un-enthralled.

'Ooh, it is. I'm so glad you think so. Most people find it quite a bore. I guess it's one of those hobbies that either you get it or you don't,' he said, suddenly looking like an eager puppy.

'Yes,' Drew said, aware that she was one of those who didn't. 'A bit like train spotting, I guess.'

'Exactly!' Steven was ecstatic. 'I can see why your mother thought we would get on so well.' He looked as if he were about to start clapping. Drew braced herself then his excitement drove him to pick up his glass instead and she breathed a sigh of relief. 'Cheers!' he said and she watched him take the tiniest sip of shandy.

She took a long swig of the gin and was already plotting the third. 'Should we take a look at the menu?' she said.

'Can we wait a little longer? I wouldn't want to rush through the evening. I'm prone to indigestion,' he said and giggled.

Fucking hell! 'Right,' Drew said, feeling the pain of an extended evening ahead. She sat back in the chair and glanced around the room. Jesus Christ! You have got to be kidding me? Esther smiled back at her and she groaned.

'Is everything alright, my love?' Steven said.

No, no, no! 'Sorry, I was just thinking about food. I'm really quite hungry. Do you think we could order? It can take a while to get served at the moment. Our head chef left recently.'

'Oh, I'm sorry to hear that,' Steven said and looked a little flustered. 'Should we have chosen somewhere else?'

'No, no, this is fine. The food is excellent, it just takes a bit longer. I can recommend the beef and ale pie,' she said, knowing it would just need heating in the microwave.

'Oh, right. I prefer sea bass or salmon,' Steven said.

Of course, you do! 'Right. I'm not sure that's on the menu. Steak, haddock and chips, lasagne,' Drew said with a shrug.

'Oh dear, that all sounds a bit heavy for my stomach. I have grumbling guts, you see,' Steven said. 'Have to be a bit careful what I eat this time of night. I'm okay up until lunchtime,' he continued.

Oh my God. Too much information! 'Salad, maybe with tuna?' Drew suggested. When she looked up she noticed Harriet and Grace had taken a seat at the table next to them. And then, Jenny and Vera entered the pub and approached the bar. She could feel her cheeks flush with indignation and glanced across at her mother, whose smile became a glare directed at Jenny and Vera.

'Salad would be perfect if the tuna is in brine but not in oil, thanks. Shall I go and order?'

Drew leapt from her seat. 'I'll go,' she said. Can I get you another drink?'

'Oh no, one half is my limit thank you,' Steven said. 'I'll probably struggle to finish this one.'

Drew grimaced and went to the bar, approaching Vera and Jenny with a wide-eyed look of despair. 'Hi,' she said.

'Who's that?' Vera said.

'Don't ask. Another G&T please, Bryan, a tuna salad if the tuna is in brine and I'll have a beef and ale pie please.'

'Right you are,' Bryan said and wrote out the order. 'I'll bring your drink over.'

'No rush, I'll wait,' Drew said, thankful for the space from the man sat at the table.

'Oh, I meant to say, there's a woman coming to the café on Friday to interview you about working life in the village if you're interested? She's a reporter for a local magazine. I can't remember what it's called. What do you think?' Vera said to Drew.

Drew smiled.

'A bit of free advertising.'

'Sure, sounds good.' Drew nodded.

'Here you go, petal.' Bryan passed Drew the drink. 'I see your mum's in. Where's Doug tonight?' he said.

'At the Duckton Arms if he's got any sense!' Drew said.

Bryan chuckled. 'Still plotting to move up that way, is he?'

'In his dreams.' Drew smiled. She took the drink from the bar. 'Wish me luck,' she said and headed back to the table.

'Good luck,' Jenny and Vera chorused.

'She doesn't look happy,' Jenny said to Vera.

'Can you blame her,' Vera said, and glared across the room at Esther, who gloated at her.

Drew leaned back in the seat, the aching silence drowning out the general hum and buzz of conversations taking place around them. She caught Harriet's pained expression and Grace's look of concern and didn't know whether to laugh or cry at the situation. And then Steven started to babble about something and she knew to cry was the front-runner. At that moment she vowed never to allow her mother to set her up again. And then thoughts of Faith drifted into her awareness and the man opposite her didn't matter anymore. She held onto the image of Faith, wearing Lycra, her breasts revealed through the thin wet t-shirt that clung to her very wet body and the soft green gaze that touched her with kindness, tenderness. And then there was the sound of Steven's voice, loudly in her ear.

'Drew, Drew,' he said. 'Are you alright, my love?'

Drew flicked her eyes open. 'Sorry, I must have drifted off.'

'Goodness, I thought there was something wrong.' He said, a hand pressed to his chest.

'Here you go,' Bryan declared and put the two suppers on the table.

'That was quick,' Steven said.

'Salad,' Bryan said with a shrug and turned away from the table.

Drew smiled and her cheeks flushed. 'Bon appétit.'

'Oh, you speak French; that's nice,' Steven said.

Drew rolled her eyes. 'That's my entire repertoire,' she said and started to eat.

'Oh!' Steven said. He sounded disappointed.

Drew ate in silence, finished her beef and ale pie before Steven had munched his way through half the salad, and sat back in the chair. She sipped her drink, hoping he would finish soon enough so she could go home. Drew looked up to see Vera approaching the table from behind Steven. She had a mischievous grin on her face and winked at Drew before stopping next to them.

'Excuse me. I'm very sorry to disturb you, both. Drew, there's report of a water leak at the café,' she said. 'I think you might need to check it out.'

Drew sat up in the seat. 'Oh, no!' she said.

'Oh, goodness,' Steven said. He looked at his half-eaten salad as if pondering whether the disaster was something he should give up his food to attend to and then opted for heroism. He stood. 'I'll come and help,' he said.

'No, no, no, it will be fine,' Drew insisted. She put a hand on his shoulder and helped him to find his seat. 'You finish your salad; it's too good to waste. It was lovely meeting you, Steven,' she said.

'Oh, umm, right,' Steven mumbled. 'Yes, it was lovely. Perhaps we could do it again sometime?'

Drew shook her head. 'I'm a bit busy at the moment, what with it being the summer season. I'll settle the bill though.' She patted him on the shoulder and headed for the door with Vera in tow. She stepped out into the muggy air and breathed in. 'Thank God for that,' she said.

'You looked like you needed a little help,' Vera said and hooked an arm through Drew's. 'I'll walk you home.'

'Mother set me up,' Drew said, as they walked.

'I guessed,' Vera said. 'Daft bat!'

Drew chuckled. 'God, that was painful.'

'Looked it. Anyway, onwards and upwards, I think you'll enjoy the conversation with the reporter on Friday. I hope you don't mind; I contacted her to see if she would run a piece on the village, the market, and your café.'

Drew squeezed Vera's arm, comforted by the fact that Vera seemed to get her better than her mother did. 'I think it's a great idea. Thanks, V.'

Vera smiled. 'You going to the meeting on Friday evening?'

Drew grinned. 'It's a three-line whip, isn't it?'

Vera chuckled. 'I guess.'

7.

Faith wandered down the track towards Duckton House and Harriet's cottage. She stared at the bright pink and white camper van in the driveway with a mild amusement before turning her attention to the beautiful landscape beyond the buildings. The hills seemed to dominate the skyline for miles to the rear of the larger house leading up to the lake, and then there was the flatter terrain of the valley to the right leading into the town of Ferndale just short of the horizon. She approached the gate to a fenced field. A chestnut horse approached and snorted at her. She held out her hand and it nuzzled, snuffling at her palm and she stroked down its nose admiring its markings. Two ponies stood together at the other side of the field, munching at the grass. She stepped back from the fence as the deep barking sound came to her and before she could think about what to do next, a black and white Great Dane leapt at her and tumbled her to the ground.

'No, Flo!' a voice yelled, getting closer. But the dog didn't respond.

Faith groaned before being silenced by the wet tongue that sniffed at her ear and slobbered over her black shirt. Then a higher pitched noise came to her and she opened her eyes to see an orange poodle yapping at her left ear and baring its teeth. Suddenly the Great Dane was being dragged away and Grace was staring at her with wide eyes.

'God, I am so sorry,' Grace said. 'Archie, away,' she said, waving her arm. The poodle backed off and ran to the field, chased by the bounding giant of a dog.

'Well that was quite a welcome,' Faith said, pulling herself to her feet and brushing her hands down her top and trousers.

'I'm really sorry, Vicar. She's not normally like that,' Grace said, and flushed, aware that Flo had greeted her in exactly the same way the first time, too. Maybe it was a sign? Did she just think that?

'It's okay, just a bit of dirt and slobber. I was passing and thought I'd say hello. Beautiful horse,' she said, indicating to the chestnut.

'Do you ride?'

'A bit; you?'

'I'm learning.'

'She's doing very well,' Harriet said and wrapped her arms around Grace's waist from behind. 'Oh my God, did Flo jump up at you?'

'Yes,' Grace said and held Harriet's hands in place.

'I am so sorry, Vicar,' Harriet said. 'She's really just a pup.' Flo would always be a pup to Harriet even though she was close to eighteen months old and as big as a Shetland pony. She smiled apologetically.

Faith smiled as she nodded. 'Call me, Faith, please.' She studied the two women before turning her attention back to the chestnut horse. 'I was just saying, this chap's a real beauty.' She stroked the horse's nose and spoke to him.

'That's Buzz,' Harriet said with pride.

'His markings are stunning,' Faith said.

'And, that's Fizz on the left, and Midnight,' Harriet said, indicating to the two black and white ponies.

Faith was nodding. She seemed to have an affection for the horses and when she turned to face the two women there was tenderness in her gaze.

'Would you like a cup of tea?' Grace said.

'I don't want to disturb you,' Faith said.

'You're not. We're just about to have a drink. Could stretch to a gin or wine if you prefer?'

Faith smiled. 'Tea would be lovely. Thank you.' She followed Grace into the cottage, stood in the kitchen and admired the quaint space. 'Have you lived here long?'

Grace shook her head. 'I only moved here recently. I used to work in London, in the events industry, but sold my flat and business.'

'That's quite a change,' Faith said.

Grace held Faith's gaze. 'It's a long story, but I fell in love with Harriet. What can I say?' She shrugged and beamed a grin.

Faith nodded. 'Love does that,' She smiled.

'What about you?' Grace said.

Faith pursed her lips and shook her head, confused.

'You've had a similar experience?' Grace said then realised she was prying. 'Sorry, none of my business.'

'It's fine. Yes, I have moved for love,' Faith said. Her smile didn't give anything else away.

'You have a love of God, though, right?'

Faith smiled. 'I think they're quite different and one doesn't preclude the other,' she said.

Good to know. 'Yes, I suppose so,' Grace said. 'So, are you allowed to be in a relationship then?' Grace felt the heat rise to her cheeks, but this was important information to know. Her duty to Drew came before any notion of political or theological correctness.

Faith held Grace's gaze with intensity. 'Yes, I am. Though that doesn't always go down well with parishioners,' Faith said and a rue smile suggested she'd been on the receiving end of disapproval at some point in time.

Grace acknowledged Faith's honesty. 'I can imagine. You'll be safe here. People are very understanding.'

Faith nodded. 'They seem to be,' she said. 'But they can change. They don't expect their Vicar to be anything other than straight, most often white and male; oh, and usually ancient!'

Grace chuckled.

Harriet came through the front door and went to the sink to wash her hands.

'We were just talking about how accepting the village are of us and Faith was saying about the challenges of being a lesbian Vicar.'

'Oh, right. That's good, very good,' Harriet said and then realised her enthusiasm might have been misinterpreted. 'I'm going to have a glass of wine; anyone else?'

'I will,' Grace said and raised her eyebrows at Faith.

'Go on then, just a small glass,' Faith said.

Grace thought Faith looked more relaxed for having shared her news with them. Excitement brewed with the possibility that Faith and Drew could become an item after all. That debacle with the man in the pub the other night had been excruciatingly painful to watch. She hadn't known what had come over Drew's mother, but the woman was certainly looking through the wrong pair of glasses at her daughter. And that wasn't acceptable.

'So, how long have you ridden for?' Grace asked and blushed instantly. 'Faith rides horses,' she said to Harriet who was looking at her with an odd expression.

'That's great. We've just started up the riding lessons on weekend afternoons. You're more than welcome to get involved if you fancy it. After service of course,' Harriet said. She was beginning to waffle and stopped, turned her attention to the fridge, and pulled out a bottle of wine.

Faith smiled.

'I'm going to knock up some lunch. Would you like to join us?' Harriet said, looking to Faith.

'Harriet's cooking is the best,' Grace said.

Faith nodded. 'How can I refuse such an offer?'

'That's what I said. Got me into a lot of trouble,' Grace said and chuckled.

Harriet slapped her on the arm. 'Take your wine,' she said.

'We'll go and do some project planning then,' Grace said and led Faith through to the living room.

*

Faith ambled back to the church cottage with the sun on her back. She took the short climb up the steep hill to the church in her stride and stopped suddenly at the sight of Esther loitering at the door.

'Hello, Esther.' The woman looked pensive, pacing up and down. 'Is everything okay?'

'Could I have a word please, Vicar?'

Faith felt the woman's distress in the aching in her heart. She couldn't help it. Empathy was her greatest strength, but it had also been her downfall over the years. She always cared for people. Even supporting some of the worst offenders who had committed heinous crimes when others would have them hung if they could. She understood the protester's passion too, but she couldn't subscribe to it. 'Yes, of course; please come in.'

Esther flustered her way through the door and followed Faith to the front pew. Faith sat and encouraged Esther to sit next to her. Esther sat, clasped her hands in prayer, and stared at the crucifix sitting proudly on the wall at the head of the church.

'How may I be of help?' Faith said.

Tears trickled down Esther's weathered cheeks and she wiped them away. 'I feel so foolish coming to speak to you,' she said.

Faith studied the proud woman, silently.

'I don't know where to start,' Esther said.

'Maybe you would just like to take time here to think, or pray?'

Esther nodded and more tears rolled onto her cheeks.

Faith sat, her breathing soft and deep, effortless, supporting, holding the space around Esther, allowing the woman to reflect. Esther would speak when she was ready and when she was Faith would be there to listen to her.

'You know, when you bring children into this world, your only wish is that they stay healthy and happy.' Esther said. 'You want to protect them; make sure they are safe and don't come to any harm.'

Faith watched Esther as she worked through her troubled thoughts.

Esther suddenly turned to face Faith. 'Isn't family important, Vicar?' she said.

Faith held Esther's pleading gaze with affection. 'Some people think so, Esther, yes.'

'Community; children, and family, surely they're important,' Esther said.

Faith nodded. She agreed in principle.

'So, when the close friends you've had for nigh on thirty years start plotting against you and your family in the most dreadful way possible, what do you say to that, Vicar?'

Faith was acutely aware of Esther's anger coming through, though it wasn't clear to what specifically she was referring. 'I can't imagine how difficult that must be,' she said.

'Close friends! Pah! I don't think so,' Esther said, shaking her head back and forth, her body set in tension. 'Close friends don't set you up like that. Close friends don't make allegations against your family and then plot against you. They don't draw your children from you and pull apart the family unit, do they? That's not right, is it Vicar?'

It didn't sound right, but Faith was still clueless as to what specifically Esther was so worked up about. As far as she could recall, Esther and Doug only had one child and that was Drew. And Drew seemed perfectly happy. A little pushed around by Esther if she were going to be quite honest, but she couldn't tell Esther that. Faith hadn't picked up any indication that there was a plot against Drew, or Esther for that matter. But, Esther had certainly got her knickers in a twist about something. 'I honestly don't know what to say, Esther. I'm so sorry you're experiencing this.'

'And then, a bloody useless husband who does nothing about it. Just moans about wanting to move to Upper Duckton. I swear it's because he fancies that trollop of a barmaid up there, with her bust all exposed as she does. He won't be the only old fool to fall for that trick. Tilly, whatever her name is. Delusional old git! I'm sorry, Vicar. I've been feeling a bit out of sorts for a time now and these things are starting to get to me. I've got no one to speak to. I've felt quite crazy with it all going on behind my back.' Esther straightened her back in the wooden seat.

'It's been a difficult time for everyone, with Elvis passing, too,' Faith said wondering if grief was a part of the problem. Though, from where she was sitting, Esther seemed to be in a more frenzied state. 'Have you spoken to Jarid?' Maybe a medical perspective might be helpful?'

Wrong thing to say!

'That man's a part of the bloody problem. How can he be impartial?'

Faith was now completely confused. She had been given the rundown of who was who in the village. How on earth was Jarid related to the problem? He was Jenny's son and the Doctor supporting the village, and Jenny didn't look like the sort of person to break up families. On the contrary, from what she had heard, she was part of a group of women in the village insistent on bringing people together. She looked at Esther, estimating her at early to mid-fifties. There was no doubting she was in menopause and that might explain the slightly paranoid and irrational state that seemed to be behind her outburst. But it wasn't her place to tell Esther what to do. She held the distressed women with a compassionate gaze and waited.

Esther glared at Faith. 'You think I'm the crazy one?' she said and stood suddenly.

Faith shook her head, stood slowly, and in a soft voice, said, 'No, I don't think you're crazy at all, Esther.' But she hadn't finished the sentence before Esther had stomped up the aisle and through the church door.

Oh dear, that didn't go too well! Faith sighed. Esther certainly seemed troubled about Drew. She got the impression that Esther was seeking an affirmation that her perspective was correct and whoever it was who was plotting against her was wrong. Faith couldn't give that confirmation. For one, she didn't have enough information and secondly, she wasn't in a position to judge anyone.

8.

Drew walked through to the counter from the kitchen and slid the tray of cakes onto the surface. She opened the back of the cabinet and started filling the empty slots on the shelf. The place was buzzing, the bustling market attracting customers from far and wide and the flow through the café had been relentless. If this reporter turned up now there would be no hope of talking to her without interruption. Where the fuck was her mother when she needed her? Had she really got the hump about Steven?

Drew had felt sorry for the poor chap, after the event. But her guilt had soon passed as she had reflected on the fact that her mother had clearly set her up with him and therefore she should accept some responsibility for its utter and inevitable failure. She had torn up Steven's business card and thrown it in the bin and with that ritual she had found a sense of release.

At some point, she needed to talk to her mother and get her to open her eyes. She had hoped not to have to go through the 'I need to tell you something' routine, but it was becoming clear that Esther hadn't sparked to the fact that she was attracted to women. She couldn't blame Esther. She had only just owned the fact herself, even though if she looked back at her behaviour over the years – the feelings for Harriet that had never really gone away – she should have accepted herself years ago. She had buried her attraction for Harriet, watched from the outside and been there to pick Harriet up when she was down. She had settled for that. But now Harriet had Grace and they were good together. And then there was Faith. Just the thought of Faith had her feeling weak at the knees and something far more disconcerting. Lust - for a woman! The, I want you to fuck my brains out until I can't scream anymore but I don't have a clue where to start, kind of lust.

Drew moaned out loud and looked up to see a couple staring at her from the seat closest to the counter. Faith's seat! She flushed, cleared her throat, picked up a cloth and started wiping down the surface; thankful the chattering noise in the café had served to limit her embarrassment. She bent down to put the cloth under the counter and when she straightened, Faith stood in front of her with a smile on her face.

'Hi, can I get a coffee, please?' she said.

Drew's throat constricted and she tried to swallow. 'Sure.' She turned to the machine and loaded the coffee grounds. With precision, she pressed the coffee and twisted the handle into the slot. She pressed a button and turned towards Faith to realise Faith had been watching her closely. 'Would you like a bun?' she said and then closed her eyes as flaming heat flashed through her cheeks.

Faith chuckled. 'They are great buns, so yes, thanks,' she said.

Drew thought she had seen the Vicar's cheeks darken and that didn't help.

Another woman approached the counter and smiled warmly. 'Hi, I'm Annie Banks, I'm here to interview Drew Pettigrew,' she said and flashed her reporter's badge.

Bugger!

Annie noticed the dog collar and said, 'Excuse me, Vicar. Sorry, I've interrupted you.'

Faith smiled and Drew felt it in the warmth that settled in her stomach.

'No, you go ahead,' Faith said.

'I just need to finish this.' Drew pointed over her shoulder at the half-made coffee.

Faith looked around the room. Another customer approached the counter, and the absence of Esther became apparent. 'Do you want a hand?' she said to Drew.

Drew looked at her and was about to chuckle. Then she realised Faith was being serious. 'You know how to do this?'

'Sure,' Faith said. 'I haven't been a Vicar all my life.'

Drew's eyebrows rose. 'Are you sure?' She eyed Faith suspiciously.

'You look like you've got an appointment and there's already a queue.' She shrugged her shoulders and smiled. 'I can handle this; I promise.'

'Great, thanks.' Drew swapped places with the Vicar. 'Do you want a drink?' she said to Annie.

'Cappuccino would be lovely, thanks,' she said.

'Extra hot, extra shot, or how it comes?' Faith said, and Drew grinned.

'Extra shot would be great, thanks,' Annie said.

Faith loaded the coffee and started to froth the milk. 'I'll be with you in a second,' she said to the man waiting at the counter who was staring at the dog collar around her neck with an amused smile.

'It's novel having a vicar serving at the café,' Annie said, taking a seat at a table.

'You should have been here when the last vicar was alive; he owned and worked the pub as well as the church,' Drew said and chuckled.

'Really?' Annie laughed.

Drew studied her. She had a soft sweet laugh and curious blue eyes.

'What an interesting village. I was just talking to the lady at the market who does readings and potions.'

'Delia.'

'Yes, that's her.'

Drew chuckled. 'Did she do a reading for you? She's usually spot on.'

Annie's cheeks coloured and she looked to the window briefly. 'She said, I need to listen to my inner voice and that love will come where I least expect it.' She shrugged and Drew sensed sadness beneath the veneer through which the woman carried out her professional life.

Drew smiled warmly.

Annie held her gaze before continuing. 'So, I got an email from a lady called Vera who said we might be interested in running an article or two on village life here,' she said, and the professional smile was back in place.

'How can I help?'

Faith approached with two coffees and placed them on the table.

Drew smiled. She hadn't been expecting a drink and was impressed by the creative swan-like design set in the creamy milk. 'Thanks.' She picked up the coffee and sipped. 'Hmm, that's good,' she said.

Annie sipped at her coffee. 'Hmm, very good.'

Faith nodded and returned to the counter.

Annie held up her reporter's badge. 'I work for a magazine called Gay Northwest, have you heard of it?' she said.

Drew choked on her drink, splattered cream across the table and then continued to cough trying to recover the air to her lungs. 'I'm. Sorry. No.' She spluttered and stuttered at the same time, said, 'Sorry, that was the wrong hole,' and then wished she'd kept her mouth shut.

Annie chuckled and handed Drew a serviette. 'We cover the whole of the Northwest of England and report on the culture of local towns and villages so that the LGBTQ community can be fully informed about the places they visit.'

Drew slowly placed the cup on the saucer. She would kill Vera! 'Right,' she said. She picked up the cup again and took another sip.

'So, tell me, what's it like as a lesbian in such a small village?'

Drew snorted into the coffee and sprayed the table, again. 'I'm so sorry,' she said, and smiled apologetically as she wiped at the spillage with the damp serviette, heat flushing her cheeks. Then, she saw Faith watching her from the counter and wanted to crawl under the table. Oh my God. 'Umm, I um, I never really thought about it,' she said, and in some small way she felt good about the indirect admission of her sexuality. 'Everyone here is very friendly. We have two female couples in the village.' She shrugged.

'Excellent. Quite the Hebden Bridge of the Northwest, then?' Annie said and pulled out her notebook and pen. She jotted something down and looked back to Drew.

*

Faith smiled as she observed the two women talking. Something had clearly tickled Drew and it was good to see her happy and laughing. She certainly looked more at ease with the reporter than she had with the man who had asked her for a date the previous week, and in Faith's mind, there was a good reason for that. There was no doubt that Drew was gay and so was the woman she was talking to; her gaydar was too good not to have noticed. The twinge in her gut was also an indicator. One that told her about her own feelings towards the attractive café owner. She had noticed Drew from the first moment of setting eyes on her and had been convinced Drew had noticed her. But Drew it seemed, was also firmly inside the closet and there was no way she was going to bust that door down. She had fallen foul of doing that once before and it had cost her; her place in the community and the woman. Some people didn't take too well to knowing their vicar was gay.

She gazed at Drew and sighed then turned her attention back to the counter, wiped down the work-surface, knocked out the used coffee grains and rinsed the filter. As she turned back to the counter, she jolted. 'Hello, Esther, can I get you a drink?' Taken aback by the woman's presence a prick of guilt reminded her of the conversation they had had earlier and her musings about Drew.

'Vicar, what on earth are you doing behind there?' Esther said, removing her coat and taking it into the kitchen. She returned to the counter, rolling up her sleeves. 'This is no place for a woman of your standing.'

Faith placed a gentle hand on the woman's arm and smiled. 'I'm having a bit of fun actually,' she said and grinned broadly. 'I used to work in a café, a few years ago now. I enjoyed it.'

Esther forced a grin to appear and Faith squeezed her arm.

'What about you and me double up, while Drew is doing the interview?' Faith said, indicating with her eyes to the table Drew was sat at.

Esther peered across the room. 'Who's that she's with?' Her back stiffened and her nose lifted.

'She's a magazine reporter.'

'What does she want?' Esther peered closer.

'I don't know. I think she's doing a piece on village life,' Faith said.

Esther mumbled something and then turned her attention to the approaching customer.

'Two Latte's please, one extra hot the other with one shot.'

'One extra shot, the other extra hot,' Esther said as she wrote the note.'

'No,' the man started.

'Got it,' Faith said and smiled at him.

'Thanks, Vicar,' he said.

'Can we interest you in a cake?' Faith said.

The man studied the counter. 'Two of those, please.' He pointed.

Esther pulled two custard cream slices out of the cabinet, plated them and by the time she placed them on the counter the two coffees were waiting for her. She took the man's money and turned to Faith. 'How did you do that pattern?' she said.

Faith chuckled. 'Would you like me to show you?'

Esther smiled and for the first time looked as though she were enjoying herself.

*

Drew had been aware of her mum arriving and settling behind the counter and it had allowed her to relax into the conversation with Annie. Seeing her laughing had also made her realise that she hadn't seen Esther untroubled for a long time. It was comforting to see but what was more intriguing was the woman who had elicited that response from her. Every so often she had caught Faith working the coffee machine, interacting with the customers, wiping down the counter. Having a vicar serving coffee had become quite a talking point. She had overheard conversations at other tables making mention of the fact and it warmed her to watch. Faith had the skills of a trained barista and there was something hot about that. She had drifted into fantasy about the two of them making coffee together and then making so much more. Faith seemed to be doing a great job of selling the cakes too. She was good. She was fucking hot. And, she was still the Vicar!

'Sorry?' she said. She'd completely missed what Annie had said.

'I'd better let you get back to work,' Annie said, smiling. 'So, you said there's a mic night at the pub next Wednesday?'

'Yes, it's open to anyone; so, you just show up on the night, put your name down for a time slot and then play. It's very popular.'

'Great, I'll come back for that,' Annie said. 'Thanks for the coffee. It was lovely meeting you.' She held out her hand and when Drew took it she held Drew's gaze and then held her hand a few seconds longer. 'I hope you'll be there.'

Drew smiled. 'I will,' she said and spontaneously pulled the woman into a hug.

'What are they doing now?' Esther said, scowling across the room at the two women in an embrace.

Faith shrugged, though her insides had done a quick spin at the physical contact between the two women. 'Saying goodbye, I guess.' She hadn't meant to sound sarcastic and as it happened Esther didn't seem to have registered the words let alone the tone.

Esther mumbled something inaudible.

'Esther, Drew's been in a meeting to talk about promoting the café. It's a good thing,' she said, and then wondered who she was trying to persuade. Faith watched Esther's eagle eyes on Drew and pondered. Drew's mother seemed hypersensitive and more than a little controlling when it came to her daughter's acquaintances. She took a deep breath and released it slowly and then smiled as Drew approached.

'Hi mum,' Drew said and smiled. 'You having fun?' she added before Esther could make some scolding response.

'We were,' Faith said, again before Esther could speak. Surely, Esther would have no choice but to mellow?

'Who was that?' Esther said to Drew, in a tone that came across as somewhere between aggressive, defensive and downright interfering.

Maybe not that mellow then!

'That was Annie. She's from the.' Drew stopped. No way could she go there. 'She's from a local magazine and they want to run an article on the village.'

'See, Esther, nothing to worry about,' Faith said and placed a gentle hand on the woman's arm.

'You can speak to her yourself. She's coming back for the mic night on Wednesday,' Drew said and shrugged.

'Oh, right,' Esther said and seemed to back down.

Faith studied Drew intently, her insides churning. Her smile felt tight; her jaw even tighter. She breathed slowly reminded of her civic duty to the community. 'That will be wonderful,' she said.

'Thanks for helping out,' Drew said to Faith, her tone soft. Her gaze lingered and then she was aware that Esther was still in the room, though thankfully the woman had her attention on pouring the foamy milk into a swan-like pattern.

'Here, what do you think? Faith has been teaching me,' Esther said, presenting the cup, with a proud smile.

Drew stared at the wavy splodge with spikes and grinned. 'Looks great, mum,' she said and when she looked up Faith's green eyes were on her.

'Right, I'd better be off.' Faith said. 'I'll see you both at the meeting later?'

Drew nodded.

'Yes, thank you, Vicar,' Esther said.

9.

'Huh hum. Huh hum.' Doris projected her voice as best she could across the room, barely impacting the chattering villagers. It seemed impossible to think that so many different conversations could go on in such a small space at the same time.

Doug looked around the table. Bloody hell, this meeting would take forever. Everyone seemed to have shown up tonight. Even Kev and Luke had pulled themselves away from the farm to attend. That was a first. They both sat gawping, wide-eyed, at the woman at the head of the table. And it wasn't Doris or Sheila they were starry-eyed over, either. Bryan was also here, which meant that the pub was shut. This must be serious. The chattering continued and Doris's feeble efforts to control the group were starting to irritate him. He leaned across the table, picked up the gavel and banged it three times on the wooden surface.

Silence came quickly and he put the gavel back.

'Thank you, Doug,' Doris said and nodded at him.

'You're welcome, Doris,' Doug said, crossing his arms. He glanced at his watch; this was going to take at least two hours. He huffed and slouched back in the seat and Esther nudged him in the ribs, so he sat back up again.

'Good evening, everyone, how lovely to see so many people here tonight,' Doris said, glancing over her spectacles around the room and smiling.

Mumbles of good evening echoed back and then the occasional sniffle and cough as people settled in their seat.

'There are a couple of things on the agenda for this extraordinary meeting tonight, but first I want us to thank the Vicar for a wonderful service for our dearly departed Elvis,' she said and started applauding.

'Here, here,' Doug said and mumbled affirmations continued around the room.

Faith smiled.

Drew caught her eye, instantly flushed, and looked away.

'Good. Right, moving on. The first item for us to discuss is a proposition from Grace and Faith, that we construct new children's activities in the park. Grace has been so kind as to draw up plans for the project, but the idea is to build a skate park and also a natural wood play area that includes climbing frames, swings, ropes, slides and bridges. We would need to raise £10,000 to cover the cost of materials. This is much reduced because Grace has managed to source support from her previous events supplier contacts so the labour for construction will be donated.'

'Well done, Grace,' Doug said, nodding his head enthusiastically.

Grace smiled at him and Harriet squeezed her leg.

'I'll propose that,' Vera said, from the bottom of the table.

'I'll second,' Jenny said, sat next to her.

'Are there any objections, in principle, to the proposed plan?' Doris said, gazing around the room at shaking heads. 'Good,' she said. 'Sheila if you could minute that, please?'

'I have, thank you, Mrs Akeman,' Sheila said, with a coy smile.

Blimey, this was going well. Doug looked at his watch. Only ten minutes in and even old Sheila Goldsworth seemed to be on top of her secretarial duties.

'Right, now on to the matter of funding the project,' Doris said.

Doug rolled his eyes. Of course! He hadn't factored in that little discussion.

'Does anyone have any ideas about how we might fundraise this venture?' Doris said.

Of course, they did! That would blow the timings.

'What about a psychic night?' Delia announced. 'I've got a few friends with different specialisms who I'm sure would love to get involved. We could do past-life regression, spirit contact with the afterlife, crystal healing, readings and all sorts of wonderful things.'

'Good God,' Doug said. 'Sorry Vicar!'

'There's lots of demand for Spiritual Healing, Doug Pettigrew,' Delia said.

'There's only one spiritual healing I know that works, and that comes in the form of a good pint,' he said and chuckled.

Faith's eyes widened, and Drew catching the look of abject horror on her face started to chuckle. She couldn't imagine any two disciplines being more in opposition than the church and the spiritual healing world, even though in some respects they shared the same goals.

'I wonder if that might be a bit tricky?' Drew said to Delia. 'You might go offending old Hilda Spencer with all that spiritual power in one room,' she said, trying to soften the blow of rejection she felt sure was going to come. She caught Faith's eyes on her; only it wasn't with the soft, tender glances she had seen before. The green had all but disappeared into the well of white. Shit! No one's told Faith about Hilda Spencer, the Duckton-by-Dale friendly ghost.

'Perhaps we could do a ghost hunt,' Delia said. 'Like *Ghostbusters*,' she added, excitedly.

'Bloody hell, she'll be talking about *Patrick Swayze* next,' Doug mumbled and Esther dug him in the ribs.

'Oh, I did love *Heather O'Rourke*,' Delia said.

Here we go. 'That was *Poltergeist*,' Doug said and rolled his eyes.

'Huh hum. If we could get back to the point please,' Doris said.

'Well done, Doris,' Doug said.

'You too, Doug,' Doris said, and glared at him.

Grace and Harriet sniggered from across the table.

'A ghost hunt could be fun. What do you reckon, Vera? We could use your place,' Grace said. She was joking and when Vera seemed to give it serious consideration, she felt the colour drain from her. She still couldn't walk into Duckton House without a chill running the length of her spine.

'That's a good idea. It's different too. There's a lot of people into the paranormal,' Vera said.

Doug was shaking his head. 'Real money-spinner that one,' he said.

'I reckon we could make over a thousand pounds,' Vera said. 'People will pay a fortune for a good ghost hunt and especially if we can throw in a couple of workshops which means Delia and her friends can offer readings and sessions. We could run a weekend event. What do you reckon, a dozen people, Jenny?'

Jenny was nodding and Delia had an excited grin on her face. Faith looked decidedly pale by comparison with her normal healthy appearance.

'There's no guarantee Hilda will show up of course. Vicar, would the church object to a paranormal night? We can advertise it locally so it should be easy to fill at short notice. I would have thought we want to get it in the diary for mid-October at the latest. That's about six weeks away. What do you think?'

Faith gazed around the room feeling the heat of several pairs of eyes directed at her. Decisions like this could be touch and go in a small community but it seemed everyone around the table approved of the idea. It wouldn't clash with Harvest Festival, which was late September. 'No, the church would not object. In fact, why don't we include the church in the hunt?' she said.

'Ooh!' Delia squealed. 'What a fabulous idea.'

'We'll take on the organising of that then,' Vera said, referring to Jenny and Delia.

'Minuted,' Shelia said and planted a full-stop on the page with dramatic effect.

Blimey, she is in good form! Doug thought, and raised his hand in deference to the rules of the summer fete meeting.

'Yes, Doug.' Doris said, with a smile.

'What about one of those impersonation singers? We could run a dinner night at the pub?' he said.

'Good idea,' Bryan said. 'We haven't had anything like that before. That would draw the crowds.'

'An Elvis impersonator?' Jarid said. 'Like a memorial to our Elvis?'

'You know he didn't like Elvis,' Doug said.

Faith frowned and Drew felt compassion towards her.

'I know, but everyone else in the village does, and Elvis was heard singing *I can't help falling in love with you* at the fete, so I don't think he would object.'

'Nice song,' Grace whispered to Harriet and got a tighter squeeze of her thigh in response.

'Are there any objections in principle?' Doris said.

Shaking heads answered the question.

'What about a British Bake-Off,' Esther blurted and then realising she hadn't followed protocol, put her hand up.

'That sounds like a good idea,' Grace said. 'Drew's buns are to die for,' she added in a serious tone and the next squeeze to her thigh had her jumping from the chair.

Drew was sure Faith had politely stifled a snigger and thankfully everyone else seemed to just be nodding in approval.

'We could run an antiques roadshow,' Esther said enthusiastically, her hand still raised. She was on a roll now. 'I know a man.'

'No!' Jenny, Vera, Delia, Harriet and Grace yelled in unison and the men in the room frowned.

'It's not that bad an idea,' Doug said and reached for his wife's hand to console her.

'We could see if *Fiona Bruce* could come and host it for us.' Delia added, forgetting why she had objected and getting caught up in the excitement.

'No!' Jenny and Vera said.

'Hmm, that idea's gaining legs,' Grace mumbled. Another squeeze and a stern but teasing glare from her girlfriend and she shrugged with a smile. 'Actually, what about seeing if we can get *Sandi Toksvig* or *Sue Perkins* for the Bake-Off judging?' she said and grinned.

Esther seemed to scowl at Grace.

'Ooh, now that sounds fun,' Jenny said and beamed at Vera.

'Easy tiger,' Vera whispered to Jenny and she chuckled.

'I think we have quite a few things to coordinate,' Faith said, hoping to ease the tension and reduce the burden of the arrangements.

'I'm happy to see if I can source someone to judge. It would attract more competitors,' Grace said. 'We'll come up with a plan and report back.'

'Oh, okay,' Faith said and smiled weakly. She was already feeling overwhelmed with the number of activities the villagers were thinking of putting on.

'I'd like to get a group of us to do a walk or climb.' Kev said.

All eyes turned to the unassuming farmer.

'Luke and me have been discussing it. We reckon we could do a four-peaks kind of challenge, maybe set up Abseiling for the kids. I can get a couple of farmers involved,' he said. 'We need to do it before the end of October, because of the weather. Maybe we could have it the same weekend as the ghost hunt and create a buzz about the place?'

Delia looked stricken. 'Luke, you can't be serious? Abseiling? You can't swim for heaven's sake.'

'Abseiling mum; hanging from a rock,' Luke said and laughed.

'You could kill yourself,' Delia said, looking suddenly quite stressed. 'I'll need to do a reading first,' she added, and dived into her handbag and started shuffling the Tarot cards.

Luke rolled his eyes. 'We'll make sure it's safe, mum. We know the instructors over Cariscarn who'll help, and Jarid will be there as the medical backup.' He nodded towards the doctor who shoved his thumb in the air in response.

'Is the antique roadshow going ahead, Mrs Akeman? I'm sorry, the last note I managed to get down was Drew's buns for the Bake-Off,' she said.

Grace sniggered out loud and then so did Harriet.

'Sorry,' they said in unison, clearing their throats and trying not to make eye contact with anyone in the room, and especially not Drew.

Drew held her head in her hands, her cheeks burning, aware that Faith was smiling at her.

'I think there was a definitive no to the roadshow, and a possible yes to the climbing, walking activity, Sheila. There's no decision on the impersonation evening as far as I can tell,' Faith said. 'The intention is to combine the walking event with the ghost hunt weekend, to create an atmosphere.'

Sheila scribbled frantically.

Doug studied the Vicar with a wry smile. She's picking up the ropes quickly! 'We could make the walking into a competition with Upper and Lower Duckton,' he said.

'That's a good idea,' Kev said. Luke nodded in approval next to him.

'We could have the gin bar running alongside the Bake-Off,' Harriet said. 'Drew and I will pick up the coordination of that.'

'I'd like to help with the Bake-Off,' Faith said and glanced briefly at Drew before settling her eyes on Harriet.

'Brilliant,' Harriet said.

'We should get that reporter along to cover the events?' Vera said. 'Added publicity and maybe she can help with advertising too?'

Faith looked to Drew and couldn't work out what she thought of the idea of the reporter being around. Her own feelings were apparent in the twisting in her stomach, but she couldn't let her desires get in the way of doing what was right for the village.

'Good idea,' Jenny said.

'I agree,' Esther said and Jenny, Vera and Delia stared at her in surprise.

'Well, that's a result. Perhaps she's coming around?' Jenny whispered to Vera.

'I bet she doesn't have a bloody clue who the reporter works for,' Vera said and chuckled. 'Haven't you noticed? She's ignored us the whole meeting.'

Delia turned the five of wands – competition, rivalry, and conflict. 'It needs to be a competition,' she announced.

The room went quiet and everyone stared at her.

'The climbing, walking, thing. It needs to be a competition. I just ran the cards,' she said, gazing at the faces as if to say what are you staring at me like that for?

'I said that already,' Doug said and rolled his eyes.

'Shall I minute that?'

'Yes please,' Faith said.

'Can we move this along?' Doug said, looking at his watch. 'We need to get the bar open.'

'Here, here,' Bryan said, glancing at his watch.

'I'll ask the reporter. She's coming to cover the mic night on Wednesday,' Drew said.

'Good, good,' Vera said and sat back with a smug grin on her face.

Esther smiled at the three older women sat to her left, but it was a tight smile, close to a grimace and her nose still sat as if she had a nasty smell underneath it.

'Thank you, everyone,' Doris announced. 'Right the second point we need to address is.' She looked at the note in front of her.

'Bloody hell,' Doug mumbled. He wasn't alone.

'We need to confirm that we plan to hold a Halloween event for the children up at the church this year and also the Bonfire night. I think November 5th falls on a Thursday, that's right,' she said, consulting her pocket diary. 'So, Halloween would be the previous Saturday.' She looked to Faith for an answer.

Faith pondered the church's principles around Halloween – it was normally frowned upon, some might think heresy, but this wonderful bunch of people didn't seem to discriminate in the same way as others might and if they could hold a ghost hunt at the church then why not Halloween. The kids always loved trick-or-treating. 'Of course,' she said and smiled.

'Excellent,' Doris said.

'We'll build the bonfire in the field down from the park again,' Kev said. 'I'll sort that with the lads.'

'I'll sort the catering for the bonfire night,' Drew said.

'Excellent,' Doris said.

'I've noted that, Mrs Akeman,' Sheila said.

'Thank you, Sheila.' Doris looked around the room. 'Is there any other business?'

Doug said a quick prayer then groaned as Grace raised her hand.

'I won't take long. Just to say, I've made enquiries about taking over the pub and it seems all is going to go smoothly on that front.'

A loud cheer went up and echoed around the room and Grace flushed. She raised her hands to silence everyone.

'Bryan will continue to manage the day-to-day operation,' she said.

'Well done, Bry. What you still doing here then?' Doug quipped.

'And I've also asked Tilly to join us behind the bar, and I'm delighted to say she's agreed,' Drew said.

'Ooh, that's good news,' Doug said. His eyes sparkled and his cheeks flushed and Esther elbowed him rather aggressively in the ribs.

'What you doing woman?' Doug retorted.

'He's got no chance,' Vera whispered to Jenny.

'What do you mean?' Jenny said. Her gaydar was crap!

'That's excellent news,' Doris said.

Sheila scribbled a note to the effect and looked up with a broad grin.

'Well, if there isn't any other business,' Doris said, glancing around the room.

'Please no!' Doug whimpered.

Bryan put up his hand. 'Just one more thing,' he said.

Doug moaned and pointed repeatedly at his watch.

'Ellena's starting the Zumba classes again from next Monday, here in the hall,' he said and beamed a proud grin around the room.

'Ooh, good.' Jenny declared, looking at Vera and Delia and nodding in approval. 'That will be better than the video in the front room.'

Vera rolled her eyes. 'My thigh's ache just thinking about it,' she said. They never made it off the couch watching the video, they're not going to cope with the real thing. There was no way Ellena was going to let them sit and watch. They'd better get practising!

Doris looked around the room. 'If that's everything, then I declare the meeting closed. Thank you, everyone.'

Thank God! Doug stood, eyed Bryan, Kev, Jarid and Luke then headed straight for the pub.

Grace turned to Harriet and Drew and smiled. 'I have no idea how the heck we're going to pull this lot off but it's going to be fun trying.' She looked at Drew and grinned. 'How're your buns?' she said.

'Fuck off,' Drew said, in jest, and then started laughing.

Faith approached the women and Drew did her best to avoid eye contact, but not before Grace had clocked a glance that had passed between the two of them.

'That seemed to go well,' Faith said.

The women nodded.

'We're going for a drink at the bar. Would you like to join us?' Grace said.

Faith looked at her watch. 'I'm sorry; I've got work to do. Maybe another night?'

Drew felt disappointment flood her, her heart landed heavily, and she sighed. She smiled weakly and noticed Faith staring at her with a different kind of look.

'Maybe I could come for one quick drink,' Faith said.

10.

'Testing, testing.' Doris's voice squeaked through the microphone, sending a high-pitched squeal around the pub.

'Bloody hell, woman,' Doug complained, poking his finger in his ear and wriggling it.

Doris moved the microphone and tried again.

'Bravo,' Doug said and raised his pint in a toast to Doris's achievement then turned his attention to the redhead at the bar. 'So, Tilly, how you finding the Crooked Billet?'

Tilly grinned. 'Oh, you know Doug, turn right at the junction and straight down the hill,' she said and chuckled.

'Friendlier than that lot though, eh?' he said.

'Why you always bleating about moving up there, then?' Esther said as she approached, clearly having overheard the conversation.

Tilly laughed at the blush that graced Doug's ruddy cheeks. He was so under the thumb! She took a glass from the shelf, pulled the lever and handed Doug another pint. 'Reckon you're gonna need this,' she said and winked.

Esther elbowed him in the ribs.

'What was that for?' he complained, feigning innocence, though his eyes had definitely been settled on Tilly's ample bosom at the time.

Esther glared at Doug and stormed out of the bar.

'Right, if I could have your attention, please.' Doris bellowed across the pub.

The hush moved from the stage area back through the room.

'If you would like to sign in for an open mic session, please approach the table. The first act will start in half-an-hour,' she said. 'We will come around the bar with voting slips just before the acts begin.' She sat back and waited. Sheila sat next to her, pen poised.

A couple of people went to the table and signed on the piece of paper. Bryan set up background music and went back to serving behind the bar.

Tilly watched the fair-haired woman approach with a quizzical gaze. She was looking around the room as if to locate someone. 'Can I help you?' she said.

'Hi, I'm looking for Drew,' the woman said.

Tilly looked into the light-blue eyes and a flood of warmth rushed to her fair cheeks, hiding the light smattering of freckles that bridged her nose. 'She'll be in shortly. Are you the reporter?'

The woman held Tilly's gaze and smiled. 'You're expecting me?'

Tilly nodded.

'I'm Annie,' the woman said, and held out her hand.

Tilly took it, felt the tenderness of the fingers wrapped around hers in the darkening of her cheeks. 'I'm Tilly. Welcome to Duckton-by-Dale. Can I get you a drink?'

'Umm.' Annie looked at the badges on the ale pumps. 'What do you recommend?'

'The Freckled Duck is a local favourite,' Tilly said. 'If you're into beer? We do a lovely chilled Sauvignon and a wide range of gins.'

Annie pondered the gin selection at the back of the bar. 'Wow, that's impressive. I'll have a G&T, please,' she said.

Tilly chuckled. 'You'll fit in well, here,' she said. 'Which one?'

'You choose,' Annie said and turned to look around the bar. She smiled. The tables were already filling and the atmosphere seemed chilled out. There was a jovial feel to the place and people were smiling in her direction and dipping their heads in polite welcome.

'Here, try this.' Tilly handed over the tall tumbler. 'I went with something a little spicy,' she said and her rosy cheeks shone.

Annie sipped at the long drink and mumbled. 'Hmm, that's nice. What is it?'

'It's the Opihr. It's crafted using exotic handpicked botanicals such as spicy cubeb berries from Indonesia, black pepper from India and coriander from Morocco,' she said and grinned with pride.

Annie studied the barwoman with interest. 'Wow, you know your gins,' she said.

'I'm just learning. Grace is the real expert,' she said.

'Did I just hear my name?'

Annie turned.

'Hi I'm Grace.' Grace held out her hand and smiled. 'You must be Annie. Welcome to Duckton.' She looked at Harriet by her side.

'Hi, Annie, I'm Harriet. It's so exciting you're here.' She smiled, leaned into Grace and snuggled her arm.

'Grace, Harriet,' Annie repeated, making a mental note of their names.

'Hi, Annie,' Drew said, and picking up from where they had left off in the café, gave Annie a friendly hug. 'We're so glad you could make it. Good to see Tilly's looking after you.' Drew smiled. 'Please, make yourself at home.' She indicated with her arms around the pub, her eyes scanning the room for one particular person. She couldn't see Faith and turned her attention to her friends. 'Gin anyone?'

'Sure,' Grace and Harriet said in unison.

'Coming up,' Tilly said.

'Are any of you singing?' Annie said.

Drew shook her head.

'Good God, no,' Grace said. 'Definitely not one of my strengths.' She laughed. 'Do you sing?'

Annie nodded then sipped her drink.

'Have a go,' Harriet said, excitedly.

Tilly put four gins on the bar. 'I'm going to sing,' she said and glanced at Annie.

Faith approached the group from behind. 'Evening, all,' she said, and as the women's heads turned towards her, her focus lingered on Drew before acknowledging the others.

'Are you performing, Vicar?' Annie said.

'Will it help with publicity?' Faith said and chuckled.

Annie tilted her head and smiled. 'It would be novel,' she said.

Grace cleared her throat. 'Annie, could we catch up later? I have a proposition I'd like to talk to you about,' she said.

Annie nodded. 'Sound's intriguing.'

'It's about the activities we are planning, to raise funds to rejuvenate our park.'

The mic squealed again and groans echoed around the pub. 'If I could have your attention, ladies and gentlemen, please. The first act will begin in ten minutes. Voting slips are at the desk if you don't have one already. Thank you.'

'Grace, Grace?'

Grace turned towards the frantic call. 'Oh, hi Delia. What's up?'

Delia's eyes darted around the bar and then she reached into her oversized handbag, pulled out a clear bottle of liquid and handed it to Drew. Delia had obviously designed the sticky label on the front of the bottle because it sat a little off centre and the font wasn't crisp and clean. 'It's homemade gin,' she said and crossed her arms with a smug look on her face. 'I've tested it with Vera and Jenny and they think it's the best yet. I thought you'd like to try it, for the gin wagon and maybe the pub. Our own local brew; what do you think?'

Grace studied the label; the word Vanilla was written at an angle running diagonally across it and in small font above the words, 'say yes to'. Grace chuckled. 'Let me guess, it tastes of Vanilla?' she said.

'How did you know?' Delia chuckled. 'It's got my special herbs in it; the new version. You should try it,' she said.

'I'll have a taste,' Harriet said.

'Me too,' Drew said and looked at Faith who shrugged her shoulders and then nodded.

'I'm game,' Annie said.

Tilly studied the reporter with a warm smile then turned to Grace. 'Shall I take that behind here then, boss?' She held out her hand and Grace handed over the bottle.

'I'll have one of those, now,' Delia said, rubbing her hands with excitement.

'Where are Vera and Jenny?' Grace said to Delia.

Delia gave her attention to Tilly pouring her gin. 'They're on their way,' she said but it wasn't like them to be late for a pub event and there was no sign of Esther either.

The background music silenced and the first act, a group of three, started to prepare themselves, tuning their instruments.

'Shall we grab a seat?' Harriet said, indicating to a table towards the back of the pub, furthest from the music. She set off across the room and the other women followed.

'So, Vicar, no sign of Hilda, then?' Grace said as they sat.

Faith raised her eyebrows and then smiled.

'Hilda?' Annie said and looked from one woman to the next.

'Our friendly ghost,' Grace said and sipped at her gin, watching the reporter turn pale. She chuckled. 'Gave me the fright of my life when I saw her the second time.'

'You've seen her, twice?' Annie said, wide-eyed.

'Yep.'

Then Annie looked at each of the women again and started laughing. 'You're kidding me, right?'

96

Faith remained silent, but the other three shook their heads in response and Annie seemed to disappear into a world of her own.

Drew reached out and touched Faith's arm. 'Hilda is friendly,' she whispered, reassuringly, though the sensation of the warm skin tingled in her fingers and sent a rush of fire to the hairs in her neck, and she let go instantly. Since the revelation at the committee meeting, she hadn't had the chance to explain to Faith about the rumours surrounding Hilda and it was clear Faith was still processing this new-found knowledge with healthy scepticism. She just didn't want Faith to be fearful though.

Faith nodded, a slight frown accompanying her thoughts.

'We're going to put on a ghost hunt in October,' Grace said. 'It's one of the things I was hoping to chat to you about getting publicity for.'

Annie looked vacantly at Grace, and sipped at the gin.

Drew looked from Faith to Annie and back again. It had never occurred to her that some people really were wary of the paranormal. She smiled at Annie and then at Faith, *I'm Coming Out* echoing in the background from the trio who clearly couldn't sing.

*

'What are you doing out here? Daft old bat,' Vera said to Esther, who was sat on the bench in the village square.

'Bugger off,' Esther said.

Vera softened her demeanour and sat on the seat next to her old friend. Jenny sat the other side of Esther and stared across the square towards the pub.

'What's wrong, Esther?' Vera said.

Tears rolled onto Esther's cheeks and she sniffled.

Jenny pulled out a clear glass bottle, with the label Vanilla on the front of it, unscrewed the top and passed it across to Esther. 'Here, sup this, it's medicinal,' she said and pushed the bottle into Esther's hands.

Esther studied the label, lifted the bottle to her lips, sniffed. Bugger it. Why not? It would be the first drink she had taken since getting drunk on the raspberry gin at the summer fete, and previously had only ever been seen with the occasional sherry at a special event, but feeling as out of sorts as she had these last weeks, the offer was too tempting to refuse. She took a sip from the bottle, started to choke, and put the back of her hand to her mouth. 'Bloody hell, what's in that?' she said and then a smile tried to form. 'Lovely vanilla taste,' she added.

'Delia's been practising with her new herbs. We're going into business together,' Jenny said. 'What do you reckon?'

She sipped again. 'Tastes very good,' she said and her features seemed to soften.

'So, come on, what's got up your nose, then?' Vera said and reached for the bottle. She took a long swig and wrapped an arm around Esther.

Esther tensed, and then relaxed a fraction. 'I think Doug's having an affair,' she said.

'What?' Jenny said, trying to hold back a laugh. He might have been a good-looking chap a few years back, but she couldn't think of anyone locally who might be interested in Doug in that way – or he in them in fact. Whether Esther believed it or not she was his one and only love. And, everyone in the village had known each other for years, so if something were going to happen, it would have already. 'Who?'

'That trollop from the bar,' Esther said.

Vera sniggered. 'You referring to Tilly?'

'Yes, redhead, big boobs, and a bigger grin with perfect white teeth,' she said and swiped the bottle from Vera and took a sip of the gin.

'No chance,' Vera said and took the bottle back again.

'What would you know?' Esther retorted.

'She's gay, Esther. You know,' she said, pointing to Jenny and then herself as if to say, just like us.

Esther pulled away from Vera's arm around her shoulder. 'Gay? With boobs like those! Looks more like she belongs on page three of *The Sun*,' she said.

'Yeah well, Samantha Fox was gay too,' Vera said and seemed to dip into a distant and pleasant fantasy.

'Oh, good God!' Esther said.

'A bit like Drew, eh?' Vera said. It was one step too far.

'Don't you dare label my Drew in that way,' Esther said and stood sharply.

Vera and Jenny stood and studied Esther.

'Why are you so against your daughter being gay?' Jenny said with a softness that she knew Vera wasn't capable of right now.

Vera's eyes narrowed, her lips pinched, and the lines that aged her cheeks deepened. Jenny smiled tenderly at her.

'How can she be?' Esther said and wiped at the tears that had slipped onto her cheeks.

'Why does it matter so much?' Jenny said. She reached for Esther's hand and squeezed it tightly but Esther pulled away.

'It's not normal. How can she have a family, and what will happen when she changes her mind? What respectable man is going to want her then?'

Vera looked as if steam would burst from her any moment. And then it did, and she shouted. 'You bigoted old fart!' She gasped. 'Seriously? We've been friends for how long? And, now you decide that being gay isn't fucking normal. What does that make us?' She pointed to Jenny and then to herself. 'What about Harriet and Grace, Tilly, Kev?'

Esther looked at her oddly.

'Yes, every one of us Esther! How about that?'

Esther didn't speak.

'Do you have any idea what happens to a child rejected by their parent because that arse of a parent doesn't agree with, doesn't understand, or doesn't fucking like the fact that their son or daughter loves someone they don't approve of? Who are you to tell Drew who she should fall in love with? Surely, it's more important that she finds love and is happy? You want to force her to try and be with a man. Why?'

Jenny reached out to Vera to calm her.

Vera backed down, took a deep breath and paced around then came to stand next to Jenny. When she spoke her tone was softer, reflective. 'My mother rejected me, Esther and I can tell you from first-hand experience it breaks your heart more than any lover can. To feel that you are unworthy, unloved by the one person you crave unconditional love from, it cuts deep and it's not an easy pain to recover from.'

Jenny squeezed Vera's arm again.

Esther was shaking her head. 'It's different. Drew's never been like that,' she said.

Vera was shaking her head. 'You really are as blind as a fucking old bat,' she said. 'She was in love with Harriet for years. Did you not see that, woman?'

Esther was shaking her head vigorously. 'That was just a schoolgirl crush. She's dated men; always men.'

Vera stared at Esther and it wasn't clear whether she felt sorry for the old woman or completely bemused by her ignorance. 'Some lesbians date men until they realise who they are,' Vera said. 'It's not easy coming out, and with an attitude like you have, how the hell is Drew ever going to be able to have that conversation with you?'

Esther was still shaking her head.

'You set her up with that bloke. That didn't go down too well, did it?'

'That was just the wrong man. She seemed to get on really well with Mitchel; he was a very nice chap, good business sense, seemed to like Drew too,' Esther said.

Vera rolled her eyes. Mitchel bats for the same team as Kev, Esther. So, yes, he's a very nice chap and I'm sure he'll get on well supplying Drew. But it won't be with anything more than the farm produce he'll be giving her, I can guarantee it.'

Esther was staring at Vera with wide eyes.

'I know it's difficult to adjust,' Jenny said. She had lived in an open relationship with Bryan for so long that she didn't understand how people could be so judgmental and discriminatory. Though, she hadn't always been as free-thinking and could relate to Esther's struggle. 'Drew seems really happy,' she said.

Esther didn't know whether Drew was happy or not. She certainly wasn't and hadn't been for some time.

'Why don't you come to the pub and have a drink with us?' Jenny said, softly.

Esther was shaking her head. 'I don't think I can face everyone.'

'You can talk to us,' Jenny said. She went to reach out to Esther again, but hesitated.

Esther looked at her, head still shaking. 'No, I can't,' she said, and walked off, leaving the two women standing, staring at each other in disbelief.

Vera shrugged.

'You were a bit harsh,' Jenny said.

'She tapped a nerve,' Vera said.

Jenny looked at Vera with tenderness. 'I know. Esther's not quite herself though.'

'She needs to lighten up. Bloody menopause if you ask me.'

'You could be right.'

'She needs to bloody men-o-pause for Drew, for fuck's sake. Leave her alone and let her find a good woman.' Vera smiled at Jenny. 'Come on, my good woman, let's get to the pub.' She hooked her arm through Jenny's. 'I need a drink.'

'Do you think she'll be all right?'

'She'll pass out when she gets home. Three sips of that gin and she'll sleep like a snoring elephant,' Vera said and huffed.

'I don't think she's all that well.'

'She'll be fine, Jen. She should see Jarid though.'

'Yes, I think so.'

*

Drew gazed around the pub. Annie was chatting and laughing with Grace and Harriet at the bar. Tilly was keeping a close eye on the reporter. Vera and Jenny were singing along with the act on stage. Delia's gin seemed to have gone down well. She felt cloaked in a contented glow that softened the edges of everything, leaving a carefree, warm sensation that had eased the tension she had felt in the presence of the woman to her side. She turned to Faith and smiled. 'Have you enjoyed the evening?' she said. God, she was gorgeous.

Faith held Drew with enquiring dark eyes. 'Very much,' and her voice seemed subtly deeper.

Drew nodded. 'It's been a good event.'

Faith smiled.

Drew felt her breath hitch in her throat. The event couldn't be further from her mind. 'Good gin.'

'Very good gin.'

Drew felt Faith's eyes on her, seeing into her deepest, darkest secrets, and then a bolt of electric energy shot through her and she found it hard to breathe; hard to think, impossible to focus on anything other than the soft, green gaze.

Overwhelmed by sensation, she closed her eyes. That didn't help! Erotic images of Faith flashed to mind and she flicked her eyes open again. Faith was still staring at her.

'Is there anything I can do?' Faith said.

Drew's heart raced. She couldn't find words other than fuck me, and that seemed a wholly inappropriate thing to say under the circumstances. 'I think I'd better get going,' Drew said and felt her heart plunge into her stomach. The last thing she wanted was to leave Faith. On the contrary, she wanted to take Faith home with her. 'I've got an early start.' She closed her eyes to try and shake off the feelings.

'Yes, I have early service,' Faith said.

There was that damn smile again. So intrusive, so... fucking, fuck me!

Faith moved to speak, and then stopped, drawn by the sweet voice coming from the stage. Drew took stock of Tilly singing and then caught Faith gazing at her again. The words, *flashing fever from your eyes* registered and then, *hold my hand don't let me fall. You've such amazing grace. I've never felt this way.* It was as if the music was speaking to them both. Drew felt the fire flaming in her cheeks and was acutely aware of Faith's flushed appearance.

And then the whole pub joined in... *Oh, show me heaven, cover me. Leave me breathless. Oh, show me heaven, please.*

As Drew broke eye contact and glanced around the pub, Vera and Jenny were singing loudly, Harriet and Grace were smiling at each other, and Tilly's attention seemed firmly fixed on Annie. Tilly was singing to Annie and Annie was entranced.

She looked back to Faith and wasn't sure if the groan that she felt in the vibration that moved through her had escaped her mouth or the woman's staring intently at her. 'I think I'd better go,' she said, her voice broken.

Faith nodded.

11.

Drew could feel her heart pounding in her chest as she approached the café. She opened the door and walked up to the counter. Esther was already working, but the place was empty of customers. She looked at Esther and sighed. She went to speak and then stopped. She took in a deep breath and blew out hard and in a fit of determination, said, 'Mum, I need to talk to you.'

'Not now, Drew, I'm perfecting this coffee-art,' Esther said, her tongue protruding from her thin lips as she tipped the jug and wiggled the foamy milk into the cup to create a pattern. 'There, what do you think?'

Drew studied the swan-like image. 'That's good mum, really good.'

A young man approached the counter. 'Can I get a flat white, please?' he said.

'Hello Mike,' Esther said. 'This is our Drew,' she continued. 'Drew, this is Mike. He's the Bancroft's boy from Cariscarn way. You know, the family with the big house. Own the milk farm.'

'Mum!' Drew barked.

'What?' Esther shrugged, shook her head.

'Sorry, Mike. I'm sure you're a very nice person and all that, but I'm gay.'

Mike's cheeks flushed, he tilted his head, raised his eyebrows and smiled.

'What she's trying to say is she's happy,' Esther said, glaring across at her daughter and then turning to face the coffee machine.

'No, mum, that's not what I am saying. Mike, I'm gay; a lesbian gay.' Drew looked from her mother's back to the white strip at the collar of the woman approaching the counter and felt the tremble take hold of her. 'Uh, good morning, Vicar,' she said, avoiding eye contact with Faith and oscillating between rage and embarrassment.

Mike's grin widened. He took a step back from the counter and watched the scene playing out with fascination.

Esther turned to face Faith. 'Ah, Vicar, I'm glad you're here. Please, will you talk some sense into my daughter?' she implored.

Faith smiled at the man and then noticed the pain in Drew's eyes. 'Esther, my door is always open to you,' she said and smiled at the older woman.

Esther stood taller. 'Thank you, Vicar.'

Drew turned away from the counter and ran into the kitchen.

'Can you manage, while I talk to Drew?' Faith said, trying not to reveal the turmoil that churned her stomach.

'Please, Vicar. I think that would be really helpful.' Esther put the flat white on the counter and addressed Mike. 'That will be two-pounds-seventy, please,' she said and held out her hand as Faith walked through to the kitchen. Another customer approached the counter, drawing Esther's attention from the conversation about to ensue in the kitchen.

Drew stood facing the sink with her back to Faith. Faith shut the door behind her to ensure Esther couldn't earwig on them and approached Drew. She stood a pace from her, her gaze gentle yet questioning.

Drew was shaking her head, and when she turned to face Faith, her teeth were clenched tightly, her eyes filled with hurt fuelled by rage. She shifted eye contact and started pacing the room.

'Drew,' Faith said, her voice soft, caressing.

Drew glared at Faith, jaw rigid, eyes wild. 'Christ, I'm fucking livid. I've had enough of her trying to fucking set me up, and not listening to me.' She groaned under her breath. 'She's

105

never been there for me. It's always been about her,' she blurted, waving her arms in frustration.

Faith studied Drew then her eyes lowered and she nodded. When she looked up, her irises were a shade darker, her focus painfully intense. 'I'm sorry you're going through this, Drew,' she whispered.

Drew held the deep gaze and felt a bolt of energy move through her, causing her mind to muddle. She stared at Faith, her thoughts shifting between her mother and the Vicar, confused feelings warring for her attention. She closed her eyes and breathed deeply and when she opened them, Faith was still looking at her with such tenderness it reached inside and caressed her. Her tone quiet, 'Was it this hard for you?'

Faith shook her head. 'No.'

Drew observed Faith, the smoothness of her skin, the line of her chin, her lips, her eyes, and then smiled. She really did feel fragile in the woman's presence, but not in a bad way. As her thoughts settled, and feeling calmer, she started to chuckle and then, with a shaking head, said, 'God knows what she's going to say about you?'

'Well, I hope He forewarns me,' Faith said and smiled warmly. 'Are you okay?'

Drew nodded, her features softer. 'I'll be fine,' she said. She avoided eye contact and started to fidget.

'Would you like me to go?'

No! The voice screamed in Drew's head. She nodded. 'I need to cook. It will get busy soon.'

Faith smiled. 'How about a Cappuccino?'

Drew locked eyes with Faith and the urge to kiss her moved through her in a tidal wave. 'Coffee's good here, apparently,' she said, her voice broken.

Faith looked at Drew for a time, and then said, 'Would you like to go for a walk with me this afternoon? We could finish at the riding school.'

Drew smiled. 'That would be nice.' Then she looked at Faith with suspicion. 'You're not going to run me up the hills, are you?'

Faith chuckled, shaking her head. 'No, I've already trained today.'

Drew stood, entranced by the sparkling eyes. Slowly, she opened the door. Esther was battling with the coffee machine. Three customers were waiting patiently. She smiled. 'I'll bring your coffee over,' she said to Faith.

'Would you like me to help serve, so you can cook?'

Drew tilted her head, warmth filling her. 'Would you, just while I get the bacon and sausages going?'

Faith moved behind the counter and smiled at Esther. 'You ready for this Esther,' she said, and Esther seemed to mellow in Faith's presence.

'Let's do it,' Esther said.

'What can I get you?' Faith said to the next customer and smiled.

Drew went into the kitchen.

*

Drew paced the small, open plan kitchen-living room space. The morning had dragged after Faith had left the café for the church. Her mother had swiftly followed so as not to miss the mid-morning service and Drew had been left wondering as to the irony of the situation. Esther could easily go to church and claim to be the good Christian, and yet, not accept her own daughter for who she was. Esther would inevitably turn to Faith for guidance, and the thought tickled her. The way the morning had panned out hadn't been as she had rehearsed coming out to her mother, but at least she could stop dancing around the white elephant in the room now and live her life. She felt better for being honest – lighter, and with a sense of freedom and liberation. She could handle whatever came next. She smiled with the renewed confidence. At least she would be free to look at Faith without feeling she was going to get caught and punished for doing something wrong, although there was still a niggle that reminded her Faith was a Vicar and there was something oddly disconcerting about that. Though Faith was definitely gay! She would let the feeling settle, rather than get wrapped up in concerns that might come to nothing. At least, telling her dad would be a breeze by comparison with Esther, and the chances were most of the village already suspected anyway – or didn't care.

It had always been her mother that had been the sticking point. She hadn't been able to speak to her about her feelings for Harriet and Esther had always tried to palm her off with this boy or that bloke over the years. She had gone along with it until she realised she didn't feel anything for the men she had dated. She had tried, believing she should make the effort to feel something, and some of them had been truly lovely, but there had never been a spark that had caused her mind to spin or her heart to ache let alone the other parts of her throb with desire.

She hadn't realised how oppressive Esther had been until the last few weeks, and in truth, she seemed to have gotten worse. It was as if she was obsessed with hooking her up to prove a point. She shook her head back and forth, sighed deeply. And then she thought about Faith's imminent arrival and started to chuckle, and her heart fluttered and her stomach flipped. The knock at the door made her jump with excited anticipation.

She opened the door with a beaming grin that wiped from her face instantly. 'Mother!' she said, and released a deep breath, feeling drowned by the aura that invaded her space as Esther breezed past her into the flat.

'I've been thinking,' Esther started.

Drew stood with her hands on her hips, glaring at the older woman. 'What?' she said with irritation.

'We should expand the café,' Esther said. 'It's too small to serve the village and someone else will open up if you don't do something about it.'

Drew's jaw dropped and she was lost for words. Seeing her mother at the door had in the first instance given her brief hope that she had come with an apology. No! Instead, she comes with an idea to expand the café, on a Sunday afternoon, and on her half-day away from work. 'We don't need to discuss this now do we?' She didn't care that her words had been clipped, her tone short. The fire that flared through her, built in intensity with every second in Esther's presence.

Another bang at the door came and Drew opened it with an urgency that betrayed her frustration. 'Yes!' she said, sternly, and then stopped. 'Sorry, I was just.' She stopped talking and held her head in her hands.

'Vicar, how lovely to see you again,' Esther interrupted. 'Thank you for a wonderful service this morning. I thought your message about family support, love and kindness was brilliant. More people need to learn that lesson, I can tell you.' She rose up in stature, crossed her arms, studied Drew with a look that said, you need to learn the lesson.

'Esther!' Faith said. She sounded as surprised as she looked. She held Drew's gaze briefly before turning her attention fully to Drew's mum.

'I don't suppose you've got time to talk, now, have you?' Esther said to Faith in a tone that seemed to carry the weight of the world and the depth of all the oceans. How quickly her temperament shifted!

Drew rolled her eyes and sucked in a deep breath.

Faith looked apologetically to Drew and then smiled at Esther. 'I could spare a few minutes, if now is a good time for you?'

Esther instantly beamed a pained smile. 'I'll come straight to the church,' she said and set off out the door.

Faith looked at Drew. 'Sorry,' she said. 'How about I meet you at Harriet's in an hour or so?'

Drew nodded, feeling something between murderous towards her mother and shaky under Faith's gaze. 'I'll go over there now, so whenever you finish.' She sounded deflated.

Faith nodded and hurried after Esther.

Drew leaned against the closed door and felt the breath drain from her. Fucking mother! Gathering herself, she set off for Harriet's.

*

Esther settled into the pew, inhaled deeply. and breathed out. 'Such a stunningly beautiful place, church, isn't it?'

Faith looked around; the old stone brickwork, hand-painted glass, inscriptions on plaques attached to the walls, the large wooden alter standing proudly overlooking military-style rows of bench seats, Jesus on the cross at the head of the church, and the table beneath clothed in white silk. 'I happen to think so, yes,' Faith said. 'There's beauty everywhere if one has a desire to see it, Esther.'

The point went straight over Esther's head.

'More people should follow Christ, don't you think? There would be fewer problems if everyone followed the same rules.'

Faith sighed. 'That would be easy. Life – people aren't made that way, though, Esther.'

'Damn shame if you ask me,' Esther said and shook her head back and forth.

'You like nature?' Faith said.

Esther nodded. 'Of course; look how wonderful it is around here.'

'What do you see in nature?' Faith said.

'Beauty.'

'What else?'

'The different seasons, each brings something different. New colours, smells, it feels different at different times of the year, too,' Esther said.

Faith nodded. 'There's a lot that changes in the course of a year.'

'Yes. My favourite season is spring. I love seeing new flowers coming to life. It's so vibrant, so pleasing to the eye.' She scanned the church.

'I like autumn,' Faith said. 'The colours change dramatically as life prepares for death. And I like winter when at its most barren, the cleansing, and preparing for new life. Every season brings lessons for us to learn about ourselves and how we live, don't you think?'

Esther nodded, though it wasn't clear that she did think, or get the message.

'Everything has to die to be reborn again,' Faith continued. 'I understand that it is difficult to accept those things we don't understand or agree with, but others must take responsibility for their own lives, too.'

Esther looked at her and frowned. 'What's your perspective on homosexuality, Vicar? What does the church have to say about it? The Bible?'

Faith felt her insides curdle as she considered the questions respectfully. 'Esther, my perspective isn't important. The church and religious texts are there to guide people through principles and conceptual propositions. Over time we've developed stories, fables and in some cases, sadly, rules that preclude large numbers of people because they don't fit what many consider to be the norm. I don't subscribe to any belief structure, religious or otherwise, that excludes or degrades another human being. I have worked with some very serious offenders, Esther, and very few have I come across who do not feel some level of remorse. And I believe even those people who, for whatever reason are unable to feel repentant, are still deserving of our compassion. It is not for me to judge others, simply to be there to help guide them. Each and every one of us needs to make our own choices, live our own lives, learn our own lessons, and, importantly make our own mistakes.'

'Do you think Drew is making a mistake, being.' Esther couldn't bring herself to say the word gay or lesbian.

'I don't know about that. But I do know it's her decision alone to make, and honestly, as a parent, I would hope to be there for my child under such circumstances.' Faith smiled, encouraging Esther to do the same. 'I'm sure she will be fine, Esther.'

'Do you honestly think so?'

Faith released a sigh and held Esther with a compassionate gaze. 'Yes, Esther, I genuinely do.'

Esther stood, turned slowly. She looked back over her shoulder. 'Thank you, Vicar. I think I understand what you're saying.' She ambled down the aisle, closed the door quietly behind her.

Faith released a long breath and sat for a moment. She hoped Esther understood. Her heart ached with a familiar feeling: that of loving someone and not being able to be with them. Even if Esther were able to accept Drew's sexuality, there was no guarantee that Esther would accept Faith in Drew's life. And what then? Would she be forced to leave the village she had already developed a fondness for, again? What about Drew? Would Drew choose Faith over her family? Could Faith leave the church to be with the woman she loved? She sat quietly, staring at Christ on the cross, waiting for the answers to come. Nothing came. She hadn't expected it to. She looked

112

around the church. Yes, it was a very special place and it could be the hub of the community drawing people together in support of each other. But, she had seen how divisive religious beliefs could be too, and she didn't want that to come to the village.

She stood slowly, rubbed at tired eyes and made her way out of the church.

*

Faith walked down the lane towards Harriet's cottage and smiled. The pink and white camper van had been removed and she had a direct view of the women standing at the fence watching two girls on horseback. The deep barking sound alerted her to the flash of black and white heading in her direction, the orange poodle hot on its heels and barking furiously, and blimey, a third dog – a Dachshund skipping along behind and barking randomly into the air.

She braced herself just in time and presented a hand to the Great Dane who pulled to a halt and nuzzled excitedly. 'Hello, Flo.' Archie barked at her feet and she leaned down and allowed him to say hello too. She stroked his curly coat and then the Dachshund's and when she looked up, Drew was standing in front of her and smiling.

'You made it?' Drew said.

Faith stood and smiled. 'I did.'

'Flo, Archie, Winnie,' Harriet called and the two younger dogs ran towards her, Winnie pottering along in her own sweet time.

'Harriet has her hands full with those three,' Faith said to Drew, smiling at the dogs.

Drew nodded. 'Flo and Winnie are Vera's but they spend a lot of time here with Archie,' she said.

113

Faith nodded and took a fleeting glance out across the field before her eyes settled back on Drew.

Drew held Faith's gaze. 'Is mum okay?'

Faith pursed her lips, squinted her eyes.

'You can't say, can you?'

Faith slowly shook her head, apology written in her eyes.

Drew nodded and a slight smile formed. 'It's okay; I understand. Would you like a drink?'

'Yes, thanks.'

Drew walked towards the paddock, Faith at her side. 'Anyone else for a drink?'

'Hi Faith,' Grace said. 'There's Pimms in the jug, beer, wine, or gin of course. Ellena, do you want a top up?' she said, addressing Bryan's partner.

'Go on then,' Ellena said. 'Hello, Vicar.' She waved at Faith before turning her attention back to her daughter on the black pony.

'Hello, Ellena,' Faith said, but the proud mum was deeply engrossed in her daughter's riding lesson.

'Well done, Luce,' Ellena said, clapping as Luce brought the pony to a steady trot. 'She's doing well,' she said to Harriet.

Harriet nodded. 'Yes, she is.'

'I'll help with the drinks,' Grace said, pressed a kiss to Harriet's lips, and headed for the kitchen.

'What would you like?' Drew said to Faith.

'Um, a small Pimms, please.' She held Drew's gaze.

Drew broke eye contact, turned and walked into the kitchen, her heart racing.

Faith felt Drew's absence, the lingering tension linked to Esther, and stood watching the two girls with a strained smile. 'Who's the other rider?' she said, minded that she hadn't seen the redheaded, freckle-cheeked girl in church.

'That's Tilly's sister, Maisie,' Harriet said.

Faith frowned.

'Tilly from the pub,' Harriet said.

Faith nodded. She turned her head and gazed at the front door of the cottage, searching for Drew.

'Would you like to ride Buzz?' Harriet said, pointing to the chestnut that was standing still, munching grass. The horse's ears flicked at the sound of his name and then he snorted.

Faith shook her head. 'Maybe another day,' she said and then noticing Drew approaching she smiled warmly. She looked delightful and yet Faith felt hollow emptiness with the distance she needed to maintain. 'Thank you,' she said, taking the drink from her. Mindful of her conversation with Esther, she broke eye contact quickly, looked towards Grace, and said, 'Where's the gin wagon?'

'In the workshop,' Grace said. 'I'm having it kitted out.' She grinned and her eyes sparkled. 'Pinkerton's Passion Wagon,' she said making out the sign with her hands, and couldn't prevent a chuckle.

'Over my dead body,' Harriet said.

'What's wrong with that?' Grace said, but she was still grinning.

'It's a gin wagon, not a passion wagon,' Harriet said and took the drink Grace offered and handed it to Ellena. She returned and put an arm around Grace's waist.

'People are very passionate about gin,' Grace said. She mocked a deflated look and Harriet started to tickle her.

'Pinkerton's Passion, eh?' Faith said and smiled.

'See, someone appreciates it,' Grace said, trying to wriggle out of Harriet's grip.

Drew watched Grace and Harriet, the light-hearted banter and affection, and when she became aware of Faith watching her, she felt heat sear her skin and dry her mouth.

Grace pulled Harriet into an embrace and rocked her closely and Harriet leaned her head against Grace's chest. Grace kissed the top of Harriet's head then looked towards Faith and Drew and smiled. 'Do you guys want to stay for a barbeque?'

Faith seemed to pause as if questioning whether she should.

Drew nodded. 'Fine with me.' She turned to look at Faith.

Grace looked from Drew's pleading gaze to Faith's unease and then watched the Vicar quizzically. She seemed to reconcile her thoughts for a moment and nodded her head.

'Thank you,' Faith said.

Harriet eased out of the hug. 'Right, let me get the girls off the ponies,' she said.

'I'll fire up the coals,' Grace said. She waved to Ellena. 'See you at Zumba tomorrow.'

Ellena waved back, though her attention was still on her daughter.

Harriet stopped the two ponies and the girls dismounted, both wearing broad grins and jumping up and down with excitement.

'Come on, girls,' Ellena said and coaxed them out of the paddock. 'Say goodbye to your sister,' she said to Luce.

Luce grabbed Harriet around the waist and squeezed tightly.

'Would you like to bring Maisie next week?' Harriet said.

'Can I?' Luce looked to Maisie who jumped up and down with enthusiasm.

'Right, let's get you home,' Ellena said to the girls. 'Will you come to Zumba, Vicar? Tomorrow evening at the hall.'

'I'd be delighted,' Faith said and looked genuinely interested.

The girls skipped their way down the lane to the main road, hand-in-hand, with Ellena following, then they all turned out of sight heading towards the village.

Drew studied Faith as if time were standing still, her heart racing in her chest, a constant tingling flow of excitement moving from the inside to her trembling hands. She would definitely be going to Zumba classes now. The image of Faith in Lycra shorts and a sleeveless t-shirt came to mind and she stifled a groan. She became aware that she had been staring and aware of Faith's dark eyes assessing her. Her chest thumped and she wondered if it was obvious.

'Faith, do you eat lamb chops?' Grace said, alerting both women to break eye contact with each other.

'Yes,' Faith said.

Drew smiled at the darkening of Faith's cheeks, her stomach doing somersaults with her vivid imagination of Faith, minus the dog collar. Minus a lot of things, actually! She swallowed, her mouth dry, brought the chilled Pimms to her lips and sipped hungrily.

'That reminds me, Hilda and Brambles were seen in Upper Duckton, yesterday,' Grace said as she wandered back to the kitchen.

'Someone caught Brambles, then?' Drew said, referring to the lamb chops, and chuckled.

Harriet laughed.

Faith frowned.

'Bodes well for the psychic night, if she's on the prowl again. Will be good for publicity,' Grace said. 'Annie's up for helping us promote the weekend.' She disappeared into the kitchen.

'That's great,' Drew said, to herself, noticing Faith's slight unease. She felt the urge to touch her arm, but held back, realising her deeper sensual desires wouldn't be satiated by such contact. On the contrary, she would be left feeling even more frustrated than she did standing just a short pace from the Vicar. So close and yet so far! She breathed in, the scent of Faith coming to her with a force so strong as to drain the power from her legs. She sipped from her drink to distract from the intense feelings and turned her attention to Grace who was carrying a plate of uncooked chops back to the barbeque.

Harriet had lifted one saddle and hooked it over the gate. 'I'll need to get some salad prepared. Feel free to wander, or sit in the garden,' she said to Faith. She went to the second pony and removed its saddle.

Faith looked at Drew and smiled. 'What would you like to do?'

Drew held the gaze, hoping Faith couldn't see the images that passed through her mind in response to the question. No words came to her. In fact, she couldn't remember the options. 'Umm,' she mumbled, her voice hoarse.

'Would you like to sit?'

Drew shook her head and swallowed.

Faith tilted her head a fraction, held Drew's gaze and smiled. 'A walk?'

Drew shook her head again.

Faith's cheeks flushed and she looked away.

When Drew followed her gaze, she noticed Grace was staring at them both.

Faith walked towards the barbeque and sat at the ornate round metal table. Drew followed her, keeping her distance and sitting in the seat furthest from Faith.

'So, how did you get into the church?' Grace asked, laying out the chops on the griddle, and then a row of sausages.

Faith turned to Grace, her focus taking time to come to her. She cleared her throat. 'I fell into it, really.' She paused. 'I went through a tough time when I was a teenager, as most do I guess. It was after I lost my family in a car accident. I was fortunate to have an amazing foster-mum and after I came through it I decided I wanted to help others. I found theology an interesting topic. If it hadn't been that, it would have been therapy, I guess.' She smiled with openness. 'Though with a name like Faith Divine, it was a close call between preaching in church and a career on the stage.' She laughed.

Grace chuckled. Faith was cool! She sipped from her drink and poked at the meat that had started to sizzle.

Drew melted, warmed by the snippets she knew of Faith's past and burning to know more about the woman who had captured her heart.

'Where were you before coming here?'

'Manchester,' she said.

'Must feel very different?' Grace said.

Faith pondered. 'In some ways, yes but there are similarities too.'

Drew noticed a shift in Faith's demeanour as she reflected on her work in the city.

Grace nodded. She hadn't missed London or her business life since taking the decision to sell her flat and move north. 'How do you like your lamb?' she said.

'Not bleating,' they both said in unison and then looked at each other and chuckled.

Grace grinned and turned the chops on the griddle.

Harriet came from the kitchen carrying a bowl of salad and freshly baked loaf of bread on a chopping board and placed them on the table. 'I hope you're hungry.'

Drew knew she was!

'Starving,' Faith said and smiled at Harriet.

Drew closed her eyes as sensual images came to her again and rendered her dumbstruck.

*

Harriet reached for Grace's hand and they watched Faith and Drew walk down the lane towards the main road and the obvious distance the couple maintained, though ambling in step.

'They've got it bad,' Grace said and grinned.

Harriet studied Grace in profile, ran a finger down the side of her cheek and tilted Grace's chin to face her. She gazed into her eyes with intensity but didn't smile. 'I know that feeling,' she said and her lips met Grace's with tenderness.

Grace moaned, deepening the kiss and pulling Harriet's body tight to her. She eased from the kiss, her mouth exploring Harriet's neck and whispered in her ear. 'Come to bed with me.'

'I thought you'd never ask,' Harriet said, her voice hoarse.

*

'It's a beautiful evening,' Drew said.

Not the weather conversation, again!

'Glorious,' Faith paused. 'I'm sorry we didn't get to go for a walk.'

Drew glanced across at her, and then to the road ahead. 'How about Tuesday afternoon? I could ask mum to cover the shop for a couple of hours. Tuesday's usually quiet.' Realising her excitement, a wave of heat filled her.

Faith looked at Drew with pursed lips and narrowed eyes. 'I have to go to Manchester on Tuesday,' she said apologetically.

'Oh,' Drew said, deflated. It hadn't occurred to her that Faith would need to take a trip so soon after arriving, and then a swell of anxiety assaulted her. 'Are you away for long?'

Faith smiled and spoke softly. 'Just the day. Some of the offenders I used to work with are having a celebration party.'

'Oh,' Drew said and glanced at Faith in profile as they walked.

'They've completed a community project,' Faith said. 'Part of an overall rejuvenation plan where they live. They have done an amazing job and they invited me to go and celebrate with them.' Faith looked at the wide-eyed gaze on Drew's face and smiled. 'I don't suppose you'd like to come?'

Drew hesitated and looked away.

'I realise it might not be possible, because of the café,' Faith said.

Drew bit her top lip and turned to Faith. 'I'll see if Harriet can help for the day,' she said, and noticed a glint appear in Faith's eyes when she smiled.

'We'll have to go on my bike,' Faith said.

Drew's eyes widened and her mouth opened and closed without any words issuing. And then she said, 'I don't have a helmet.'

Faith studied her and the urge to trace the shape of her face, her jawline, down her neck and continue down her body, overwhelmed her. 'Huh-hum, I have a spare one,' she said, her voice affected. She shook off the image that had her mind spiralling. 'Have you ridden before?' she said, and then flushed.

'No,' Drew said, and the innocence in the tone touched Faith making it hard to swallow.

Faith smiled reassuringly. 'I won't go any faster than you're okay with?'

Drew smiled. 'I think I'm okay with fast,' she said and it was unclear to Faith to what she was referring.

'You're welcome to come with me.' Faith said, getting back to the topic. 'My mum might be there and if not, we can drop in and say hi.'

Drew swallowed. 'Are you sure it will be okay?'

'Yes. Her place is like an open house most of the time. She'd be lost without people traipsing through and stopping for something to eat. I think you'll like her.' She was nodding her head. She knew Andrea would love Drew. Who wouldn't?

Drew was nodding. 'Okay, let me speak to Harriet and mum,' she said.

Faith stopped at the path up to the church. 'I'll see you tomorrow then.' Drew grinned and Faith admired the softness in her eyes. 'I'll be in first thing for coffee. Are you going to Zumba?'

Hell yes! Drew nodded. There wasn't a cat in hell's chance of her not making that session. In fact, she'd be betting half the village would be turning out if they had any idea the Vicar would be showing up in shorts and a vest. She cleared her throat. 'Yes,' she said.

'Good,' Faith said and turned up the steep path to the church.

Drew watched, not wanting Faith to leave. 'Thanks for talking to mum,' she shouted, for want of something to delay the Vicar.

Faith turned and smiled. 'You're welcome,' she said.

When Faith continued up the path, Drew felt the sting in her chest spread through her in a wave of excitement. She cleared her throat, pulled her gaze from Faith then set off at a pace towards her flat.

Faith smiled as she turned the lock to the door of the church cottage.

12.

'V! V!' Jenny shouted.

'What?' Vera said, heading quickly towards the panicked cries in the bedroom.

'I'm stuck. These bloody spandex are too tight,' Jenny said, trying to pull the elasticated pants up. She was puffing and her cheeks flushed as she looked up at Vera's broad grin.

'Just let it all hang out,' Vera said and chuckled.

'Make yourself useful and pull them up at the back, will you?' Jenny said straining as she tugged at the front and turned her back to Vera.

'Jesus, Christ,' Vera moaned as she tried to leverage the pants over Jenny's hips. 'Breathe in,' she said.

'How the fuck's that going to help get it over my hips?' Jenny moaned.

'Stop bleating woman,' Vera said, trying to grip the elastic and heave it higher. 'When did you last wear these? They must be three sizes too small.'

Jenny huffed and yanked at the material. 'There,' she said with a smug grin. And then her face changed colour. 'Jesus!' she said, wobbling the flesh that hung over the top of the pants. 'I feel as though my tits are in my throat.'

'That's because they are,' Vera said, looking Jenny up and down. 'In fact, you look like you're about to pop. How are you going to dance when you can barely breathe?'

Jenny tried to move and struggled. 'Oh my God, I'm dying,' she said and frantically grabbed at the top of the pants to try and pull them away from her body. 'I now know what an apple feels like going through a presser.'

The colour of her cheeks was starting to clash with the bright pink of the cotton headband that kept the sweat from her eyes. Beads of perspiration had formed above her top lip and she seemed to lack focus.

'You don't look good,' Vera said. 'Take them off.'

Jenny pulled desperately at the pants. 'Fuckers won't move,' she said.

'Lie down,' Vera said and helped Jenny stagger to the bed.

Jenny screamed as she tried to sit and failed. 'I can't bend.'

'Just flop back,' Vera said stifling a chuckle.

'It's not fucking funny.'

'I know, we're going to be late for Zumba.'

Jenny allowed herself to fall like a plank to the bed and groaned. She tried again to pull at the pants. Vera grabbed at the sides, trying to help force them off, but it was as if Jenny had grown inside them and they weren't budging an inch.

'Bloody hell, they're super-glued.'

'I can't breathe,' Jenny said, her chest quite literally pressing against her throat. 'Go and get the scissors.'

Vera went to the kitchen, returned with the scissors, and handed them over. 'You sure you don't want me to cut it?'

'I've got it,' Jenny said and slid a blade beneath the material stretched across her stomach. She tried to snip but the thick elastic seemed to defy the blades. 'Bugger!' She tried to snip again and they still wouldn't penetrate the material. 'Call Jarid.'

'What?'

'He'll have a scalpel, or Kelly will. See if Kelly can pop around. She'll be going to Zumba.'

'I told you not to put those bloody things on,' Vera said as she left the bedroom.

Jenny lay staring at the ceiling and empathised with a beached whale. 'And bring me a drink.' Jenny shouted. 'All this exercise already, I've built up quite a thirst.'

Vera returned with two glasses of hooch. 'Kelly's on her way in ten.' She looked at Jenny with tenderness and smiled. 'Do you have any idea what you look like, woman?' Vera chuckled.

'Help me up,' Jenny said and grabbed another pillow to prop under her head.

'Here,' Vera said, handing over the glass. 'How does it feel?' She studied the cream coloured elastic pants that looked as though they had seen better days. There was more of Jenny poking outside the top of them than there appeared would be tucked behind the material. Everything had risen upwards and Jenny looked like a cartoon character; exaggerated in all the wrong ways. And yet, the sight was deeply endearing and her heart sang with joy.

'How do you think it feels? Like a bloody sardine rammed into a tin can,' Jenny said, navigating her bosom to get to her mouth and sipping at the drink trying not to spill it. She swallowed then rested her head back. 'That's better.'

'Looks hot,' Vera said and smirked.

'Bloody boiling,' Jenny said and wiped at the moisture on her lip.

Vera teased a finger up Jenny's thigh. 'I mean a sexy kind of hot.'

'Good God!' Jenny exclaimed. Her cheeks seemed to darken suddenly and then it looked as if she had stood under a shower.

Vera grinned, teased a little further.

'No! Get off, I'm having a hot flush,' Jenny said and started flapping her hand in front of her face. 'Oh my God, it's excruciating.' Water blossomed on her cheeks and she continued to moan.

Vera went to the bathroom and returned with a cold wet flannel and a towel. She pressed the cloth to Jenny's face tenderly and smiled. 'You still look hot.'

'I am fucking hot,' Jenny yelled.

Vera chuckled. 'I love it when you get all feisty.'

The doorbell rang and Vera went downstairs aware of Jenny still moaning and groaning on the bed.

Kelly entered the bedroom, studied the patient and smiled. 'Ready for Zumba then?'

'Just get these bloody things off me, please. I can't feel my legs,' Jenny said.

Kelly approached the bed and studied the pants. 'Right, you need to keep very still.' There's no room between your stomach and the material.'

'You're fucking telling me.'

Kelly took the sharp blade, eased the pants sufficiently to create an opening and snipped the material. Slowly she continued to snip down the front to groans of relief from Jenny. Then she stopped so as to spare the woman her dignity and started from the leg working her way up both sides until the material was loose enough to be able to be removed.

'Oh my God, thank you.' Jenny pulled herself up to sit, her body finding its natural position about a foot lower than it had been and breathed deeply.

'You should be able to manage from there,' Kelly said. She looked at her watch and stood. 'Don't be late.'

'Give me ten minutes.' Jenny waved at her dismissively, finished the drink and recovering herself before getting into her loose track-suit bottoms for the Zumba class.

Kelly and Vera went down the stairs chuckling, saying something about not sharing this with the rest of the group.

*

Drew couldn't take her eyes off Faith as she entered the hall. The t-shirt that fitted her body revealing parts that Drew wanted to touch, taste, and explore. Faith's smooth, toned legs beneath the tight black shorts were particularly alluring. Drew felt her breath stick in her throat, her heart racing in her chest, the energy sapped from her legs. How the hell was she going to get through the session?

She had intentionally taken a spot at the back of the hall to ensure she could see Faith no matter where she was, now though she wondered if she would be better at the front where she could concentrate on the instructions. She couldn't look away from the sexy, hot, delicious woman, but then became aware of Grace and Harriet's eyes assessing her. When she looked towards them they were smiling knowingly and Drew felt heat consume her. And then Faith was walking towards her and smiling, and she melted.

'Good evening,' Faith said.

Drew tried to swallow; tried to remove her eyes from the breasts that tantalised her senses. 'Hi,' she said. 'You look,' she started to speak then cleared her throat as she found a different word to the one that had popped into her head. 'Fit.'

Faith smiled with tenderness. 'Thanks.'

Drew noticed Faith's eyes take her in.

'You look good, too,' Faith said. 'Can I work-out here?' Faith indicated to the floor-space next to Drew.

Fuck! Drew nodded. Words were so difficult to get her tongue around, and again she became aware of Harriet and Grace eyeing her.

Faith placed her bottle and towel close to Drew's and started to stretch.

Drew became lost in the sweet perfume that drifted to her with Faith's movement, and hadn't realised she had been watching with an open mouth until Delia, Jenny, Kelly and Vera came through the door and stole her attention. She had to confess to being mildly relieved that her mother hadn't shown up with the other women and was close to praying that she would stay away from the class.

'Evening all,' Vera said. 'Sorry we're late, we had a minor an incident to attend to. All good now, though.'

Jenny glared and her and she chuckled. So much for keeping it quiet.

The women who assumed their places in the room and gave their attention to Ellena.

'Right. Good evening ladies,' Ellena said. She started up the music and took centre-stage. 'It's been a while, so we'll take it easy for the first session. Kelly, no pushing too hard.' She smiled at the Vet with a bump that came from being five-months pregnant. 'Right, follow me, everyone, let's get some simple movements going,' and she started walking on the spot.

Within a short time, they were all walking on the spot, though not everyone was in step and not everyone's knees lifted to the same height as Ellena's. Delia's steps seemed particularly tiny, and Jenny was struggling to stay in one place. Then Ellena started moving her arms in wave-like movements to the sky. The coordination of two different body parts seemed to challenge Jenny and she moved to alternating, between lifting her legs then waving her arms. It was a totally different action from the rest of the room, but Ellena smiled and encouraged her nonetheless.

'And arms out to the side,' Ellena announced, demonstrating the rolling style dance movement.

Jenny swung her arm to the left and caught Delia, square in the face. 'Oh shit!' she said as Delia groaned and held her nose. She stumbled towards her to help.

Delia swatted the attention away and moved further from Jenny's reach.

Ellena looked in the direction of the incident and nodded to confirm they were okay. 'And, stepping to the side reaching to the front, squeezing the air with your hands,' she said, keeping the rest of the group focused on the routine.

Jenny stepped to the side and punched to the side, narrowly missing Vera who was still reaching into the air and walking on the spot.

Faith was keeping up with Ellena; she had clearly done this before.

Drew's eyes were on Faith and in truth, she didn't know what the moves were supposed to be and didn't care.

The music changed and Ellena shifted to another pattern of movement that involved rolling her hips, stepping out, ankle rotations in a balanced pose, and then hands, arms and shoulders moving in another wave-like routine. Jenny didn't stand a chance and slumped to the floor puffing. Vera was struggling with her balance and tottering with any change in direction, and Delia was still walking on the spot with tiny steps and reaching into the air. The music moved on to another track and another set of movements that involved a coordinated foot pattern, bending into a squat-like position, lunges and a three-hundred-and-sixty-degree spin. That was Vera out.

'I'm buggered!' Jenny announced to Vera who nodded in agreement. She slumped to the floor, reached into her bag and pulled out her blue sports water bottle and swigged from it. She held it out to Vera who glared at it.

'Water? For fuck's sake, woman. I need a proper bloody drink after that,' Vera said.

Jenny chuckled. 'I decanted,' she said. 'Can't be seen doing exercise with a glass bottle. It's a health-and-safety risk,' she said and swigged again.

'In that case!' Vera sat, took the bottle, and took a long drink then handed it back. They sat watching Ellena in admiration.

'Oh, to be twenty years younger,' Vera said. She reached out and took Jenny's hand and squeezed.

'And thirty-pounds lighter,' Jenny said and chuckled.

The women watched with intrigue, Delia eventually joining them for a drink, until the music stopped.

'Drinks break,' Ellena said, and Jenny, having been given express permission, took another swig of the hooch.

'We should be drinking water, you know?' Vera said, taking another sip.

'Bollocks to that,' Jenny said, taking another mouthful before offering the bottle to Delia.

'I concur with Jenny,' Delia said. She took a sip and looked around the room, her attention settling on Drew chatting to the Vicar. 'Esther spoke to the Vicar, you know,' she said.

Jenny and Vera looked towards her blankly.

Delia nodded. 'About Drew.'

'Jesus Christ,' Vera said, shaking her head. 'Why doesn't she leave well enough alone?'

'Apparently, the Vicar agrees with Esther,' Delia said.

'What do you mean?' Vera said.

'Homosexuality is a crime, according to the church.'

Jenny and Vera looked towards Faith who was laughing with Drew, Harriet and Grace. They frowned.

'Faith said that?' Vera said.

'According to Esther, the Vicar said Drew is making a mistake and it would be easier if everyone followed the rules of the church.'

'Is that so?' Vera said, feeling the irritation rise up her spine and settling in a ball of fire in her head. From what she had seen of the Vicar, she couldn't imagine for one minute those words had come from her lips. After seeing Faith and Drew chatting at the mic night, there was no doubting she liked the ladies, though she couldn't tell whether the Vicar's calling came before her carnal desires? Or whether she might even be celibate?

'Apparently, Faith did say we should have compassion for criminals,' Delia said. 'I think Esther took some comfort from that.'

'Oh, my good God,' Vera said, shaking her head. 'What a load of twaddle!'

'I know, so I did a spread for Esther. I'm not getting on with the rune stones. They're too vague and the only thing that keeps coming up is about having faith.' She shook her head. 'I need something more to work with than that.'

'What came up?' Jenny said and sipped at the bottle.

'The Tower,' she said and studied Jenny and Vera with serious intensity. 'It means radical change and destruction.'

'Yeah, well Esther's going to do a bloody good job of destroying her family if she carries on the way she is,' Vera said, snatched the bottle from Jenny and took a long drink. 'Bloody old fool.'

'There's going to be a bust-up,' Delia said, turning her attention to Drew.

Jenny and Vera followed her gaze and stared.

'Drew looks happy,' Jenny said.

'Yes,' Vera said. 'We need to talk some sense into Esther, before it's too late.'

'She's not going to listen,' Delia said and reached out, taking the bottle from Vera and sipping. 'The Hierophant keeps coming up, too; tradition and conformity, morality and ethics. And if she thinks the church is on her side, she's not going to change her perspective. You know how stubborn she is.'

Vera was shaking her head, watching Faith watching Drew and everything became crystal clear. She had been blinded by the fact that Faith was a Vicar and consumed with the irritation that Esther had brought to the surface. Damn! A smile grew into a broad grin. 'I don't think there's any danger that the church is on Esther's side.' She said. 'Esther has heard what's suited her, delusional old bat.'

131

Delia and Jenny frowned at Vera.

'What do you mean?' Delia said.

'Look,' she said, indicating towards Faith and Drew.

The two women watched and then looked back at Vera, both shaking their heads.

Vera rolled her eyes. 'They're into each other, big time.'

Delia's eyes darted towards the Vicar and Drew again and she squinted. 'Really?' she said, shaking her head. 'I'm not so sure.'

Even Jenny was frowning. 'The Vicar?'

Vera closed her eyes and shook her head. 'You two can't see what's in front of your noses.'

Delia watched the two women and after a moment's silent reflection, said, 'Faith!'

Vera smiled. 'Yes, Faith!'

'But Faith's a Vicar?' Jenny said.

'I know, fooled me too,' Vera said and kissed Jenny on the nose.

'Ooh, I'm not sure that's a good idea,' Delia said. She was still shaking her head.

Vera was nodding. 'Oh, yes, believe me, that's a very good idea,' she said and chuckled. She couldn't wait to see what Esther would have to say about that.

The music started up again and the older women groaned. They remained seated, continued to watch the session, the younger women, and especially Drew watching Faith.

13.

'Thanks for helping out,' Drew said as Harriet and Grace settled behind the counter. Both had agreed to manage the café for the day and Drew was under strict instructions from Harriet to not rush back and to enjoy the trip. She certainly planned to do that. Nervous anticipation made her feel jittery and her breathing was short and shallow. The thought of sitting on the back of a motorbike filled her with thrill and dread in equal measure. She trusted Faith implicitly, but it was the idea of sitting on the vibrating machine clamped to the woman of her dreams that caused her a problem. Just the thought of it sent shivers of desire through her. And then she turned towards the opening door of the café and her stomach somersaulted. Faith appeared in the same black leather trousers and jacket she had arrived in. She was carrying another leather jacket and approached holding it out to Drew.

'It should fit,' Faith said and smiled.

Drew felt her insides dissolve. 'Thanks.' She put on the old jacket and the scent of Faith overwhelmed her. When she turned to Harriet her cheeks were flushed, her eyes glazed with lust.

'Very hot,' Grace said, with a teasing smile and received an elbow in the ribs from Harriet.

'Have a fab day,' Harriet added.

Faith nodded and smiled at the two women behind the counter. Finding her voice, 'Thanks,' she said.

Drew followed Faith out the door and stood at the side of the red Ducati unsure of what to do next. Faith handed over a helmet and Drew squeezed it onto her head. Damn that's tight! Oh my God, Faith's perfume was everywhere. She fiddled with the chin straps, struggling to connect the two ends. When Faith reached out and took over, the sensation of Faith's fingers at her throat caused her breath to stall. She watched Faith studying the clip, immobilised.

'There,' Faith said, connecting the clasp. She picked up her own helmet and secured it then turned to Drew.

Drew gasped at the green-eyes locked onto hers, revealing the masked smile.

Faith seemed to hold her gaze and then nodded her head as if to say, are you ready? Then she slung her leg over the machine and settled into the seat. She turned the ignition and revved the engine then left it idling. She motioned to Drew to get on the bike and indicated to the peddles.

Drew climbed on the back her knees raised and pressed tightly to the sides of the bike, and tensed. Her preconceived thoughts about sitting on the back of the vibrating machine, up close and personal, became reality in a moment of excruciating bliss that resulted in a groan escaping her.

Faith tilted the bike to one side and Drew grabbed at her waist. She released the stand and turned to Drew. 'You ready,' she shouted.

Drew nodded and Faith turned to face the road. She squeezed the lever, flicked the gear into first and eased the bike forward. Drew clung on despite the fact that she could walk faster than the bike was moving. Slowly, Faith increased the speed and eventually Drew relaxed and started to enjoy the thrill. She didn't let go of Faith's waist though and was acutely aware that she was more than enjoying the shape of the woman beneath the leather jacket.

*

By the time Faith pulled up at the community centre, every cell in Drew's body hummed. She stood from the bike and removed her helmet, feeling the world was still moving around

134

her, and then Faith was staring at her with a gaze that rested so softly it caressed her.

Faith removed her helmet and revealed her beautiful smile. 'Sea-legs?' she said.

Drew lifted her hands; they were trembling. 'A bit wobbly.'

Faith nodded. 'I didn't scare you, did I?'

Drew sensed the concern in her voice. You scare me on so many levels! She shook her head, cleared her throat. 'No, it just vibrates a lot.' She smiled.

Faith seemed to release a long breath and held Drew in her gaze as if reassuring herself. 'We can put these indoors,' she said referring to their helmets.

Drew looked towards the community centre, nodded, and followed Faith. The smell of fresh paint hit her as they entered the changing room area, dumped their gear, and then there was the aroma of cooking and spices as they approached the small kitchen. 'Food smells good,' Drew said.

'They're great chefs,' Faith said. She snuck through the door and approached the slim African man and a larger woman from behind.

Both turned and grinned with bright white teeth and sparkling eyes. 'Hey, Faith,' the man said and pulled her into a tight embrace.

'Faith my darling,' the woman said, pulling Faith into her ample bosom and squeezing her tightly.

Faith stood back after being let go and looked to Drew. 'Reggie, Madge, this is a friend; Drew.'

Drew smiled and approached the couple with a hand outstretched.

Ignoring the hand, both Reggie and Madge greeted Drew in turn with as warm a welcome as they had given Faith, then they smiled at her with an approving gaze.

'Lovely to meet you,' Reggie said. 'We're so glad you came,' he said to Faith. 'The crew will be chuffed you could make it. We're expecting a good crowd.' His grin beamed and seemed to light up the space around him.

Faith looked at the disorganised state of the kitchen. 'I wouldn't miss it for the world. Do you need a hand?'

'We're on track, but potatoes need peeling if you fancy it?' Madge said, pointing.

'I'll do it,' Drew said looking from Reggie to Madge and then to Faith. Faith held her in her gaze and she felt acutely aware that the way Faith looked at her hadn't changed in the presence of the couple now watching their interaction closely. There was something disconcerting about the intensity, but at the same time, something honest that reached into her heart and she felt it aching with desire.

'Faith, hey man!'

Drew turned to the youth at the kitchen door, with his big white smile misshapen by the scar running the length of his face.

Faith met him with a wide smile and a ritualistic greeting of hand slapping and fist punching. Drew watched with a curious gaze.

'Cliff, hey, how's things,' Faith said, standing back and studying the youth. 'You look good.'

'I'm cool, man, real cool. We done good, Faith, real good. Come, shoot baskets with us?' He was hopping from foot to foot as he spoke, eager for Faith to join him. 'Come. Come and see the crew.'

Faith looked to Drew who smiled and nodded at her, and then back to Cliff. 'Sure,' she said and followed him out.

Drew turned to the potatoes and started peeling.

'Have you known Faith long?' Madge asked.

'Not long,' though she felt she had known Faith forever, or maybe she just wished she had.

'She's a good woman,' Reggie said. 'You'll see.' He was nodding his head in sync with his thoughts.

Drew had already seen.

'Do you play basketball?' Madge asked.

Drew shook her head.

'Skateboard? Climb?'

Drew shook her head. She would have felt inadequate if it hadn't been for the kind smile that graced the older woman's face and the twinkle in her eyes that reflected a passion for life.

'You'll be doin' them things by the end of the day,' Madge said and when she laughed the hearty sound caused Drew to chuckle with her.

Drew's pace of peeling slowed.

'Why don't you go watch, have a go?' Reggie said. 'We can get this done in good time.'

Drew felt a flutter of excitement and grinned.

The old man smiled. 'Go. Turn left out the door and follow the building around.'

Drew dropped the peeler and left the kitchen, unaware that the two chefs were looking at each other and smiling in affirmation of their assumption that Faith and Drew had a good thing going together.

Drew approached the basketball court with a coy smile. She sat on the bench seat at the side of the court and watched. Faith looked to be holding her own, making passes to Cliff who passed to another guy. She ran around the back of a girl from the opposing team and collected the ball again, turned, jumped and threw the ball high. It bounded off the backboard, collected by Cliff, who reached up and slammed the ball into the net. Cheers and high-fives passed between the three players and the other team threw the ball in from the side of the court and started an attack into the same net.

Drew caught Faith's attention with her gaze and she faltered in her defence, the opposing girl skipping past her and shooting. Another cheer went up and Cliff threw his hands in the air.

'Girl, where d' you go?' he jested to Faith and glanced across at Drew and winked. 'Next hoop wins,' he announced.

Drew saw Faith look flustered for the first time. It was cute and she flushed at the obvious admission of guilt she had seen in Faith's response to Cliff. Then she saw Faith give her a look that sent a tingling sensation down her spine and coloured her cheeks further.

Faith took the ball and ran to the side of the court. Giving the game her full attention she threw the ball to Cliff, moved into a space, received the ball, passed again, dodged past the girl, and set up a shot for the other man on her team that everyone referred to as A-J. High-fives went around again and Drew received a quick glance and smile from Faith.

As Faith approached the bench, wiping the sweat from her brow, Drew felt the tingling move through her again, settling low in her core.

Faith tilted her head; her gaze was soft. 'You want to play?'

Drew did, but not basketball! She hesitated.

'It is hot,' Faith said, looking to the blue sunny sky.

The view was hot from Drew's angle too! 'Maybe later?' Drew managed to say, but it didn't sound like her voice, and Faith grinned knowingly.

'Here,' Cliff said, handing Faith a bottle of water and then passing one to Drew.

'Thanks,' Drew said.

'Want me to show you around?' he said.

Drew nodded and stood.

'This way,' he said, and led them around to the skate park area.

The first thing that struck Drew was the wall that ran the length of the park, which had been hand painted. A wide range of colourful images, in different art forms, brought life to the otherwise grey-space. 'That's beautiful,' Drew said, gazing at the wall.

'The crew built, designed, and painted it,' Cliff said. He sipped at his water, admiring their work and then turned to Faith. 'You bring your board?'

Faith shook her head, sipped at the water.

Cliff put an arm around Faith's shoulders. 'You can borrow mine.'

Drew turned her attention to Faith and studied her. The soft sheen still forming on her skin from the basketball, the sparkle in her eyes that mirrored her smile and the love that radiated from her to every member of the crew. It was clear they all loved her too. Wow!

Cliff looked to Drew and she flushed. 'Do you skateboard?' he said.

Drew shook her head. She was beginning to feel inadequate and hoped it didn't come across to Faith because she was also enjoying watching Faith with people who clearly knew her well.

'Faith's a great teacher,' Cliff said and smiled at Faith.

Faith nodded. 'If you want?'

Drew smiled, her insides shaking. The possibility of close contact with Faith, Faith touching her in any way, filled her with a feeling that she had no words to describe. She couldn't be that close to her. She didn't trust herself. Fuck the dog collar. She was well over that! 'Maybe later?' she said.

Cliff nodded and continued to the high-ropes.

Faith smiled.

'You climb?' Cliff said to Drew as he guided them both towards the tall climbing wall.

How difficult can climbing be? Drew nodded.

'Cool,' Cliff said, grinning.

A group of young children were lined up waiting for a free slot. Another harnessed youth was managing the children on and off the activity.

'Hey Leroy,' Faith said.

'Hey, Faith.'

The man approached Faith, slapped hands and fists and then pulled her into a full embrace. 'You're looking cool,' he said.

'You look good, too,' Faith said and slapped him affectionately on the arm. 'This is Drew,' she said, indicating and smiling at her. Then she looked to the top of the wall.

'Hey Drew,' Leroy said, pulling her into a brief hug.

'This looks great,' Faith said.

'Kids love it,' Leroy said. He looked at Drew and then Faith. 'You coming to the disco tonight?'

'We have to get back,' Faith said, but she didn't look at Drew.

'Man! Everyone's hopin' you'd be doing DJ for a session,' he said and clicked his fingers in a slapping movement of his hand. 'Man!'

Faith looked to her feet, avoiding Drew's gaze. Cliff looked at Drew and half-smiled as if sending the message that she might have some influence over the outcome.

'You ready to climb?' Leroy said to Drew.

Drew looked up, tried not to baulk at the height of the wall, felt bad about refusing the other activities, and nodded her head. This was safe – no contact with Faith! 'Sure,' she said.

'Hey kids, what you say we let our lady-guest have a go?' he said to the children waiting patiently in line.

Drew was expecting a barrage of complaints and instead got a healthy cheer that made her feel even guiltier for feeling shit scared of the idea. Leroy urged her towards the wall, slipped a harness on her and unhooked a youngster who had just finished a descent. He hooked Drew to the safety rope and stood back from the wall.

Drew's heart pounded in her chest. How difficult could this be, really? The hand and footholds were obvious and her limbs were longer and stronger than most of the children watching her. That was the point though; they were all watching her. She put her foot on the lowest rung, reached up and heaved herself to the next foothold. She reached up again, realised her fingertips were already screaming at her, found another foothold and pushed up, taking the weight off her hands for a moment. The words of encouragement helped, and looking either straight at the wall or slightly ahead of her seemed to keep her nerves in check. Her heart still thumped with the strain and she took a deep breath before finding the next handhold.

By the halfway point her legs felt like jelly and her fingers trembled. Without thought, she looked down and froze. Even knowing the safety rope was taking the strain didn't help the feeling of impending doom from consuming her. Faith's smile faded, replaced by a look of concern.

'Drew, look up,' Faith shouted and pointed. Her heart was trying to break out of her chest watching Drew trying to be brave. It was irrational; the safety rope was safe! The urge to protect Drew was strong though, and the tension she felt had more to do with her desire to hold the woman close and explore every part of her than it had anything to do with Drew climbing or falling.

Drew turned to face the wall, heart thumping, legs weak, and then, she let go.

A cheer went up and Drew realised she was floating down to the ground, supported by the safety rope. Her heart slowed and by the time she landed on the ground on her feet, she was grinning like a Cheshire cat.

'You did real good,' Leroy said, approaching her with a beaming grin and a high five. 'You want to go again?'

Drew shook her head. Her thighs throbbed and her hands still shook and as much as she might love to have a second go, the chances of her improving on the first attempt she knew would be slim. And, a line of wide-eyed children waited patiently. 'Maybe later, thanks.'

Leroy unhooked her from the harness and she walked towards Faith.

Faith went to move towards Drew and stopped. 'Well done,' she said and grinned. 'Quite the climber, eh?'

'I don't think so.' Drew shook her head with a beaming smile.

'You did brilliantly.' Faith gazed at Drew with genuine admiration.

They walked back to the centre in comfortable silence, leaving Cliff to return to the skate park. 'This is an amazing space,' Drew said.

'The crew built it, with a little help from sponsor companies. But they did all the fundraising and engaged supporters, coordinated the work.' She paused. 'It always amazes me what people can achieve when given the opportunity and resources.'

Drew got the impression Faith was underplaying her own input to the project. 'And having others believe in them,' she said.

Faith turned to Drew and smiled. 'Yes.' Her voice was softer, quieter.

'Would you like to stay for the disco?' Drew said. 'I can see if Harriet will open the café first thing if we need to stay over.'

Faith stood and held Drew in her gaze. 'I'm sure mum would put us up for the night, or I can find you a hotel room if you would prefer? I know the crew would be chuffed, but if you need to get back, that's fine. I didn't plan on staying when I asked you to come with me.' She shrugged.

142

Drew nodded. 'It's okay with me. I'm intrigued to hear the Divine DJ Vicar in action,' she said with a coy smile, and then flushed.

Faith laughed. 'It's been a while. I'll call mum and let her know.'

Drew stood admiring the shining jet-black hair, the lighter green irises, that reflected the early autumn sun. The touch of hazel and darker green around the outer edges had Drew entranced. There was a healthy glow in Faith's cheeks and soft lines that shaped beautifully almond eyes and then the kissable lips, slightly moist, enticing and very, very dangerous. Fireworks sparked through Drew and she ached with desire. Spending the night with Faith was an opportunity she wasn't going to refuse. Sod the café. If Harriet couldn't open up tomorrow then the customers would just have to wait.

14.

Drew watched Faith on the stage, headphones covering one ear, talking and laughing with the man behind the old-style turntable. She had observed her all day, talking to old friends, acquaintances, listening attentively to their stories. It hadn't escaped her notice that Faith had declined to skateboard and she thought knew why. Faith hadn't come here for herself. She was here for the people she served, and there was nothing subservient in that. On the contrary, she found the quality in Faith deeply alluring.

She hadn't thought it possible for her feelings for Faith to grow stronger, but they had. She had never wanted anyone in the way that she wanted Faith. It was a need so excruciatingly delicious, she wondered if it would ever be satiated. She hoped not. The thought of Faith's hot skin pressing against her own; the soft breath at her ear, on her neck; the delicious taste of her, had driven her to near the boiling point as the day had progressed. The idea of staying away from Faith as the night closed in was becoming harder to sustain. When Faith had approached earlier and whispered into her ear, she had darn near wet herself. She hadn't got a clue what Faith had said but she had nodded and smiled and Faith had looked at her with vivid intensity before being dragged away by another excitable youth wanting her attention.

Faith was scratching a record on the turntable and people were cheering and dancing. She looked engrossed in the music, and happy.

Drew continued to stare, sipping from her water. She didn't even have alcohol to blame for her feelings. Faith had told her, many of the youngsters were in rehab so the crew had agreed to the community space being designated an alcohol and drug-free zone. It was self-monitored and self-managed. The energy was electric; pure, innocent, and alive.

The record came to an end and the main DJ took over and as everyone applauded Faith, she took a bow, raised her hands and applauded the audience and stepped off the stage. She managed to make a quick, unhindered, path to Drew and stood in front of her grinning. 'What do you think?' she shouted, her eyes scanning the room.

'It's fantastic,' Drew shouted back.

'You will let me know when you've had enough?' Faith shouted.

There was something in Faith's look that filtered through Drew and as she held her gaze the intensity in Faith's eyes left her breathless.

Faith seemed to read Drew's mind and her smile confirmed her wishes. 'Shall we go?' Faith said.

Drew looked around the room.

'They won't be expecting me to stay,' Faith said.

Drew nodded. The movement was slow but certain and her eyes didn't waver from Faith. She hadn't realised she had been biting her lip until a sharp pain came to her. She felt the heat in her chest spread through her.

Faith looked around the room; people dancing, chatting, and laughing, and smiled. 'Come on,' she said and made her way to the exit.

Drew followed Faith into the changing room leaving the loud music in the main hall, a slight rumble accompanying them into the empty space. As the door closed behind them, the sound diminished further and Drew became aware of the fact that they were alone. Drew moved to take her jacket from the peg at the same time Faith reached for it and when their hands touched an electric shock fired through Drew. She gasped and jerked away, aware that her hands were shaking and her insides vibrated with urgent desire.

'Sorry,' Faith said and Drew noticed the dark eyes focused intently on her.

She cleared her throat, broke eye contact, took the jacket from Faith and put it on. 'Thanks,' she said, her voice barely a whisper.

Faith lifted her jacket from the peg and put it on.

In the silence, Drew could feel her heart pounding in her chest.

Faith picked up the helmet and turned towards the door.

Drew released a breath and followed her.

Climbing onto the bike, Drew moaned as Faith revved the engine. The vibration through the seat was doing nothing to help her composure and as she stared at the back of Faith, the scent of the woman inside her helmet in the balmy night air, the jacket clinging to her skin, she felt sure she might pass out if she held Faith around the waist.

And then Faith accelerated and Drew clung on for dear life. The only thing scarier to Drew was being halfway up a rock-climbing wall. And then an image of Faith lying naked next to her came into her mind's eye. No, that was scarier!

Within twenty-minutes Faith pulled into the driveway of a large detached property and stopped the bike in front of a double garage. She removed her helmet, switched off the engine and rested the bike on its stand. She moved as if to hold out a hand to help Drew off the bike then retracted it.

Drew climbed off the bike, took off her helmet and studied the house. 'Wow!' she said. 'That's pretty.'

Faith followed her gaze. She had always loved the large Georgian property with its whitewashed walls, simple symmetrical design, astragal bars of a square design in large windows that had always led to a light airy feel inside the house. But more than that, she had loved her life here with her mum and the other children that had become her siblings over the years. 'It is,' she said. 'Come on.' She walked towards the front door and rang the bell.

The woman who answered the door greeted Faith with open arms. 'Faith!' she said.

'Hey mum,' Faith said and planted a kiss on the woman's cheek. 'Mum, this is Drew,' she said, looking to Drew and encouraging her to come closer. 'Drew, this is Andrea.'

'Hello, Drew,' Andrea said and pulled her into a welcoming hug. 'Faith has told me a lot about you. I'm sorry I couldn't make it to the park today.' She led Drew into the house.

'Thank you for having me,' Drew said.

Andrea smiled, eyed Drew up and down with affection and then squeezed her arm. 'You are very welcome my darling. Are you hungry?' She looked from Drew to Faith.

'We ate at the centre,' Faith said. 'Sorry, it's a fleeting visit. We hadn't planned to stay over and need to leave first thing as Drew has to get back to the café and I've got a service.'

'Of course.' Andrea smiled at them both. The two rooms on the right are ready for you,' she said. 'I'll see you in the morning.'

'Thanks, mum,' Faith said and kissed her cheek again. She looked to Drew as if to say, are you coming and Drew nodded.

'Thank you,' Drew said, and followed Faith. They climbed the stairs and entered the first bedroom. The scent of fresh clean linen came to Drew and she stared at the inviting large double bed, the white quilt with a floral print across the lower quarter of the material and matching pillows.

'There's a shower through that door,' Faith said. 'I've got some spare clothes here you can use.'

Drew held Faith's soft gaze and noticed the intensity shift in the narrowing of her eyes. She seemed to wince, take a long deep breath and look to the ceiling before settling back on Drew with a little more reserve.

Drew watched Faith swallow and when Faith lifted her hand to rub at her forehead, Drew noticed she was shaking. Drew's heart skipped a beat with the sudden surge of lust that she felt sure was a mutual feeling. She took a step closer, hand outstretched. 'Is everything okay?' she said in a whisper, scanning Faith, seeking reassurance.

Faith lowered her hand to her side, faced Drew and released a long breath. She tried to smile but it was tainted with gravity, and Drew became aware of the racing pulse at Faith's neck. Faith went to speak, but the words wouldn't come.

Drew frowned, apprehension causing her heart to thud uncomfortably. Had she read the signals incorrectly? 'What is it?' she, stepping closer.

Faith blinked repeatedly, pulled her lips into her mouth to wet them, and then spoke in a silky-soft tone that struggled not to break. 'I think I'm in trouble.'

Drew squinted, nodded her head slowly, studied the flushed cheeks, the dark gaze and soft lips. She became aware that Faith was watching herself being watched.

'Yes,' Faith said. 'That kind of trouble.'

Drew inched closer until she was barely touching Faith and the electric current that exposed her, the heat of Faith burning her skin, caused her to gasp. And then Faith smiled with such desire, Drew could barely breathe, and yet she had never felt more alive. Drew inched closer until she could sense Faith's breath on her. She held Faith's gaze answering the unanswered question, then her eyes closed and Faith's lips touched hers with such tenderness. She couldn't prevent the guttural groan that escaped her. She fell into the soft kiss that caressed her with unhurried movements. So tender! And then Faith's hand was holding her head and pulling her closer, the other hand in the centre of her back, caressing her. Faith's tongue was exploring and dancing with hers. Drew moved effortlessly with the rhythm of it, savouring the touch and taste she had longed for. Faith's kisses became gentle and she moved away. When Drew opened her eyes, the dark intensity she saw filled her with urgency and she found Faith's mouth with such crushing need that they stumbled together. Faith eased back again and rubbed a thumb across Drew's moist lips.

'I've wanted you for so long,' Drew said, her voice broken. She reached up to touch Faith's hair, her hand trembling. She traced the line of Faith's jaw, noting the prickling effect the touch was having on Faith's skin, moved across Faith's lips and down her neck. 'You're so beautiful.' She held Faith's unwavering gaze. 'I want you to stay with me.'

Faith's lips twitched into a coy smile. She took Drew's hand and led her to the bathroom. She stood in front of Drew and removed her top and Drew's eyes refused to budge from the delicious breasts revealed through the lacy black bra. When Faith unclipped the bra and allowed it to fall, Drew gasped. And when Faith started to unbutton her jeans, she watched wide-eyed until they too hit the ground.

Drew studied the naked athletic form she had imagined. But she had never envisioned this! Urgently, she removed her clothes and stood facing Faith; Faith holding Drew's gaze firmly, reassuringly.

Faith took Drew's hand and walked her into the shower. She turned on the water, shuddered as the cold spray hit her back and then when the warm water came, she pulled Drew closer and smiled. She tipped soap into her hands and placed them on Drew's shoulders, the spray providing a soft shower of mist that fell lightly.

Drew groaned.

Faith moved the soap down Drew's arms, into her hands, interlinking with her fingers, leaned in and kissed her lips, then spread the soap up her arms and across the top of her chest. Slowly, she slipped her hands around the outside of Drew's breasts, underneath and then cupped them. Drew gasped. Faith placed another kiss to Drew's lips and ran the soap across Drew's nipples with her thumbs.

Drew jolted and groaned, encouraging Faith to kiss her harder.

Faith slipped her hands around Drew's back, down to her buttocks and pulled her into her. She held Drew's gaze, her hands moving over the top of Drew's hips and jolting Drew when she slid down the inside of her hip. Faith paused.

Drew stared into Faith's dark eyes, willing her to move lower, to where she longed to feel the sensual touch.

Faith moved to the outside of Drew's hip and down the outside of her leg. She slid her hand up the inside of Drew's leg and paused teasingly. Faith stared at Drew and then her mouth closed in on Drew's with tenderness as her hand settled between Drew's legs, and she mumbled inaudibly.

Drew moaned, kissed Faith harder and pulled her closer. Faith pressed her to the shower wall and Drew shuddered as the cool tiles found her hot skin.

Faith stopped kissing, looked at Drew then kissed her again, her hands exploring Drew's body with greater intensity.

Drew held Faith's head in her hands, bit down on her lip, teased her with her tongue and as Faith met her touch for touch she felt caressed by Faith in every cell of her tingling body. The sensation left her sapped of strength yet filled with yearning and when Faith stopped kissing her she opened her eyes and stared.

Faith watched Drew in silence and moved away from her. She picked up the soap, washed her own body, her gaze never leaving Drew's lips, ragged breathing, hazy gaze, and flushed cheeks. She turned off the water, took Drew by the hand, and led her out of the shower. Handing her a towel, taking another for herself, she admired Drew as they dried.

Drew followed Faith to the bed, and before they slid beneath the sheets, Drew had claimed Faith's mouth, and she was exploring Faith's nipple with her fingertip.

Faith groaned, conceding willingly to the erotic touch.

*

When Drew blinked opened her eyes, Faith was staring at her.

'Morning,' Faith said.

Drew moaned and then a broad smile appeared and she reached up and stroked Faith's face. 'Morning,' she said, her voice groggy from the lack of sleep. She turned onto her side and noticed she ached in places she hadn't ever before, and then chuckled. 'Christ, what did you do to me?'

Faith tilted her head. 'I hope He wasn't here.' She smiled, looking around the room, teasingly.

Drew groaned and closed her eyes. 'Oh my God. That was the best sex I've ever had.'

Faith started to chuckle. 'I think He probably knows.'

When Drew opened her eyes and smiled, she noticed a different intensity to Faith's gaze. And then Faith leaned towards her and expressed that intensity in a deep, tender kiss that Drew didn't want to end. And when it did, reality dawned and Drew felt a strong sense of emptiness fill her.

'How do you feel?' Faith said, studying Drew with concern.

Drew smiled. 'Fucking amazing. You?'

Faith wore a tight smile, her dark green eyes searching. 'A little scared.'

The smile slipped from Drew's lips and she held Faith's cheek tenderly in the palm of her hand. 'About what?'

'You.'

Drew felt a lead weight drop into her stomach. The fear of not being with Faith was something she didn't want to consider. 'I'm good.' Drew brushed her thumb across Faith's lips.

Faith's gaze was unrelenting, and then she smiled. 'Good.' She moved closer, pressed a kiss to Drew's forehead. Looking into Drew's eyes, her tone gentle, 'We need to talk,' she said.

'Yes.' Drew paused. 'But one thing I know is that I want to be with you.'

Faith nodded. 'Good.' She eased out of bed and dressed. She opened a drawer and pulled out underwear and a t-shirt. 'Here,' she threw the clothing at Drew and smiled. 'We can grab a quick bite and then get back to the café before nine.'

No wonder Drew felt cheated of sleep. It was only 6 am! 'God, I am so tired.' She flopped onto her back, and yawned.

'He hears you, but we've got to head back soon.' Faith smiled. 'I've got a service at ten.'

Drew lifted her head off the pillow and gazed at Faith. The idea of Faith the Vicar seemed all shades of odd after the night of lovemaking they had shared. But that odd was a very different kind of odd to previous thoughts that had Drew questioning the merits of getting involved with a woman of the church. She tilted her head. Maybe she could develop a fetish for the dog collar look after all? She flushed at the thought and eased herself out of bed.

Faith watched Drew dress with an intense gaze and a gentle smile. 'You look good,' she said, admiring the snug fit of the t-shirt against Drew's chest. She closed the space between them and met Drew's lips in a languid kiss. She eased out of the kiss and when she spoke her voice was groggy. 'I don't want to rush back either, but I can't miss work.'

Drew traced the line of Faith's cheek, held her gaze with deep affection and sighed. 'I know,' she said and every part of her ached to feel Faith's touch again. The next time they made love wouldn't come soon enough. And then she remembered the bike ride home. Fuck! How the hell was she going to cope with the vibrating seat and Faith sitting so close to her throbbing crotch for the best part of two-hours?

'Let's eat,' Faith said. 'Or I'll pass out.' She smiled, plucked the unused plastic liner from the laundry basket, tossed in their dirty clothes from the previous day, and led Drew down the stairs and into the kitchen.

15.

'Hello Grace, Harriet, where's Drew?' Vera said, approaching the counter with Jenny and Delia at her side and looking towards the kitchen door.

Grace grinned and her eyes sparkled. 'She stayed overnight with Faith,' she said, not making a huge effort to sound nonchalant.

'I knew it,' Vera said and nodded at Grace. 'I'll have one of those fat white coffees with a picture of a swan on top please.'

'Oh, that sounds good. Me too,' Delia said.

'Make that three,' Jenny added. 'Any buns?' She studied the brownies, flapjack, millionaire's shortbread and chocolate chip cookies but no Chelsea buns. Not a cherry in sight.

'We sold out yesterday and I haven't managed a bake yet this morning. It's been very busy,' Harriet said.

'So, where did Drew and Faith skip off to?' Vera said, digging in her purse for the money.

'Manchester.' Grace said.

'She went to look at a community project that Faith has been involved with. There was an opening ceremony,' Harriet said.

'I bet there was,' Vera mumbled and chuckled.

'Take a seat. I'll bring these over. What about cakes?' Grace said.

'I'll have flapjack,' Vera said.

'Me too,' Jenny said.

'I'll get a brownie please,' Delia said.

'Brownie, this early,' Vera said and turned up her nose.

'There's never a bad time for chocolate,' Delia said and marched to a table and sat. She dipped into her handbag and removed the rune stones.

Vera sitting next to Jenny watched as Delia pulled a stone and studied the handbook.

'I thought they weren't working?' Vera said.

'I'm persisting,' Delia said and swatted a hand at her.

'What's that?' Jenny said.

'Uh-oh,' Vera said, her eyes drifting to the café door.

Delia was lost in her reading. 'GEBO,' she said. 'The gift of harmonic relationships.'

'Well that's not what's heading in this direction,' Vera said, nodding towards Esther as she approached.

Jenny turned to face the woman and sighed. 'Oh dear!'

'Morning Esther,' Vera said, her tone confident and forthright.

Esther smiled a tight-lipped smile that made her nose turn up even further than normal. She looked towards the counter; Grace and Harriet studying her intently, both a fraction wide-eyed, waiting.

'That's good,' Delia said, still with the stones and her reading.

Vera cleared her throat and nudged Delia.

'Oh hello, Esther. I was just doing a reading for Drew,' she said, drawing Esther's attention. 'GEBO. It means harmonic relationships.' She grinned.

'Twaddle,' Esther said, turned to the counter and looked towards the kitchen door. 'Where's Drew?'

Grace held Esther's gaze and smiled as if butter wouldn't melt in her mouth. 'She's with Faith.'

Esther nodded. 'Oh, right.'

That news seemed to go down well!

And then Grace couldn't help herself. 'They went to Manchester and haven't returned yet,' she said, studying Esther's response intently, Harriet nudging her in the arm.

Esther looked from Harriet to Drew. 'Manchester?' she said, shaking her head.

'To visit one of Faith's community projects,' Harriet added with a smile.

'Umm.' Esther pondered. 'I thought she might try to get Drew to see some sense. That's good.' She looked across at the three elder women. 'It's an intervention,' she added, in an authoritative tone for all the women to hear.

'I bet it was an intervention all right,' Vera said in a whisper and chuckled.

Grace grinned and Harriet muffled a snigger.

'She'll be back soon. Can I get you a coffee?' Grace said.

'Oh, umm, yes, I will have a Latte, please,' Esther said, with a smug grin on her face.

Grace turned to the coffee machine and continued preparing the drinks. The sound of the motorbike revving outside the café caught her ear and she watched. There was something about the way Drew held onto Faith as she climbed off the back of the bike that resonated. Drew removed her helmet, went to remove the jacket and was stopped by Faith. The two women stood talking for a moment and then Drew turned towards the café. And at that moment, Grace knew without a doubt. There certainly had been an intervention, but not the type that Esther might wish for. She smiled, squinted her eyes and when Drew entered the café she turned her attention to the drinks.

'Drew!' Esther said, looking her daughter up and down as she approached the counter. 'Good heavens. You look...' Esther faltered.

'Mum!' Drew said, barely making eye contact with her mother.

'Morning Drew,' Vera said. 'You look positively radiant. Good night, I take it?' she said and winked.

Drew's cheeks shone and her smile broadened. 'Yes, thank you, V. It was.' She paused in thought. 'It was a very enlightening day.'

'You look well,' Jenny said.

'Thank you.' Drew studied the women whose eyes were locked on her and it occurred to her that they had gathered specifically for her return. She shook her head with an amused smile and turned to the two women behind the counter. 'Thanks for looking after the café,' she said to Harriet and nodded in appreciation to Grace.

Harriet smiled and a knowing look passed between Harriet and Drew.

'We need more buns,' Grace said to Drew and raised her eyebrows.

Drew flushed. She looked at Harriet. 'Can you give me half-an-hour?'

Harriet nodded.

Esther watched her daughter. She certainly seemed to have benefited from the Vicar's intervention. That had to be a good thing. Maybe she should speak to James Featherton, the farmer from the other side of Broadermere. He might be interested in going on a date with Drew.

Grace passed a coffee across the counter to Esther, clocked her vacant gaze. 'She seems to have had a good time,' she said. 'Looks happy.'

Esther was still staring at the kitchen door, through which her daughter had made a rapid escape. 'Hmm!' she said, lacking interest in the conversation. She took the coffee, handed over the money and sat at a table by the window. The bike had long since disappeared. Thank goodness for a Vicar who could keep her daughter on the right path.

'Silly old fart,' Vera said and studied her coffee. 'You need some practice at this coffee art, Grace,' she said stirring sugar into indecipherable pattern.

Grace smiled. 'Gin's more my thing,' she said and chuckled. 'In fact, I was thinking.' She stopped speaking and looked towards Harriet. She hadn't even discussed the plan with her. She hoped she wouldn't mind her asking the other women without consulting. 'I was wondering,' she started, again. Harriet was giving her a glare but the softness and sparkle in her dark eyes told Grace she knew she was about to find out something for the first time. 'The wagon will be ready on Friday. How about we have a party at ours to celebrate?' She smiled coyly at Harriet who smiled at her with her head on a tilt and then gave her attention to Vera, Jenny and Delia.

'Ooh, that sounds wonderful,' Delia said.

'Great plan,' Vera said, rubbing her hands together.

Grace nodded her head towards Esther and Vera nodded. 'Esther, would you like to come to a party on Friday evening? Celebrate the new gin wagon. It will be a bit of fun,' she said, trying to persuade Esther to lighten up.

'I'll think about it,' Esther said.

'Come on, Esther,' Vera said. 'How long are you going to carry on this charade?'

Esther stood sharply, glared at Vera then stared in Grace's direction. 'If that woman is going, then I'm not,' she said and stormed out of the café.

'ISA. Ice,' Delia announced, looking at the stone in her hand. 'Frozen in time.'

'Bloody right she is,' Vera said. 'She's the bloody original ice queen! She needs a bit more than divine intervention. We need a proper plan.' She nodded to Jenny and then studied Grace.

And then the café door opened.

'Morning Vicar,' Vera and Jenny said, in unison.

'We were just talking about divine intervention,' Vera said. 'And whether one might be possible for Esther?'

Faith smiled. 'Oh!'

'She seems to think you saved her...' Jenny elbowed Vera in the ribs. 'Ouch!' she complained.

Faith's cheeks darkened with the eyes of the women in the café on her, assessing her. She had seen Esther marching across the street to the corner shop as she had approached; she didn't look happy. A wave of sadness filled her and she cleared her throat. 'Is Esther okay?' she said, to no one in particular.

'She's frozen in time,' Delia said, with certainty.

'She's a silly old fart, is what she is,' Vera said, with equal passion.

'She'll come around,' Jenny said, her gaze filled with compassion towards the Vicar.

'We're having a gin party next Saturday. Would you like to come?' Grace said.

'I'll go and help Drew with the buns,' Harriet announced and went into the kitchen.

Faith stood, staring from one woman to the next, her gaze settling on Grace.

'Would you like a drink?' Grace said.

'Um, thank you. Cappuccino,' Faith said.

Grace turned towards the coffee machine with a smile that could be seen through the slight rocking of her shoulders.

And then Drew walked through the kitchen door and stopped, her soft gaze caressing Faith, her cheeks burning. She seemed to struggle to swallow, looked uncharacteristically flustered, and positively radiant.

'I was just saying, gin party next Saturday. Faith's coming,' Grace said and Faith looked at her and smiled as if to say, I know what you're up to.

Grace shrugged and turned back to the coffee.

'Sound's great,' Drew said. 'I need a coffee.'

'I'll make it,' Grace said, and Harriet came through from the kitchen.

'I just need to sort the baking,' Drew pointed over her shoulder to the kitchen and Grace stifled a chuckle.

'Can I talk to you?' Faith said to Drew.

Vera looked from Drew to Faith to Drew again and then smiled and nodded at Jenny. 'Oh, they've got it bad,' she whispered.

Delia started clapping. 'GEBO,' she said, nodding in affirmation.

'Sure,' Drew said. She turned and entered the kitchen, followed by Faith.

'They're definitely an item now,' Vera announced.

'Yep,' Grace agreed.

'How exciting,' Delia said.

Jenny looked worried. 'What are we going to do about Esther?' she said.

Harriet sighed. 'I don't know.'

Jenny reached out and took Vera's hand. She understood why Vera's patience had been tested by Esther's response to Drew. It was as if forty years had passed and nothing had changed with some people's attitudes towards sexuality and same-sex relationships. Vera had suffered as a young woman growing up with a mother whose violent objection to her sexual preferences had led them to an estranged relationship her whole adult life. Surely, that wasn't necessary today? The fact that one of her dearest friends had reacted badly after years of apparent acceptance of her and Jenny's relationship had really touched a nerve. It had taken all her guile to talk Vera into going some way to forgiving Esther, but if Esther kept up this pretence for much longer, she wouldn't be able to stop Vera from speaking her mind. And that would be the end of any relationship with Esther and would drive a rift through the village. It would be hell!

'Perhaps Faith can talk to Esther?' Jenny suggested.

'Like that's going to work,' Vera said, shaking her head. 'Can just imagine that conversation!'

'Might be a bit tricky, since she's part of the problem?' Grace said.

'What problem?' Delia said, reaching for her cards. 'Shall I run a spread?'

Vera put a hand on Delia's arm. 'No need for the cards, Delia, love! Grace means the problem as Esther sees it. There isn't a problem, except that old bat's bigoted mentality.'

'She's just worried,' Jenny said. 'It can be different when it's your own,' she said. She had felt a twinge of concern when she first realised Harriet was gay, but that had been years ago and Harriet had been very young. Her worries had, for the most part, been about how Harriet would be treated at school and by others as she grew up, rather than about her being a lesbian.

Vera harrumphed and bit down on her flapjack.

'Let me try and speak to her?' Jenny said.

'Good luck with that,' Vera said through a mouthful of chewy oats. She had lost patience with the stubborn old goat.

*

Faith took in a deep breath and released it slowly. 'How are you feeling?' she said. She was holding back on smiling, her gaze intense.

Drew looked at her quizzically and smiled. She reached for Faith's hand, intertwined their fingers, and studied them, savouring the feel of Faith against her skin. 'I'm good, you?' She looked up.

Faith's intensity darkened. 'I think your mother is concerned for you.'

Drew rolled her eyes, withdrew her hand and turned away, faced the window and paused. She lowered her head. 'I've been gay for a very long time,' she said, her back to Faith. 'I have tried to date blokes. I have tried to fit in with my mother's wishes and desires, knowing that being a lesbian would crush her world.' She turned to face Faith, tears welling in her eyes.

'I've really tried.' Her voice broke. She paused, looked at Faith and took in a deep breath. 'I was in love with Harriet, you know.'

Faith nodded. She knew they were close friends, but she hadn't known exactly the history they shared. The news didn't come as a surprise.

'I kissed her once,' Drew said.

Faith felt that! A sharp irrational stab to the chest, and she challenged it with an accepting nod of her head.

'I wasn't right for her,' Drew said in a whisper and we've never talked about it since. 'She's my best friend and there's never been anyone since. And then you walked into the café,' she said. Tears slid down her cheeks, but her eyes held the conviction of her intense feelings towards Faith.

Faith felt the urge to reach out and pull Drew into her arms. She had felt a connection from that very first moment too.

'I've never felt more certain about anyone in my life, Faith,' Drew said in a quiet voice, and she took a step closer to Faith. She locked onto Faith's gaze and saw vulnerability deep inside, and stepped closer. When she felt Faith's breath on her cheek, her eyes closed and when Faith's tender lips touched hers, her heart thundered in her chest and she wrapped her arms around Faith's waist.

And then the kitchen door flew open and Drew opened her eyes. Faith was stood a short pace from her, smiling, her cheeks flushed, her eyes sparkling.

'Sorry, how are the buns doing?' Harriet said.

'Shit!' Drew said and darted for the oven. They should have been out by now. She pulled out the tray and stared at eight over-browned looking cakes. 'Bugger!' she said.

Faith chuckled.

'Not yet then?' Harriet said and headed back into the café.

'I need to let you get on,' Faith said.

'I don't want you to go,' Drew said. She held Faith's gaze, saw into her soul and her stomach danced. 'I think I'm.' Drew was stopped from speaking by Faith's finger, pressed to her lips.

'I think you need to cook more cakes,' Faith whispered. She lifted Drew's chin and pressed a kiss to her lips and when she moved away Drew felt the urge to go with her.

Drew stopped Faith just short of the door into the café. 'Will you come around for supper later?'

Faith nodded 'Will you bring your buns?' She raised her eyebrows when she smiled.

Drew glanced down at her chest and then back at Faith's beautifully seductive smile. 'I'm sure I can manage that,' and there was a glint in her eyes when she smiled.

When Faith went into the café, Drew released a long breath, her heart racing. And then she stared for some time at the overcooked buns before throwing them in the bin. She stepped into the café and smiled at Harriet, aware that Faith had already disappeared as had Delia, Jenny and Vera. That thought brought a sense of relief. 'I can manage.'

Harriet squeezed her arm and smiled. 'Everything good?'

Drew gazed from Harriet to Grace. 'I think so.'

Grace smiled at Harriet and Harriet smiled at Drew, but it was a considered smile, reserved. She too was concerned about Esther.

16.

Drew's heart was racing before the knock at the door. By the time she opened it she was fit to burst. 'Hey,' she said, distracted and giddy at the sight of the dog collar, the green-eyes, and supple lips that seemed to quiver. She hadn't noticed that before and stared at them, the urge to lean in and kiss them becoming stronger by the second.

'Hey,' Faith said, her voice gravelly. She pulled her bottom lip between her teeth waiting for an invitation into the flat.

'Sorry, come in,' Drew said, stepping back, and when Faith moved past her, the scent of her caused Drew's cheeks to flush and her heart to thump.

Drew closed the door and when she turned Faith moved towards her and claimed her mouth in a delectable kiss that left her powerless and wanting. She moaned, savoured the lips, the tongue, the minty taste on Faith's breath. The scent of soap, and then the sense of Faith's hand pressing into her lower back, the fingers pulling her blouse free from her jeans and bringing goose bumps to her hot skin. She moaned again, pressing herself against Faith.

Faith eased out of the kiss and looked into Drew's eyes. 'I've found it very hard to concentrate today.'

Faith's tone revealed her desire as much as her eyes, which were darker than Drew had ever seen them. Faith's hand moved from the small of her back onto her hip and then Drew was thrust against the door. She gasped, captivated by Faith's intense gaze, and with a submissive – yes, please take me now – look she groaned loudly when Faith's thumb teased the sensitive area on the inside of her hip. The fiery gaze assessing the impact of every move, every sensation registering in Faith's responsive touch, Drew felt the burning at her core, which reminded her. 'I've burned two consecutive trays of buns today,' she said and gasped as Faith's free hand palmed her breast, the thumb toying the aroused nipple beneath the material.

'Really?' Faith said, her tone dripping with seduction. 'I can't imagine that,' she said. She pressed her lips to Drew's neck. Drew's groan came loudly to her, and she kissed down her collarbone beneath the blouse to the centre of her chest. Faith lingered there, inhaling and tasting Drew.

Her hand at Drew's hip moved down and her fingers started exploring the soft flesh there, teasing Drew into spasms.

'God,' Drew moaned as another tremor seized her.

'He really can't help you now,' Faith whispered and took Drew's nipple into her mouth.

Drew became acutely aware of the shirt against her sensitive skin and Faith biting and taunting her, the hand at her hip moving lower. She wanted Faith in direct contact with her and pulled away. Studying Faith with a deep intensity she took her hand and led her into the bedroom.

'You answered my prayers,' Faith said with a cheeky smile.

Drew smiled. She was enjoying this fun, sexy side of Faith and then it dawned on her that she wanted to know every part of the gorgeous woman intimately, every ounce of her, and every aspect that made Faith Divine who she was. A wave of nervous anxiety stirred in her stomach and when Faith's lips closed around hers the feeling became swept up in an emotional cocktail of love, lust and longing that was more powerful than Drew had imagined possible. At that moment she had never felt more certain of anything in her life, nor had she felt more vulnerable.

Faith eased out of the kiss and gazed into Drew's eyes. 'You're shaking,' she said.

Drew nodded. The previous evening, she had lost all sense of control, driven by the anonymity of being somewhere unfamiliar, where she too was unknown, and a feeling of liberation had come with that. Now, here in her home, surrounded by those she loved and cared for, there was something qualitatively different, perhaps revealing, about the impact of their intimacy. She could feel her mother's hurt and distaste, the support and encouragement of the other women, the conflict, Faith's desire, her own new-found true impulses. Being at home made explicit something she had denied for years; something she had never thought she would express to the world.

Faith held her, pulled her closer and then brought her into a reassuring embrace. 'It's okay,' she said. She kissed Drew with such tenderness, smiled with such compassion and held Drew in her arms with such strength. 'You're okay,' she whispered.

The hot breath and words softly spoken, the gentleness and love she felt coming from Faith, moved Drew to unreserved passion. She eased out of the hug, studied Faith with unwavering certainty, and unbuttoned her shirt. She unhooked the bra and allowed it to drop to the floor. She unbuttoned her trousers, stripped naked, and stood proudly before Faith, staring at her. 'I want you,' she said and closed the space between them. The kiss landed clumsily, taking Faith backwards and crashing them onto the bed. Drew pulled back and gazed at Faith. 'You're so fucking hot in that collar,' she said and grinned.

Faith flipped Drew onto her back, stood, removed her clothes and moved on top of her. 'That's much better,' she said before claiming Drew's enticing lips.

Drew moaned, the softness of Faith against her skin causing her centre to throb unrelentingly and she cried out, 'Jesus Christ!'

166

'He's got no chance,' Faith said, and then deepened the kiss, her hand resuming its position at Drew's hip and causing her to buck. She thumbed the sensitive area, drawing another jolt and a deeper groan, her own arousal growing.

Faith moved her hand lower, finding the hot wet centre, the scent of Drew drawing her deeper. She covered Drew's nipple with her mouth, kissed and tugged at the puckered bud with her teeth. She slipped her fingers into the silky texture between Drew's legs and felt Drew open to her.

'I want you inside me,' Drew said.

Faith teased the wet, swollen centre, and then slipped inside her, the silky, soft flesh reacting to her subtle touch and eliciting a groan from her lover. Drew was bucking, tensing around her fingers, and then expanding, and every shift was guiding Faith. She moved slowly at first, and then more urgently and deeply.

Drew dug her fingers into Faith's back, pulled her closer. She groaned at the feel of Faith's breasts, the nipples firm against her skin, her hips thrusting and rocking with the rhythm that was driving her to a delicious peak. The vibrations came lightly at first, then the burning, and then a sudden bolt that fired through every cell and awakened her, releasing a guttural scream. She stopped moving, and the aftershocks continued to bathe her. She started to chuckle, opened her eyes and held Faith's gaze.

'You look beautiful when you come,' Faith whispered.

Drew reached up, pulled Faith to her and planted a tender kiss with lips that still trembled. When she looked into Faith's eyes no words would come and she studied her in wonderment.

Faith swept the damp strands of hair from Drew's face, traced the line of her eyebrow, her temple, her cheek, her lips; sensing the softness, admiring her. 'Beautiful.' She smiled with deep esteem.

Drew felt affected by the genuine adoration. No one had ever looked at her in that way. Never! The feeling turned her inside out, upside down, and she never wanted it to go away. 'I want to make love to you,' she said.

Faith smiled and then continued to explore Drew's body with an unhurried, delicate touch, watching with curiosity as Drew's skin reacted and her breathing faltered. 'Later,' she whispered. 'I want to discover all of you.'

'Oh my God,' Drew mumbled under her breath.

Faith looked into her eyes and smiled.

*

Drew had never eaten past midnight, but then again, she had never been so awake; so alive, at that time of night either. That she would be up at 5 am starting to prepare for a long day in the café hadn't entered her thoughts. She sipped at the glass of water and watched Faith attack the chicken with enthusiasm. She loved everything about Faith.

Faith stopped chewing, swallowed and held Drew's gaze, suddenly serious. 'I'm still worried about your mum,' she said in a quiet voice.

Drew sighed, she slumped back in the seat and gazed to the ceiling. 'I know.'

'It's going to be difficult for me to talk to her,' Faith said.

'Good,' Drew said and looked at Faith with an uncompromising stare. 'I don't want her poisoning you with her bigoted attitude.'

Faith pursed her lips. 'It's also my job to help counsel.'

Drew was shaking her head. 'Please don't let her get between us,' and when she held Faith's attention her eyes were glassy.

Faith brushed the tear away. 'I won't let that happen, but I can't break up family either.' Her tone was soft, filled with compassion.

Drew moved away from the hand. 'Do I have any choice in that?' She held Faith in a determined look, feeling the frustration building.

Faith lowered her gaze to the table. 'Yes, of course,' she whispered. When she looked up, Drew saw the pain clearly. Faith's eyes were less focused, more distant. She felt it, deeply.

'This has happened to you before?'

Faith took a deep breath and nodded.

Drew reached across the table and took Faith's hand. 'I'm not your past Faith. I'm capable of making my own choices.'

Faith nodded again. 'I know, it's just.' She was trying to do the right thing.

Drew continued to stare at Faith as she processed her memories. The event had clearly left its mark. 'Do you want to talk about it?'

Faith sighed and a wry smile appeared. 'My ex-girlfriend, Nadia, her mother happened.'

Drew nodded. 'Disapproving?'

'Yes. Very much so. I was younger. She couldn't accept that I was both a Vicar and lesbian, and the fact that I was sleeping with her daughter was more than she could tolerate. She made life very difficult for us and I decided it was best for everyone if I left. It was before Manchester and it was my first job. I wasn't ready to deal with the conflict of a divided community or being responsible for breaking up a family unit.'

'It must have been difficult.' Drew felt her frustration melt, her heart ache with sadness.

'Impossible, and I wanted to please too many people.' Faith shrugged, but there was sorrow in her demeanour that Drew hadn't seen before.

'Were you in love with her?'

Faith nodded. 'At the time.'

'How did she take it?'

'Not well.' Faith hesitated. She didn't want to share the fact that Nadia had come at her with a baseball bat and that she had narrowly escaped a serious beating. 'She met another woman, shortly after.'

Drew shook her head. 'How did her mum react to that?'

'Badly. Nadia left town and went to live with her girlfriend. I'm not sure what happened after that.'

'I'm sorry,' Drew said.

Faith seemed lost in thought.

'There have been other lovers since, though?' Drew said.

Faith shook her head. 'I've always steered clear of getting involved. It seemed easier and I'm happy with my work.' Faith smiled.

Drew frowned. She felt something oddly disconcerting at the admission of abstinence and Faith's smile came across as incongruent, or at least she had sensed it that way. Given how she felt about Faith, she couldn't imagine not wanting to have someone in her life. She shook her head. 'What about us?'

Faith released a long breath and Drew wondered if she were trembling, avoiding Drew's gaze. And when Faith looked at Drew, the sadness came through again.

'I don't honestly know,' Faith said.

Drew stood suddenly and went to Faith. Faith stood and gazed into her eyes and when Drew placed her hand on Faith's chest and felt the heavy thud of her heart, she closed the space between them and Faith's breath faltered. 'Tell me this isn't a reflection of how you feel?' She watched Faith's quivering lips.

Drew took the lip into her mouth and nipped it, eliciting a quiet groan from Faith. 'Tell me you don't want this?' She studied Faith with a hard, focused gaze, and then kissed her with urgency and tenderness in equal measure, a hand on Faith's head and pulling her into the kiss, the other around her waist bringing them together at the hip. When she released Faith and stared into her dark eyes, she slipped a hand between Faith's legs and watched her react. 'And this,' she whispered. 'Tell me you don't want me, Faith.' Her voice was broken but she needed to know the truth. 'Because, this is me.' She took Faith's hand and guided it into the warm silky wetness between her legs and Faith groaned. 'This too. This is what you do to me.'

Faith took Drew with a fiery kiss that swept the breath from her and then Faith's arms were around her body and Drew was moaning, consuming her with her mouth and hands.

Drew, filled with frustrated desire, pulled out of the kiss and stared at Faith. 'Don't try and tell me you don't feel this, Faith.' She gazed longingly, shaking her head. 'Please, don't.' A tear spilt onto her cheek and Faith kissed it away. Then Faith kissed her with tenderness and held her in her arms.

'I'm sorry,' Faith whispered. 'I do feel it.'

Drew eased out of the hold. 'Please don't try and push me away with some lame excuse about my mother. I choose you, Faith. If you don't feel the same way then fine, but that has nothing to do with Esther.'

Faith looked at Drew with sincerity and nodded. 'I choose you,' she said in a whisper.

Drew took a moment to register the words, then a cautious smile appeared and as she relaxed her grin widened. 'You do?' Her fingers lazily teased the erect nipple beneath Faith's t-shirt.

Faith smiled, held her gaze. 'I do.'

Drew gazed and as her smile grew, it lit up her eyes. 'Good. That's settled then.'

17.

'Can I get a Latte, extra hot, extra shot,' please?' the man said. His tall frame made the café counter look small and his exuberant manner infiltrated the small space. 'You must be Drew?'

Faith turned from the coffee machine and smiled at the man who must have been in his mid-thirties. He had a ruddy complexion and a broad grin that disappeared as he registered the collar at her neck. 'No, I'm Faith.'

Drew entered through the kitchen door with a tray of assorted cakes and smiled at the man. 'Can I help?'

Faith smiled at her and started preparing the drink.

Drew smiled at the man who still had a slack jaw and wide-eyes.

'Umm, I'll take a flapjack, thanks. Are you Drew?' he said, gazing at her.

'Yes.'

'Hi, I'm James. Your mum said you'd be here. I hope you don't mind.'

He stopped speaking as Drew raised her hand, palm facing him. 'Let me stop you right there. James, isn't it?' She paused as he nodded. 'You see this gorgeous woman?' She looked at Faith.

James followed her gaze. 'Um, yes,' he said. His chirpy demeanour had disappeared and he seemed to have dropped a couple of inches in stature.

'This is Faith. She is my lover.'

James swallowed, his ruddy cheeks darkening as his eyes shifted from one woman to the other. 'Oh,' he said.

Faith placed the coffee and cake on the counter and smiled warmly.

'Thanks,' James said. He delved into his pocket and pulled out the money.

'James, would you do me a favour?' Drew said.

'Um, yes, sure,' he said, with the eagerness of a guilty puppy needing to please.

'Would you kindly explain to my mother that I am a lesbian and any efforts from her to hook me up with handsome young men like yourself will simply drive an irreconcilable wedge between us,' she said.

James's eyes widened. He hadn't been expecting that. 'Oh, um… sure.'

'I have tried, James, Lord knows I have.' Drew shrugged.

Faith turned her head, smiled at James and nodded. 'Believe me, He does know, James.'

James swallowed.

'But, I'm sure you know what mothers are like? She's not listening to me,' Drew continued. She smiled at him. 'Be sure you use my exact words, James. Your daughter is a lesbian.'

James looked at Drew and Faith passed the bun across the counter. 'How much is it?' he said.

Drew grinned. 'This is on the house, James. You have a great day now. Mum will be in the shop across the road.' She pointed to the corner shop directly opposite the café.

James moved in stunned silence, sat at a table and sipped at his coffee.

Faith turned to Drew and grinned. 'That was a bit naughty.'

'She needs to get the message,' Drew said, and then Grace approached.

'Hey,' Grace said, her tone upbeat, meeting Drew's gaze with a smile.

'Two Cappuccino's and a Latte,' Drew said to Faith.

'You still coming tomorrow?' Grace said.

Drew nodded. 'Absolutely.'

'Faith?'

'Definitely,' Faith said.

'Good day?' Drew said, referring to Grace and Harriet's market stall.

'It's been manic.'

'That's good. You'll be selling gin next week,' Drew said and laughed.

'That's not a bad idea,' Grace said.

'Has the passion wagon arrived yet?' Drew said and grinned.

Drew looked at the clock on the wall, which read 2.20 pm. 'In about an hour-and-a-half.'

'Two Cappuccinos and a Latte,' Faith said and slid the takeaway cups across the counter. 'Can't wait to see it. What name did you go with?'

'That's a secret until the great reveal, later,' Grace said and beamed a grin.

James stood and shuffled towards the door.

'Bye, James. Remember to speak to mum now,' Drew said, waving at him.

He nodded, and in a trance, wandered across the road to the shop.

Grace was shaking her head. 'What was that about?'

'Another date set-up,' Drew said, with a shake of her head.

Grace frowned, pointed from Drew to Faith. 'I thought you two were.'

Faith nodded. 'We are,' she said, cutting Grace off.

'Phew,' Grace said. For a split-second, she thought she'd been dreaming. Then she shook her head with thoughts of Esther's persistence. 'She's still not on board, then?'

Drew pursed her lips. 'Nope. But she's going to have to budge because I'm not.'

Grace nodded. 'Good on you.' She studied Drew and smiled at her determination. Coming out to her own mum hadn't been easy. She hadn't taken it that well either, but Nell had quickly come around and had never tried to set her up with dates in the same way Esther seemed insistent on doing with Drew. 'Mothers, eh!'

Faith smiled and her eyebrows lifted a fraction. There had been moments in her life where she had longed for her real mother, and then again there were times when she had wondered if she would have had to go through the same pain as she had seen others endure. Families were tricky. She had been lucky on that front. Her foster-mother had always been supportive and for that, she would be eternally grateful. 'See you later.'

Grace nodded and headed to the door. She opened it just as Doug approached the café. 'Hey, Doug.'

'Ah-right Grace,' Doug said. He had a pained expression and looked agitated, and Grace noticed James leaving the shop in a hurry. She held the door open and looked to Drew with raised eyebrows as Doug passed her and entered the café.

'Dad.' Drew said. 'Coffee?'

'I need a bloody double Brandy,' Doug said. 'That bloody woman's driving me nuts,' He shook his head. Then he caught Faith's presence. 'Sorry, Vicar.'

At least Doug was behaving normally. His only response when Drew had told him she was gay was to say, 'Live and let live.' She had kissed him on the forehead and nothing had changed between them.

'She wants to move to Upper Duckton.'

'What?' Drew stared at her father and tried not to snigger. Doug had been on about moving to Upper Duckton for the best part of fifteen years and Esther had flatly refused. The change of heart was completely out of character for Esther and only down to one thing.

'Yep. Says, there's nothing here for her now and she can't condone behaviours she doesn't agree with.' He rolled his eyes.

'Right!' Drew said, trying to curb the anger that balled in her chest.

'James just came in the shop,' Doug said.

'I know, I sent him,' Drew said.

Doug hesitated, looked to Faith and back at Drew. 'So, it's true, then?' He looked back to Faith and smiled.

Faith had turned from the coffee machine. She mirrored his gaze with affection.

'Yes, it is,' Drew said.

Doug was nodding and looked back to Drew. 'That's good,' he said. 'You two are good together.'

Drew released the breath she'd been holding and felt her shoulders relax. She met Doug's smile with a broad grin and then moved around the counter and pulled him into a full-body hug. 'Thanks, dad.' When she let him go he had a glassy look in his eyes.

Faith slipped the coffee across the counter. 'Thanks Doug,' she said softly.

Doug shrugged. 'Don't worry, she'll get over herself.' He pondered over Esther. 'She's all bluff and thunder.'

Drew wasn't so sure.

'So, are you moving?' Faith said.

Doug shook his head. 'Nah. Not now Tilly's working here.' He broke into a hearty chuckle.

'You know you've got no chance, dad,' Drew teased.

'I know, she's on your team.' He sighed, picked up his coffee. 'Can't stop an old man admiring a nice pair of buns, though.' He winked and Faith chuckled again.

Drew flushed and grimaced.

Doug gazed at the cake stand, longingly. Esther had him under strict instructions to diet. Bugger that! 'I'll take one of

176

those, please.' Drew handed him a toffee slice and he headed towards the door. He turned and looked to Drew. 'I'm going for a walk, so she can't leave the shop until I'm back,' he said, referring to Esther. 'She's going to need time to adjust, Faith. Gay is one thing, being gay and a Vicar is beyond her comprehension and especially when she's emotionally deranged.' He shook his head and sniggered as he opened the door.

Faith frowned.

'Menopausal, I'm sure of it,' he said with a nod of his head. 'That's got a lot to do with it. She never used to be quite this... unreasonable.' He stepped into the street and turned right, heading towards the Crooked Billet.

Drew wasn't entirely convinced. Her mother had certainly tried to guide her choices over the years. Maybe it was just his way of coping with the woman he loved dearly?

Faith looked to Drew with a sympathetic smile.

Drew nodded. 'I'm glad they know.'

'Yes,' Faith said.

'I'm looking forward to seeing the gin wagon,' Drew said, in need of a positively distracting thought.

Faith watched Drew sigh, the pensive look in her eyes revealed the inner turmoil that would be hard to shake until her mother settled. She had seen it before. 'I think a glass of Delia's gin would be well timed,' she said, and smiled and then Drew looked at her adoringly and the smile softened and flowed through her in a warm wave. She couldn't deny her feelings for Drew, and every effort to do the right thing by Esther would be to do the wrong thing by Drew. Maybe she should have stood up to Nadia's mother all those years ago? Maybe she should speak honestly to Esther?

*

'Jenny, Jenny, open up,' Delia shouted, banging on her front door for the third time.

'I'm coming,' Jenny yelled, pulling the Lycra shorts up over her hips and stomach. She opened the door, red-faced, sweat beaded on her forehead.

'What in the blazes are you up to?' Delia said.

'I'm just trying on these new shorts,' Jenny said and puffed. 'They're still too bloody tight and they're two sizes bigger than the last ones,' she said, tugging at the waist.

Delia gazed at the elastic at full stretch and then focused her attention on Jenny. 'They do look a bit cosy.'

Jenny waved a hand at her. 'Anyway, you're early.'

Delia stepped into the house and wandered uninvited into the dining room. 'Well,' she said, clasping her handbag in front of her.

'Well, what?' Jenny said, starting to pull the pants down.

Delia looked away. 'I've just been to the shop and Esther is fuming.'

'Oh, good God! What now?' Jenny strained, heaved the shorts over her hips and stood with them clinging to her knees. 'Thank fuck for that,' she muttered, referring to the relief and took in a couple of deep breaths.

'Well, apparently, she tried to set Drew up on another date,' Delia said.

Jenny rolled her eyes.

'Anyway, James, that's his name. He turned up at the café and Drew announced to him that the Vicar, that's Faith.'

'I know who the bloody Vicar is,' Jenny blurted.

'Drew said, Faith and she are lovers. Told James to tell her mother that,' Delia said, and smiled, eyebrows raised.

'Ha!' Jenny started laughing and then stopped. 'Does Doug know too?'

'Doug walked out the shop and left Esther to it, apparently,' Delia said. 'Looked as though he'd had enough.

Walked straight across to the café then spent the rest of the afternoon in the pub.'

'I need to speak to her before she does something stupid,' Jenny said.

'Drew?'

'No, Esther,' Jenny said in a frustrated tone.

'We've got the party now,' Delia said.

'Yes, I'll talk to her tomorrow,' Jenny said. 'Now, help me out of these damn things, will you?' Jenny sat on the floor and Delia grabbed the elastic waist and tugged towards Jenny's feet.

'They're glued on,' Delia said, puffing with the strain. 'I think you need a size bigger.'

'I'm not wearing a bloody size eighteen, in bloody Lycra,' Jenny said with indignation. She got to her feet and staggered to the kitchen and retrieved the trousers she had removed. She brushed her hands down her top and cleared her throat. 'Right, you ready?'

Delia nodded with an enthusiastic smile. 'Let's go and party.'

*

Drew and Faith walked down the lane leading to Duckton House and Harriet's cottage in silence, keeping a respectable distance between them. The deep sound of Flo's bark echoed and then Archie's higher pitched yap came. Faith stopped, braced herself for their approach, and then relaxed when the dogs didn't appear. As they moved closer to the cottage, the camper van came into sight.

'Hey,' Grace said, approaching from the other side of the van. 'What do you think?' She indicated towards the spruced-up wagon and grinned.

'I think the rainbow roof is a bust,' Drew said, and chuckled.

'Pinker Gins, eh?' Faith said, reading the sign above the serving hatch.

'You like the name?' Grace said. She sipped from her drink.

Harriet approached. 'I love the name,' she said. She slipped her arm around Grace's waist. 'What can we get you? I hear a celebration is in order.' She grinned and went around the other side of the wagon and appeared at the hatch. 'I understand Vanilla is very popular drink around these parts,' she said with a wink.

Drew sniggered.

Harriet giggled and she looked as though she had sampled a couple of glasses already. 'We have other gins of course, but this one comes highly recommended.'

'Is that the one from the pub?' Faith said.

Drew reached out and took Faith's hand and squeezed. 'Yes, I'll have one, please.' She smiled at Faith.

'Me too,' Faith said and rubbed her thumb across the back of Drew's hand. She let go to take the drinks and hand one to Drew.

'The others are in the garden,' Grace said, looking to where the barbeque was in full flow, Vera at the helm.

As Drew and Faith approached the smoking grill, Delia collared them and smiled. 'Don't worry about Esther,' she slurred. 'Rest assured, things are happening exactly as they should.' She sipped from the glass in her hand. 'We just need to have faith.'

'She's already got Faith,' Vera shouted and chuckled.

Drew linked an arm around Faith's and squeezed. 'Yes, I guess I do.'

'Come on love-birds,' Vera shouted. 'Let's get this party started.'

Faith sipped from the gin and smiled at Drew and then indicated to Doug who stood smiling at the two women.

Drew walked over to him. 'Didn't expect to see you here.'

'I'm only staying for the one,' he said and winked. 'Otherwise, the pub 'll go out of business.' He chuckled and raised his glass to them. 'Wanted to raise a toast to you both,' he said, and his cheeks darkened.

'Thanks, dad.' Drew placed a kiss on his cheek.

'Welcome to Duckton-by-Dale, Faith,' Doug said and raised his glass.

Faith nodded. 'Here's to you,' she said and met his toast with her own.

'Well done, you two,' Bryan said, approaching from the kitchen. 'I can't stop, gotta get to work. Might see some of you after this,' he said, scanning the garden.

'I reckon it'll be men's night in the bar tonight,' Doug said and chuckled. 'We can get some practice in for the next quiz night.'

'Ah-right,' Bryan said. 'Your best player's here.' He indicated to Grace.

'That she is,' Doug said, with affection. 'I'm so glad she stayed.' He paused, gazed around at the women at the party. 'Quite like the fact that we've got our own Hebden Bridge here. It's unique.'

'It's not unique, you delusional old fart,' Vera shouted. 'There's already one in Hebden Bridge.' She started laughing and Doug chuckled.

'I'll come with you,' he said to Bryan and finished his drink.

Drew squeezed Faith's hand, locked onto Faith's dark eyes, noticing the light that seemed to highlight the slight tints of hazel, and smiled.

'So, it is true.'

The voice came from the side of the gin wagon, bringing instant silence to the garden. It wasn't a raised voice, but the tone of disapproval didn't go unmissed by the group. Esther glared at Drew then scanned Faith briefly with a look of contempt. 'Call yourself a woman of God,' she said, her tone vitriolic.

'Come on Esther,' Vera said, approaching the woman with open arms. She was definitely more than half-cut. 'Stop this nonsense.'

That was the wrong thing to say!

Esther turned towards Vera and glared. 'You're the ringleader of this immoral behaviour. How dare you speak to me?'

'Esther, come with me,' Doug said, reaching for Esther's arm.

She shrugged him off. 'You, you're spineless. You should be doing something about this, not allowing this debauched behaviour. She's your daughter for heaven's sake,' Esther was enraged.

'Esther, I think you should go before you say something you really regret.' Doug said.

'I'm done with you,' Esther said, staring at Drew. 'I brought you up well and look at you now.'

Drew felt the urge to release Faith's hand but Faith was gripping her tightly.

The other villagers looked on in shock, no one speaking. In the silence, the dogs barked.

Faith stood perfectly still, squeezing Drew's hand, fully aware of the impact Esther's outburst would be having on her. She wanted to scream at Esther, but that wouldn't help anyone. She bit down on gritted teeth, breathed deeply through her nose, gripped Drew tightly, and prayed.

Whether Esther had simply seen enough or just finished with the tirade of abuse wasn't clear, but she turned sharply and walked away from the house at a pace.

Drew turned to Faith, tears flooding her eyes.

Doug came to her with open arms. 'I'm so sorry she said those things. I know she didn't mean it. I'm going to have a word with Jarid tonight and see if he can see her.'

Drew eased out of his embrace and nodded.

Faith could see the raw hurt in Drew's pained expression. She had learned long ago that things should never be said in anger, but clearly, that was a lesson Esther was yet to grasp. She wrapped her arms around Drew's shoulders and squeezed. 'Shall we go home?' she whispered.

Drew pulled back and looked at Faith. 'Do you mind?' she said, her tone weary and dejected, tears slipping onto her cheeks. She wiped at them with the palm of her hand, cleared her throat, tried to regain her composure.

Faith looked towards the path Esther had taken, shaking her head. She took a deep breath, turned to face Drew and nodded, lips pinched.

Vera's dark eyes had narrowed to a pinpoint, her eyebrows bunched, and she was glaring with gritted teeth in the direction of the main road. Her face had turned beetroot red and her hands were shaking. She looked as if she were unable to breathe and about to explode. Jenny was trying to get her attention and console her. Delia was studying the cards she had laid out on the table, and Sheila Goldsworth approached the garden from the large tented greenhouse with Doris and Neville at her side.

'Your beans are coming on a treat,' Neville said, oblivious to the dark energy that had descended on the party. 'Measuring in at eight point four three centimetres on average. I measured ten in a random sample across five plants.'

Doris cleared her throat to get his attention but he remained oblivious.

'Cucumbers are still going strong,' he continued.

'Neville,' Doris said, trying to alert him to stop talking.

'Can I grab some of those ladies' fingers, Harriet?' he said.

'Neville,' Doris yelled.

'What's that dear?' Neville said.

Doris eyed him with a look that could kill.

He squinted as he looked towards Harriet, and then to Grace. 'What did I say?'

Harriet smiled warmly and walked towards him. 'Would you like to take some away with you tonight?' she said softly and went into the tent, followed by an excited Neville.

Vera took in a deep breath, turned to face Jenny and slurred, 'I swear I'm going to kill that woman.' But there was something other than anger in her tone; something more akin to deep regret.

Jenny tugged Vera into her arms and whispered, 'No, you're not. I'll go and talk to her and let's see if she'll go and see Jarid. She's getting worse and it's not like her.'

Vera harrumphed.

'Right, let's get some music on,' Grace said and clapped her hands. She turned the meat on the barbeque. It was going to take a lot to shift the sombre atmosphere. And then she turned towards the gate to the paddock and blinked. Her jaw relaxed and she blinked again. 'V, Jenny, look.'

Vera and Jenny turned and stared into the dark night. 'Hilda,' Vera called out and waved.

Drew snapped her head towards the vision.

Faith followed her gaze searching for the ghost she had heard about.

Delia turned the cards and grinned. 'The Knight of Cups, following the heart, the romantic,' she said, not that anyone was listening. The group had congregated at the gate, all eyes searching the field beyond the paddock.

'Did you see anything?' Faith said to Drew.

Drew shook her head.

Faith smiled at her softly, brushed a thumb gently over her damp, red, puffy eyes. 'Let's get you home.'

Drew nodded.

18.

Drew woke to the unexpected banging at her front door. Faith mumbled something and turned over. She looked at her phone. 1.15 am. The banging came again and she groaned, stepped out of bed, put on her dressing gown and descended the stairs. She opened the door to her father's wide-eyed, ashen appearance.

'What is it?' she said, blinking and trying to stem the anxiety that had imploded in her chest.

'It's your mother,' he said.

Drew closed her eyes, a kaleidoscope of emotion lighting her up. When she opened her eyes, Doug's worried gaze caused a further surge of panic. 'What is it?'

'She's been taken to hospital,' Doug said.

Drew blinked, working the information through a sluggish brain and the emotional soup that any mention of Esther elicited. She was still feeling raw from the earlier assault and frustration came easily.

'I thought she was having a heart attack,' Doug said. 'The medics said they thought her heart was okay, but they've taken her in for tests because she was also talking nonsense.'

'She's been talking nonsense for a long time,' Drew said. Sympathy just wasn't coming to her. She rubbed at her temple and brow.

'What is it?' Faith said, arriving at Drew's side, rubbing at her eyes.

'Mum's been taken to hospital,' Drew said.

Faith looked to Doug with concern. 'Is she okay?'

Doug shrugged. 'The ambulance has just taken her to Ferndale. I thought you should know. I'm going over there now.'

Faith looked to Drew. 'Do you want to go?'

Drew shook her head. 'No.'

'Right, I'll leave you be,' Doug said. 'I'll find out what's happening and let you know.'

'Thanks,' Drew said and watched him walk away.

'Are you sure you don't want to go?' Faith said softly.

Drew shook her head. 'No, I'm not, but I just can't face her. I feel so angry, so hurt. I'm worried.' Drew turned to Faith, the confused pain evident in the sheen that lightened her eyes and the tight smile that was a lousy veneer for her conflicting thoughts and feelings.

Faith stroked her face with kindness, and gently tucked the hair behind her ear. 'I'm here, whatever you decide,' she whispered. 'We can bike there in fifteen minutes, if you change your mind.' She pulled Drew into her chest, breathed her in, and held her close and when Drew started to shake in her arms she pulled her closer and whispered into her hair. 'I'm here, Drew. I'm not going anywhere.'

Drew softened, eased out of the comforting embrace and stood with closed eyes. Torn between wanting to be there for her mother and wanting to avoid the pain the woman had inflicted, a sense of duty and love competing with her will, she nodded. 'Will you take me, please?' she whispered.

'Yes,' Faith said softly. 'Of course!'

*

'Heartburn?' Vera said to the assembled group of women, with the same disdain Drew had felt as she stood at her mother's bedside in the hospital at 2.30 am that morning.

'Yes,' Drew said, wearily, yawning as she handed out their drinks.

'She has high blood pressure, and they are looking at putting her on a mild anti-depressant. Apparently, she talked to the doctor about the situation with me and she's been advised to explore HRT.'

'Ha! Good on him,' she said.

'It was a female doctor,' Drew said, and smiled.

'Good looking?' Vera said and winked at Drew.

'Not so much,' Drew said and smiled at Faith.

'Well, hopefully, they'll give her something for her sanity,' Vera said. 'She's been unrecognisable recently.'

'It does help knowing hormones might be a part of the problem,' Drew said. And she meant it. The idea that her mother's behaviour had some foundation over which Esther hadn't any control did bring some small comfort and in that she had found compassion for her mother.

'Ageing sucks,' Vera said.

'I'll second that,' Delia said.

'Cakes. We need cakes,' Jenny said. 'Sugar is good for the soul.'

'Coming up,' Drew said.

'It's not good for those Lycra's though,' Delia reminded Jenny.

'They're going back to the shop,' Jenny said with a dismissive wave. 'Got a pair of tracksuit bottoms. I don't think that Lycra material stretches like it should.'

Vera studied her. 'Did you tell them about the spandex?' she said.

'Spandex?' Delia said with a frown.

Jenny flushed.

'These were Lycra shorts,' Delia said.

Vera looked at Jenny with raised eyebrows. 'Shorts, eh?' she said and a wicked grin appeared with the glint in her eye.

Jenny slapped her on the arm. 'Eat your bloody bun,' she said, pointed at the cake arriving at the table, the cherry on the top glistening.

Vera grinned, picked up the bun and took a large bite.

'That reminds me,' Jenny started. 'I was thinking we should do a Zumbathon to raise funds for the playground.

Alongside the Bake-Off, music, the gin bar, and a bouncy castle for the children. What do you think?' She sipped at her coffee.

'You didn't last five minutes at Zumba last week,' Vera quipped.

'I'm in training,' Jenny said and slapped her on the arm again.

Grace pondered the idea. Harriet was nodding. 'I think that's a great idea,' Grace said. 'It wouldn't take much to advertise it. I'm sure Ellena could encourage her clients, too.'

All the women around the table were nodding and then Vera chuckled. 'Hasn't been minuted, you know!'

Grace laughed. 'I'll let Doris and Sheila know. We can minute it retrospectively,' she said. 'Is everyone in agreement?'

The women nodded again.

'I'll speak to Ellena,' Jenny said.

'We need a plan,' Vera said to Delia and Jenny.

'Annie has put an editorial piece out about the ghost hunt and we've had half-a-dozen bookings already.' Delia said.

'That's very good,' Vera said and hungrily bit the cherry off the bun, causing Jenny watching, to blush.

'I've got nine entries for the Bake-Off. We can only take twelve for the first round. They will need to make a sweet dish that doesn't involve an oven because we can only get four ovens for the final,' Harriet said.

'Bloody hell, there's a challenge!' Vera said.

'We've got camping and barbeque equipment, so there are options, just no ovens. It will be exciting,' she said, enthusiastically.

Vera looked at her unmoved. She couldn't see the excitement in that at all!

'Luke says they've got four teams signed up for the running. The route is mapped out and they've got the local support services involved. He's managed to get the Farmer's Association to sponsor it too,' Jenny said. 'They're trying to get another four teams and should have that confirmed by the end of the week. They'll set off at 9.00 am and should all be finished by 1 pm. Bryan said about offering lunch at the pub, but if we're running a barbeque in the park, everyone could congregate there? I'll speak to them.'

'That's awesome,' Grace said. 'Is there anything we've missed?'

'Can't think of anything,' Harriet said. 'Who's doing Zumba tonight?'

All the hands in the room went up.

Harriet looked at Drew. 'Do you think we could get your mum involved?'

Drew sighed. 'I don't know. I think she got quite a fright, but she's a long way from changing her attitude.'

'I'll go and talk to her,' Jenny said to Harriet and squeezed her daughter's arm. 'We need her back in the fold.' She nodded at the women around the room.

'Agreed,' Vera said. 'She needs some of your herbs, that's what she needs,' she said to Delia.

'I've been working on the perfect pick-me-up,' Delia said. 'I'll bring some round and you can take it to her.'

'I'll bring some flowers over for her this afternoon, mum,' Harriet said.

'That'll be nice. I'm sure she just needs to know we're here for her. She might even fit into those Lycra pants I bought. I haven't sent them back, yet. What do you think?'

Delia looked at her and frowned. 'I think they'll drown the poor woman.'

Vera laughed. 'You leave my chumpkins alone,' she said teasingly to Delia and when she laughed again Jenny thumped her on the arm.

Drew smiled at the women, heartened by their concern for her mother. Perhaps she should speak to her too. She looked to the door as it opened and her smile broadened.

'Watch out, here comes our happy Vicar, looking all bright and gay,' Vera quipped and burst out laughing.

Jenny chuckled and received a stern look from her daughter.

'Morning Vera,' Faith said and laughed. 'Didn't see you at service, yesterday. I meant to say, I think God's missed your witty presence.' She stared at Vera with a glint in her eye. 'Maybe tomorrow? We have a short service ten-thirty 'til eleven. Perfect for those of a certain age, and with a short attention span.' She grinned and winked at Vera who held her palms up in submission.

Grace and Harriet sniggered. Grace couldn't imagine Vera in church under any circumstances.

'Do you know, I think I'd like to go to that,' Jenny said. 'Do you think Esther will be there, Faith?'

'She used to come to it,' Faith said and pursed her lips.

'Ah, yes,' Jenny said, acknowledging that Faith was now part of the Esther problem. 'I'll see if I can get her back there. She used to enjoy church.'

'Yes, she did,' Faith said. Her smile held compassion and a hint of remorse.

'Right, I need to get on,' Jenny said and stood.

'Me too; I'll get those flowers picked and bring them to the house,' Harriet said.

'I'll start organising the barbeque and gin, and I'll get Tilly to liaise with Annie. We've only got three weeks,' Grace said.

'I think Tilly's been liaising with Annie just fine,' Vera said. 'Annie's been in the pub three times since the mic night.'

'How'd you know that?'

'Doug said.'

Grace chuckled. 'That's good.'

*

191

Jenny stood at Esther's front door, pulled down the blouse that had crumpled on the short walk from her house and juggled the large bunch of flowers, the Lycra pants and tonic in a bag tucked under her arm. She blew out a puff of air before wrapping the doorknocker. She stepped back and waited, feeling slightly on edge at facing Esther uninvited. She banged again and the door opened.

'Jenny!' Esther said. She stood in the doorway, staring at Jenny, the flowers in her arm, the conciliatory smile on her face.

'You look tired,' Jenny said, taking in the pallid cheeks and dark rings around Esther's sunken eyes.

Esther opened the door fully. 'I'm exhausted,' she said, her tone softer. 'Come in.' She turned, followed the short hallway to the back of the house and went into the kitchen. 'Do you want a cup of tea?'

'Please,' Jenny said and handed over the flowers. 'These are from Harriet... and Grace,' she added deliberately. She still felt uncomfortable, waiting for an irrational blast of anger from Esther, but something about the woman's fragile state and the resignation in her admission of tiredness gave her hope that Esther's barriers were down. 'Delia sent you a pick-me-up, too,' she said, pulling the bag from under her arm and placing it on the small wooden kitchen table. 'Her special herbs and the Vanilla gin. Works wonders,' she said.

Esther smiled weakly and laid the flowers on the surface. 'That's kind of her.' She plucked a vase from the cupboard, filled it with water and arranged the flowers, filled the kettle and turned it on and then leant on the work surface waiting for the kettle to boil staring out the kitchen window into the garden. 'It's been a beautiful day,' she said.

'It has. We're hoping the heat-wave holds for the fundraising weekend,' Jenny said with enthusiasm.

'Yes,' Esther said. The kettle boiled and she poured the water into two cups, mashed the tea-bag, lifted it and added milk. She placed a cup of tea on the table in front of Jenny and sat facing her. She sipped at her drink.

Jenny studied her friend. 'How are you?' She searched Esther's grey-blue eyes. The fire that had become so familiar wasn't there and concern filled Jenny. Esther had lost her spark.

Esther shook her head and slowly sipped at her tea. 'Confused.'

Jenny nodded, looking for permission to speak. 'It's hard when it's your own.' She sighed.

Esther looked at her as if she hadn't been expecting Jenny to understand her situation. Jenny had lived in an open relationship with Bryan for as long as she could remember and then having hooked up with Vera, she hadn't considered that Harriet coming out would have affected her in the slightest.

'I know. It's hard to think I might have struggled when Harriet came out, but I did. Bryan introduced me to a lifestyle that was fun and worked for us, but it was still unconventional and went against my own upbringing. Some things are deeply ingrained in us, but that doesn't make them right. It just means it can create a negative reaction that defies logic,' she said. 'I was worried about Harriet, especially being so young. What if she had made the wrong decision? Was she too young and what would her friends say? Those questions still went through my mind, along with the fact that Bryan and I were sure to get the blame for her turning out the way she did. Imagine how bigoted I felt having those thoughts. It was hard at the time, Esther.'

Esther sighed, her fragile hands around the cup in the saucer, beginning to shake. 'I didn't know,' she said. 'You've always been so assured.'

'I had to adjust. Now, I wouldn't bat an eyelid. But this was more than twenty years ago. I wasn't much past being a kid myself. At one point I thought, hoped even, that Harriet and Drew would get together.'

Esther looked at her quizzically.

'I suppose I assumed it would make things easier, protect them both,' Jenny said. 'They were always such good friends at school. In my naivety, I thought they would make the perfect match and we wouldn't have to worry about outsiders hurting either of them. Drew is like a daughter to me, too.' She chuckled. 'I realise how odd that sounds under the circumstances.' She reached across the table and took Esther's hand. 'We've all been friends for such a long time, Esther. I hope we can put the last few weeks behind us, and move on.'

Esther didn't pull her hand away, which was a good start.

'I think Elvis's death came as a big shock to us all, too,' Jenny said. 'It's hard losing someone you love. But, you haven't lost Drew and love is the most important thing; not the out-dated rules we were brought up with.' She held Esther's gaze with a compassionate smile.

'I think I have lost her,' Esther said, in a whisper. 'Why would she want me in her life now? I was obnoxious.' She was shaking her head. 'I don't even want to be around me.'

Jenny squeezed the limp hand. 'Because you're her mother and you love her dearly and you care about her so much it has led you to be a proper dafty-pants. She will understand,' she said with affection and let out a nervous chuckle.

Esther's chuckle was almost a muffled huff, but it was there and a major breakthrough. 'Faith is a good person, I know that,' Esther said.

Jenny wasn't expecting that admission. 'Yes, she is,' she said, feeling slightly tense as she awaited some kind of vitriolic counter comment.

'She's a Vicar,' Esther said.

Here it comes! 'Yes, she is, and a good one too.'

'Don't you see the problem with that?' Esther said and held Jenny's gaze as if looking for the truth.

Jenny shook her head. 'No, Esther, I don't see a problem with that. But I understand it's not what we're used to. That we haven't been brought up thinking openly about relationships doesn't make that relationship wrong. It just makes it different.'

Esther sighed. 'I know. But it's so hard.'

Jenny nodded. 'It can be. Change is difficult to accept. And it will be much harder if you lose Drew, your friends, the villagers who are also your family. No one else cares, Esther. They see Drew and Faith as family too, and everyone misses you.'

Esther studied Jenny. 'Really?'

Jenny nodded.

'What about Vera?'

Jenny grinned. 'You obviously tapped her buttons, but she's been your friend for long enough. She knows it's not like you; not deep down.'

Esther looked at Jenny and blinked repeatedly. 'But it is, isn't it? Otherwise, I wouldn't have said those things,' she said softly.

Jenny didn't have a response. She pondered. 'We can say hurtful things when we feel threatened, Esther. It doesn't make them true. It was just a reaction to your concern for Drew. I guess the real question is how do you feel now?'

Esther's expression was hard to read, a mix of remorse and uncertainty. 'Maybe?' She still felt the conflict as if it were the Great Wall of China sitting between her thoughts and feelings. Knowing the logic that who Drew loved didn't matter was very different from the feeling that it was wrong. And, the feeling was so strongly deep-rooted. She toyed with the idea of acceptance and it slammed straight into that wall and then the thought of losing Drew and her friends brought overwhelming sadness. 'I need help,' she said.

'Talking helps,' Jenny said. 'Why don't you talk to Drew? Focus on her happiness, not what you think is right.'

'That's easier said than done.'

'I know.'

'But, I know I'll lose everything if I don't.' Esther sighed, wiped a tear from her cheek then looked at Jenny with a tight smile. 'Thank you for coming.'

Jenny felt the tension subside. She squeezed Esther's hand, released it and pulled out the pot of herbs from the bag. 'Right, let's get some of these down you,' she said. She pulled out a clear bottle with Vanilla handwritten on the label.

'What's that?' Esther said.

'It's that new formula you tried the other night in the square,' Jenny said. 'Delia's pick-me-up herbs and the gin; it's all delicious. Where are your glasses?'

Esther shook her head. She had forgotten about the incident in the square. 'On the sideboard.' Esther pointed to a pair of black-rimmed spectacles.

'No, your drinking glasses.' Jenny chuckled and started opening the cupboards on the wall.

Esther studied the label, opened the screw-top lid, and sniffed. 'This smells like vanilla,' she said.

'Tastes like it too.'

'I don't remember.'

Jenny returned with two small glasses and a teaspoon. She spooned in the herbs and poured a shot of gin over the top. Stirred and handed a glass to Esther. 'Think of it as a double dose of medicine,' she said and knocked back her drink in one hit. 'Ooh, that is good. I think it's better than the raspberry gin liqueur,' she said and grinned.

Esther sipped at the glass then took a longer sip, and then finished the drink. 'That is lovely,' she said and her eyes had a sparkle about them. 'Taste's familiar.'

After the third glass, Esther's cheeks had a rosy complexion and she was smiling. 'I've been such a bloody stubborn fool, Jen' she said.

'Ah, nothing that can't be solved,' Jenny said. 'That reminds me, I brought these around for you.' She pulled out the Lycra shorts and held them up.

Esther squinted at the elastic strip-like clothing. 'What's that?'

'Lycra shorts. They're for Zumba. You'll need a pair for the Zumbathon we're doing for the fundraising.'

'Zumbathon?'

'I'll explain when we're at the group tonight,' Jenny said. 'What group?'

'The group you missed last week. Mondays with Ellena.'

'I'm not sure I can do it after this.' Esther pointed to the empty glass on the table and the half-empty bottle of gin.

'I doubt you'll be able to do it without.' Jenny chuckled. 'Takes the pain away. I'll come by at seven.' She stood, not giving Esther the chance to refuse. 'Make sure you're wearing those pants, they'll keep everything in check.' She straightened her top. When Esther stood, she swayed and Jenny pulled her into a full-on busty embrace. 'I've missed you. You, old fart,' she whispered.

'I've missed you too,' Esther said.

Jenny moved away and smiled. 'Make sure you eat something.' She nodded at Esther. 'Seven, remember?'

Esther smiled. 'I'll have a little kip first.' She tottered up the hall to let Jenny out the door.

Jenny stopped and held Esther's gaze. 'Promise me you'll speak to Drew; listen to her. She knows what she's doing.' Jenny nodded her head in affirmation.

Esther sighed. 'I promise.' She closed the door behind Jenny. As she wandered into the living room, a tear trickled onto her cheek, and as she sat, a trail slid down her face. 'Such a fool,' she muttered.

Jenny headed home with a skip in her stride, a satisfied smile on her face. That went quite well. Maybe that was SOWILO in action. Delia had said, a path to self-awareness. Seeing that which makes you destructive to yourself and others, seeking change to heal and be complete. Well, Esther certainly seemed to have turned a corner, and Drew certainly seemed to be on a path of self-knowledge, too. Maybe the rune stones weren't too far off after all?

19.

Jenny opened the hall door, but it was Esther who walked in first. The room was empty of people though the music player sat next to Ellena's water bottle at the head of the room. The lights were on, so somebody must be around.

Jenny followed her into the room. 'Oh, we must be early,' she said though she didn't seem surprised.

Both women turned their heads when the door opened again.

Drew walked into the hall, Faith at her side, and seeing her mother, stopped.

'I'll leave you two to it then?' Jenny said and grabbed Faith by the arm and led her out the door. As she closed the door behind her, Delia, Vera and Ellena appeared from the side of the building, Vera giving a thumbs-up to Jenny. Jenny mirrored the gesture and the women gathered at the entrance, Vera and Jenny with their ears pinned to the door.

'What are they saying?' Delia said.

'SShhh! I can't hear,' Vera said.

The women stood in silence, waiting, listening.

'Mum!' Drew said, her heart pounding, her mouth dry. She studied the fragile-looking woman with detachment. She hadn't been convinced of the meeting, but Vera had insisted that Esther wanted to talk to her. Her mother looked tired, worn-down, and older than she had noticed before. The oversized t-shirt hung loosely over her narrow hips, the Lycra's hung loosely around her thin legs.

'Drew,' Esther said. She hadn't planned to have the conversation with her daughter right now; she hadn't fully thought through what she needed to say.

Drew looked at her. 'You don't need to say anything, mum.'

Esther shook her head. 'No, I do,' she said. 'I just hadn't expected...' She stopped talking, looked straight at her daughter and sighed. 'You've always been a good person, Drew.'

'It's okay, mum.' Drew was aware of the tightness in her jaw, her discomfort with the compliment when she was still feeling cross with Esther.

'You have. You are kind, considerate, loving, and I've always been so very proud of you.' Esther cleared her throat, held her daughter's gaze. 'Remember the time you nursed Harriet when she got a cold and took her fruit to school for a week. You were 6 years old. She was your best friend,' Esther said, softly. 'I always thought that was all it was, friendship. I didn't know you had...' She paused. 'I didn't know you had different feelings for her.'

Drew felt the heat in her cheeks, broke eye contact, and looked towards the back of the hall. She wasn't sure she was ready for this kind of chat and more to the point she didn't know what to say. She said nothing.

'I'm sorry, Drew.' Esther said, in almost a whisper. 'I'm sorry I didn't see you; take notice of your needs. I.' She stopped again. 'I did what I thought was right. It was all I knew. I'm not good with change, never have been. That's not meant as an excuse, it's just who I am.' Esther looked around the room and back to Drew. 'Are you happy?'

Drew held her mother's gaze, nodding, the tightness dissipating with the brave admission. 'Yes,' she said, her voice broken.

Esther nodded. 'It will take some getting used to,' she said. 'But, I need to adjust.' She paused, studied Drew, her top lip quivering. She cleared her throat. 'Will you help me?'

Drew stepped up to Esther, held her arms open and clamped her mother in a tight embrace. 'I'm sorry I didn't say something years ago,' she said. She kissed her mum's head and whispered 'I love you, mum.'

Esther received the hug with the protective distance she had always maintained between them and when Drew let her go she straightened her t-shirt and cleared her throat again.

Drew smiled at her mum's reticence. She had never known her be any different, but there was no doubting the love Esther felt in the glassy eyes that rested on her. 'Thank you,' she said.

'What's happening?' Doug said as he approached the hall.

'Sshh!' Delia said and flapped a hand at him.

'Esther's sorry she didn't take notice of the newt when Drew was a kid,' Vera said.

'What newt?' Delia said with a frown.

'She's not good with money, and something about exercise not being for her,' Vera added.

Delia's frown deepened.

Doug rolled his eyes. 'Bloody hell. Is this what you're up to?'

Ellena chuckled excitedly. 'It's an intervention,' she said, proudly. She'd never been involved in one of the women's fixes before. This was fun!

'Hang on. Esther's just asked if Drew's happy. Oh, wait, what was that?' Vera stood away from the door and addressed Doug. 'Is the business going bust?' she said.

'What?' Doug said. 'Bloody woman's lost the plot.'

'She's asking Drew for a loan,' Vera said and put her ear back to the door. 'Drew's saying, she loves Esther. That's good,' Vera said.

And then the door flung open and Vera tumbled into Jenny who tumbled into Delia who took out Doug. Doug stumbled into the laurel hedge that lined the path and slid to the ground.

'Bloody hell,' Doug mumbled. 'I came for Zumba, not some bloody combat class.' He pulled himself to his feet with a helping hand from Faith.

Drew shook her head, knowing full well the women had been snooping at the door. She turned her gaze to Faith and felt warmth flood her. God, she was gorgeous. She smiled and walked towards her.

Esther stood in front of Vera.

Vera straightened her t-shirt and cleared her throat. 'Esther,' she said, the gruffness in her voice softened by the embarrassment of having been caught out.

'You, silly old fart,' Esther said and smiled.

'I'm in good company,' Vera chirped back and opened her arms.

The contact between them was brief, but it meant everything.

'Right, come on everyone, it's Zumba time,' Ellena announced and clapped her hands.

*

'Who wants gin?' Vera said.

'No, I'll have a pint,' Doug said. 'Bloody hell that was exhausting.' His cheeks still flushed from the exercise and a thin layer of moisture covered his skin.

'So, what about the Zumbathon?' Vera said to him. 'You up for it?'

He nodded. 'Count me in. Bryan will do it too.'

Bryan chuckled as he pulled the beer and handed it across the bar. 'Ellena puts me through my paces enough already,' he said with a glint in his eye and a broad grin that made his cheeks shine.

'I bet she does,' Doug quipped. He had been happily admiring Bryan's other half at the front of the room until the boxing jab-like movements she had introduced into the routine. At that point, Esther had lost control of the Lycra pants she'd been gripping at her waist and they had landed at her ankles. The image had never been the same after that! He hadn't realised Esther possessed a pair of red frilly lace knickers, let alone worn them. He had made a commitment at that moment. He would be attending Zumba classes every week.

'Gin's coming up,' Tilly said, placing two drinks on the bar.

Vera handed one to Drew and one to Faith. 'Esther, what are you having?'

'Say yes to Vanilla,' she said and smiled at Jenny. 'Just one though.'

'Good on you,' Vera said.

'Coming up,' Tilly said handing over another two gins.

'So, Zumbathon is on,' Vera said, raising her glass in a toast.

A cheer went up.

Drew looked to Faith and raised her glass.

Faith smiled and gave her a look that said, is everything okay?

Drew smiled, longingly.

'Vicar?' Doug interrupted, oblivious to the intimate moment Faith had been trying to share with his daughter.

Faith cleared her throat, sipped her drink. 'Yes, Doug?'

'How are you at quizzes?'

'Um, okay I guess, why?'

'There's one next Wednesday. Could do with you on the team,' he said.

'Um, right,' Faith said.

'Good, very good,' he said and turned back to the bar. Faith overheard him saying to Bryan, 'We're gonna win this year, divine intervention, give me another pint, Bry,' and she smiled.

'Sounds competitive,' Faith said to Drew.

'Oh yes!' Drew said and held her gaze. She leaned in and whispered, 'You have amazing eyes,' and when she backed off, Faith's cheeks were flushed.

'Ah-right, love birds,' Grace said and watched Drew's colour shift. 'So, you're officially out now,' she said to Drew and beamed a grin. She raised her glass. 'Cheers to that!'

Harriet nudged Grace in the ribs. 'Leave them alone,' she said and dragged Grace away.

Faith looked at Drew and smiled. 'They'll stop teasing eventually.'

Drew looked around the room, spotted her mother studying the rune stones that Delia had laid out in front of her, Vera's hand resting on her shoulder. She held Faith's gaze, looked into the green eyes and beyond. 'Can we go home, I'm shattered?' she said.

Faith nodded. She left her half-full glass on the bar and turned towards the door.

'I'll just say goodnight to mum,' Drew said. 'I'll catch you up.'

Faith stepped out of the pub onto the cobbled street and took a deep breath. The balmy autumn evening held a slight chill, the sky dark, clear, allowing the stars to be seen. She took in the café just a few doors down, the curb she had parked her bike at on that first day, across the road to the small cobbled square and the corner shop that Doug and Esther owned. Her eyes wandered along the back of the square, the Duckton-by-Dale community clock on the wall of the old bank building with duck prints embedded in the brickwork either side of it. She smiled. It was a quaint village.

She tracked back across the square and nodded at the woman sat on the bench seat, the white poodle sat perfectly to attention at her side. The woman waved to her and she waved back. She didn't recognise her from any of the services she had conducted. It didn't matter though. People were friendly here and in the surrounding villages, there was always a warm welcome no matter who you were. She felt the slight breeze on her cheek and turned towards the pub door as it opened and smiled.

'Hey,' she said to Drew and held out her hand.

'Hey,' Drew said and took it.

'Your place or mine?' Faith said.

'Yours,' Drew said. The thought of staying overnight at the cottage caused a slight twinge of something close to guilt, and then a wave of excitement swept it away and her stomach somersaulted at the thought of Faith standing naked... except for the white collar around her neck. Her heart raced at the image and then fire shot through her. Faith was looking at her and she wondered if she could read her mind, and then Faith's attention shifted to the square, she was waving and Drew felt mildly disappointed. 'Who are you waving at?'

'The woman over there,' Faith said.

She looked across at the empty bench seat. 'What woman?'

'The silver-grey haired woman sitting on the bench, with the poodle.' She pointed.

Drew looked again. Nothing. 'I can't see her,' she said and smiled.

Faith frowned, looked at Drew with suspicion.

Drew's smile broadened and her eyes widened. 'I can't, honestly. It must be Hilda.' Sometimes I see her, sometimes I don't.' Drew shrugged, secretly warmed by the fact that Hilda had appeared to Faith.

Faith stood motionless, processing the image, her jaw relaxed, eyes unfocused. 'The ghost-woman?'

Drew squeezed Faith's hand, held her gaze, and smiled. 'Yes, Hilda Spencer, with a poodle,' she said in a whisper. 'Did you know, that means someone's going to move into the village, to stay? Sometimes she's seen with a sheep and sometimes the person seeing can't tell which it is. There's always a meaning, allegedly, depending on what she's walking, and some people think it doesn't matter either way.' She shrugged and looked at Faith. 'So, if it's a poodle, someone's moving here to stay.' She grinned.

Faith gazed at her then smiled. 'I guess that would be me.'

'Will you?' Drew said.

Faith's eyes narrowed.

'Will you be staying?' Drew needed certainty.

Faith looked into Drew's eyes with unwavering desire and with a hoarse voice said, 'Yes, I will. I've already confirmed with my boss.'

Overcome with passion, Drew held Faith in a lingering, deep kiss in the full darkness of Duckton-by-Dale high street, with only one onlooker: Hilda Spencer.

20.

Jenny ticked the last two arrivals off the list and Delia showed them up the stairs.

'Dinner and a full briefing will take place in the dining room at 7.30 pm,' she said. She led the women in their mid-fifties into the bedroom.

'This is just the quaintest, Ingrid,' the taller of the two said to her friend. She had an American accent and studied the room as if it were a newly excavated precious jewel of historical interest.

'I told you it would be perfect,' Ingrid said to her.

Ingrid turned to the woman and smiled. 'And there are real ghosts here?'

'Yes,' Delia said. 'There are. And we have a full schedule of activities over the weekend,' she added. 'Welcome to our inaugural Duckton-by-Dale Festival. We hope your weekend will be filled with psychic sight and ghostly goodies,' she added, remembering the slogan Annie had insisted they use in the event marketing. The campaign had certainly worked, they were already fully booked for a second event they had added that would run across Halloween weekend.

'Awesome,' the tall woman said.

'You'll have loads of material for your book,' Ingrid was saying.

'You're an author?' Delia asked, addressing the tall woman.

'Yes, ghost stories and paranormal romance. I'm S R Lewis,' she said. 'Please, call me Sarah.' She smiled.

'Oh, how exciting,' Delia said not knowing who the hell S R Lewis was.

'When do we get to see the real thing?' Sarah asked.

Delia felt flustered at the thought that Hilda might not appear. They had built up the event with the certainty of a sighting, which Annie had suggested, and now they had to deliver. 'No one ever knows precisely,' she said. That was the truth.

'Man, I'm so thrilled to be here,' Sarah said. 'Ingrid, this was such a find.'

'Well, I'm sure we can get a refund if we don't see any ghosts, right?' Ingrid said, directing the question at Delia.

Delia mumbled noncommittally. 'We'll see you both at dinner then,' she said and left the room hastily.

She ran down the stairs and into the kitchen and puffing, said to Vera, 'We need Hilda to appear or we'll have to refund.'

'We've got a plan,' Vera said, peeling potatoes and looking relaxed. 'Beef-and-ale pie is in the oven. Are you set up for readings in the living room? I've swapped the sofa and table around so the table is in front of the stag. Make sure you sit with the stag's head behind you.'

'Right, right,' Delia said and darted across the foyer heading for the living room.

'Jenny, put an extra shot of Vanilla in the punch will you,' Vera said. 'We need this lot seeing things.' She chuckled.

Jenny giggled and emptied half a bottle of gin into the large crystal-glass bowl. Then stood cutting the strawberries into small pieces, her hazy gaze shifting between Vera and the fruit. She smiled dreamily, watched Vera working with focused passion, enjoyed the warmth and comfort of her presence and started to wonder...

Vera tipped the chopped potatoes into a large pot. 'Do you think there's enough?' she said studying the pot. She turned and noticed Jenny staring at her oddly. 'What?'

Jenny smiled at her softly. 'Nothing,' she lied.

'What do you think?' Vera said, studying the pot again and scratching her head. 'I haven't cooked for this many people in donkey's years.'

Jenny approached the stove and looked into the pot. She could feel Vera's arm against her breast and a tingle stirred her, bringing colour to her cheeks.

Vera noticed the change. 'You having a flush?' she said.

'No,' Jenny said and placed a hand around Vera's waist.

'Oh!' Vera looked completely taken off-guard, unsure as to whether to focus on the potatoes or the love of her life that seemed to be propositioning her over a hot stove. Opting to take care of their guests, 'Is there enough?' she said.

Jenny squeezed the flesh around Vera's stomach. 'Plenty,' she said and before Vera could speak again, Jenny's lips had closed in on Vera's and silenced her in a tender kiss.

Vera stood immobilised by the passion in Jenny's touch, minded of the Lycra shorts and the beautiful woman squeezed into them. She had loved Jenny for more years than she could remember. When Jenny moved away and looked into Vera's eyes, Vera was lost for words.

'I was wondering,' Jenny said.

'Right,' Vera said. The potatoes were bubbling and water was spitting over the top of the pan, and then voices came to her from the foyer and Jenny was staring at her with a strange look in her eye again. The beef-and-ale pie needed to come out of the oven. They needed the punch in the living room already.

'Vera, are you listening to me?' Jenny said, reaching up and stroking her face with tenderness.

'Yes, sorry.'

'I was wondering...'

'Yes, you've said that,' Vera said. 'We need to get the punch out for the guests.'

'Do you love me?'

Vera sent Jenny a look of abject horror. 'Of course, I do,' she said. 'What on earth makes you think I don't?'

Jenny stood gazing, smiling. Vera looked frazzled and confused. The potatoes continued to spit and the gentle aroma of burned pastry started to filter through the air.

'Fuck! The pie's burning,' Vera said, flung open the oven and whipped out the tray.

Jenny giggled.

'Have you been supping too much punch?' Vera said.

Jenny shook her head, though she had had a couple of gins before she had left the house earlier. She had been thinking a lot about Vera and their life in the last few days, with what had happened between Esther, Elvis's death and Faith coming into the village. She just felt the timing was right.

Vera wiped the moisture from her top lip and looked at Jenny with exasperation. 'Jen love, we're about to serve dinner, we need to get the evening's entertainment on the go and you're asking daft questions and staring at me like some love-struck teenager. What am I missing?'

Jenny dropped to her knees and looked up at Vera, longingly, her head perilously close to Vera's crotch.

Delia stepped into the kitchen, studied the scene and leapt towards Jenny. 'What on earth? Did you faint?' she said, with a wide-eyed, concerned gaze.

Jenny turned and smiled at her. 'Give me a minute, Delia,' she said.

'Oh! Right-oh,' Delia said, and with a bemused look on her face marched back through the kitchen door.

'Stand up woman,' Vera said, reaching for Jenny's arm. 'Did your legs give way or something?' She looked Jenny up and down with bewildered bemusement. 'I need to get the spuds off the boil love. What's wrong?'

'Vera Iris Thistlethwaite.'

Vera frowned. Jenny never used her full name. She opened her mouth to speak but was stopped by the words that echoed around the kitchen.

'Will you marry me?'

'Oh, my good God,' Vera said, her hand stabbing at her chest.

That wasn't the response Jenny had been expecting. She tried to get to her feet and realised she was stuck. Her knees wouldn't move and her right leg felt as though it was going into a cramp. She tried again to move and the muscle spasm gripped her. She screamed out and Vera reached down to help her. Tugging on Vera for support, Jenny tried to stand, lost balance and brought Vera down on top of her.

'Good heavens,' the tall American woman said, staring at the two women sprawled out on the kitchen floor, and pressed her hand to her mouth. And then her hand dropped and she grinned. 'What an adventure we have here. Ingrid, take a look. This really is the Hebden Bridge of the Northwest just as the advert said. How wonderful.' She clapped her hands.

'Oh, my good God,' Vera mumbled again, trying to lift herself from Jenny amid two pairs of quizzical eyes. She reached out a hand and helped Jenny to her feet.

Jenny tugged down her blouse, smiled at the two women at the door and hobbled to pick up the crystal bowl. 'I can recommend the punch,' she said. 'If you head to the living room, I'll bring it straight through.'

The two women disappeared and when Jenny looked at Vera there was a dark intensity to her gaze and her cheeks looked quite flushed.

'Are you serious?' Vera said.

'Absolutely.' She walked back to Vera and met her lips with a fervent kiss.

'V, they're starting to arrive in the living room,' Delia said in a loud whisper. She looked at Jenny. 'Sorry to disturb you.'

Vera pulled Jenny into her arms and looked at Delia with an unhurried gaze. 'We're getting married.'

'Good,' Delia said. 'Now can we get the punch into the living room?'

Jenny chuckled. 'It's coming.'

'Is that pie burned?' Delia said, studying the blackened edges of the pastry topping.

'Nah. It's just a Duckton-by-Dale special,' Vera said and moved to the stove to rescue the potatoes. 'Make sure I get a glass of that punch. I think Jen's been on it all day,' she said to Delia. She chuckled and grinned with affection at Jenny then tipped the potatoes into the large sieve.

Jenny poured a glass of punch and handed it to Vera then took the bowl into the living room.

'Evening ladies,' she said. 'Please help yourselves to the punch. Dinner will be served shortly.' She placed the bowl on the table and left the room.

Delia took her place at the table under the stag as per the instructions, and said, 'If anyone would like a quick reading before the food arrives?' She shuffled the deck of cards with an encouraging smile.

*

'That was scrumptious,' Sarah said. 'The most interesting and intense flavours,' she said, referring to the beef-and-ale pie. 'I need that recipe.'

Ingrid was taking notes and nodding furiously.

She stood from the table and staggered to the couch, facing the deer. Ingrid slumped on a couch seat, sipped at her drink. 'That is such a beautiful specimen.' Her American drawl sounded lazier than it had been earlier.

'It's a five-point antler,' Vera said proudly. 'Worth a good look,' she said and she gazed at the beast with mild amusement.

The deer's eyes moved and Sarah blinked then stared harder.

'He always looks as though he's looking right at you, no matter where you are in the room,' Vera said. 'It is thought his spirit is still close to him.' She pondered the deer with her head on a tilt, receiving a wide-eyed glare from Delia who'd never heard that story in the time the stag had been mounted on the wall.

'Really?' Sarah said, her gaze intensifying as she continued to stare. She jumped suddenly. 'Did you see that, Ingrid. Its eyes moved, I swear they did.'

Ingrid looked at the beast on the wall through a punch-induced haze and shrugged.

Three women sat at the table in front of the rune stones and looked up at the deer. The other women, standing chatting, stopped and looked at the American woman looking at the deer. One rolled her eyes at the proclamation and then they all carried on with their conversation.

'There, again,' Sarah said emphatically and stepped closer.

Jenny froze as the woman approached and tried not to blink. It was one thing shifting her gaze from one woman to another through one of the deer's eyes, it would be something else if the deer were perceived to have winked at them. That would certainly blow her cover. Her eyes started burning. The American woman had moved closer and was staring at the deer intently. Her attention shifted from the glaring gaze to the broad grin on Vera's face, standing two paces behind the American. She tried to stifle a giggle and, damn. She blinked.

'It winked,' Sarah asserted loudly and pointed at the deer while appealing to the other guests in the room.

The noise was sufficient distraction and Jenny ducked away, swiftly fixing the deer's eye back in place. She leaned against the wall, her heart racing, stifling the giggles. This was exciting!

'It did, it did,' Sarah insisted. She was pointing at the deer's eyes. Ingrid had slumped in a seat and was sipping at the punch. She really didn't give a shit if the deer's eyes had moved or not. If her boss thought they had, that was good enough for her.

'Ingrid, did you see that?'

'Yes, Sarah,' she said and raised her glass.

The chatter in the room started up again and Delia tried to focus the group at the table back to the rune stones. Another group sat around a map of the village with every sighting of Hilda ever recorded plotted with pinpoint accuracy. 'When do we go to see the church?' A young woman with fair hair and curious blue eyes asked.

Vera noted the time, the darkness that had fallen, and smiled. 'In about an hour, we'll take a tour around the village and finish at the church.'

The young woman nodded, looked out the window and made a note in her notepad. 'It's not quite a full moon, is it?'

'That's tomorrow,' Vera said.

The woman nodded.

One of the women at the table squealed with joy. 'Oh, thank you,' she said to Delia.

Delia smiled at her and then looked to Vera with a knowing gaze.

'Would anyone like a cup of Duckton's finest herbal tea? It's our very own special blend.'

The women in the room nodded, all bar Ingrid, who was topping up her glass with the punch.

Vera went to the kitchen. She put on the kettle, turned towards the fridge, and jumped. 'Jesus Christ, woman, you scared the life out of me,' she said staring at Jenny.

'How did it go?' Jenny said. She was wearing the purple raincoat and carrying a lead, a silver-grey wig perched on her head.

'Freaky,' Vera said.

'That's good, isn't it?' Jenny said and fiddled with the wig. 'I'll head off and be at the church in an hour.'

'Good.' She closed the gap between them and placed a kiss on Jenny's nose. 'You look all shades of hot,' she said and chuckled.

The boiling kettle distracted them and Vera made a large pot of tea and took it through to the group.

Jenny disappeared out through the hunting room and into the side garden. She ambled down the path to the back of the house and set off across the field, for appearance's sake. It would add credibility if she were spotted by other villagers across the fields, Vera had said. She smiled with her musings about Vera and their wedding as she wandered to the other side of the village.

By the time she turned to head back, the purple raincoat was suffocating and sweat beaded on her forehead. When she reached the church, she was puffing and in the middle of a full-on hot flush. She stood at the far end of the graveyard looking out over the fields, her back to the church trying to recover her breath, flapping the opening of the plastic mac to get some air to her flaming body. And then she heard the women's voices and her heart pounded with the thrill and exacerbated the breathing problem. She froze and even though she had the urge, she couldn't look over her shoulder for fear of being recognised. She thought she might explode!

'Oh my God, there's two of them,' the American voice echoed. 'And look, one has a poodle!'

Two! Jenny's heart skipped a beat and it took all her will power to not look round.

'Ingrid, Ingrid! Did you get a picture?'

Vera stared from one version of Hilda to the other and grinned. Well I never, Hilda had shown up. She waved at the woman facing them and the woman waved back.

'Where?' Ingrid said, searching the darkness. She couldn't see anything.

'There, there!' Sarah said, pointing frantically.

'Ah, yes, got that one,' Ingrid said and scanned the graveyard. 'Where's the other one? I can't see anything,' she said. 'I can't see a poodle.'

'I can see them,' the fair-haired woman said in a quiet voice.

'I can only see one,' the other voices chorused. They seemed quite disappointed.

Jenny stood perfectly still and then decided to wave her arm.

'That one's waving. Oh man, this is so cool. Did you get a picture, Ingrid?'

'Yes,' Ingrid said, sounding quite bored and knowing she only had one image of Hilda in the frame, and no dog.

'Let's go inside the church?' Vera suggested, hoping to give Jenny time to escape.

The group followed Vera into the building and Jenny headed home, exhausted with the stress of it all. As the group left the church and headed down the road to Duckton House the women were still chattering excitedly about seeing Hilda Spencer. And for the two women in the group who had seen, her long-lost sister, Agnes Avery.

Vera closed the front door to Duckton House with a beaming grin. The night had been a huge success. Tomorrow they would encourage the women to take a wander around the events at the park during the day and that evening they would take the group to the Crooked Billet and talk about the history of the area and undertake more readings. Then come back to the house for a late-night séance. She deliberately hadn't bled the radiators so there would be plenty of strange noises throughout the night to keep the group entertained.

She headed back to Jenny's with one thought on her mind. Lycra shorts. Very tight, Lycra shorts. And then the thought of a wedding came to her and bathed her in abject fear. Fuck! Had she agreed to marry Jenny? She smiled at the thought of Jenny on her knees in the kitchen looking at her with doe-eyes, the burned pie and being pulled to the floor, and the fear eased and a soft warm feeling stayed with her until she slipped into bed and snuggled up next to the snoring woman of her dreams. God, how she loved Jenny!

21.

'Is that Mary Berry?' Delia said to Jenny looking over Jenny's shoulder in the direction of the Bake-Off tent.

Jenny glanced over. 'Looks like her; older than I imagined,' she said wiping the sweat from her brow.

'Is that possible?' Delia said, and frowned.

Jenny chuckled.

Both women sipped water, then looked at each other and pulled a face at the thought of getting back to the Zumba. Delia scanned the park as if looking for something, or someone.

Esther joined them with a skip in her step. 'Zumba is great fun,' she said, looking as fresh as a daisy. 'Is that Mary Berry?' She pointed.

Delia nodded and Jenny shrugged.

'Those pants are a better fit,' Jenny said to Esther.

Esther looked down at the Lycra, clinging to her slim legs and waist.

'They sure do,' Doug said and pinched his wife's bottom. His leggings didn't look as appealing!

Esther let out a muffled squeal and smiled at him. 'Doug found them at the sports shop in Ferndale,' she said. 'They're two sizes smaller than the other ones.'

Jenny mumbled something about obviously getting her pants from the wrong shop.

'Where's Vera?' Esther said, looking around the park.

'She'll be bringing the ghost hunt group over shortly,' Delia said and grinned excitedly.

Esther nodded then looked from Delia to Jenny. 'Two Hilda Spencer's, eh?' she said and smiled.

Jenny's cheeks darkened and she sipped at the water. 'According to some,' she said.

Esther looked from Jenny to Delia and back again. 'Hmm.'

The music started up, calling the Zumbathon back to action. 'Great to see so many people here,' Delia said wandering back to the dance area.

'How is that woman so full of energy?' Jenny said, referring to Ellena who was smiling and chirpily guiding the group with a dance routine that involved moving forwards, sideways and backwards, and then reversing the sequence.

'Only three hours to go,' Delia said and chuckled.

'I'm going to need to pace myself,' Jenny said. She looked to Esther who was diligently following the instructions and looking spritely.

'I thought you were, already,' Delia quipped. She stepped forward, went to change direction, and stepped on Jenny's foot.

Jenny yelped, bent down to clamp the pain, lost her balance and plunged straight into Esther sweeping her feet from the floor in what looked like a scrum-half tackle.

Esther landed in a crumpled heap on top of Jenny who was moaning at the pain in her foot and now her hip.

'Ooh, err, Esther. Are you making a move on my lady?' Vera said, approaching with a bottle, four glasses, and a beaming grin.

Esther chuckled, clambered to her feet, held out a hand to Jenny and pulled her up. She started following Ellena's steps again and glanced at Jenny. 'You needed to change direction, Jen,' she said, undeterred.

Jenny huffed, lifted her hand dismissively and said, 'I need a drink.'

'I thought you might need this by now,' Vera said, handing over the gin.

'Where's the group?' Delia said, looking around the park for the tall American woman and her sidekick.

'They're in the Bake-Off tent with Mary Berry,' Vera said and sipped at her drink.

'We really got Mary Berry?' Jenny said. She dabbed the sweat from her lip with the cotton wristband and sipped her drink

'Nah, that's an impersonator Grace found,' Vera said. 'But they don't know that. Sarah what's-her-face is positively ecstatic. She watched the American Bake-Off and loved it.' Vera chuckled. 'She'd had Ingrid take half-a-dozen pictures before I'd left the tent.'

'That's good,' Jenny said and wiped at the moisture that had burst onto her cheeks.

'Makes up for the fact that only one ghost appeared in the photos Ingrid took last night. Boy has she been bleating at her for messing that up.' Vera held Jenny in her gaze and chuckled. 'How does it feel to be immortalised as Hilda Spencer?' she whispered.

Jenny chuckled. 'I feel a bit of a fraud, actually. Did you see Hilda?'

Vera nodded. 'And Brambles,' she said.

'Ooh, that means Faith will be staying,' Jenny said. She finished the drink.

'That's what I figured.' Vera said. 'You know, I think those stones were right.'

'Yes,' Jenny said. 'Things have happened exactly as they should.'

'I meant the faith bit.' Vera smiled, turned towards the café tent and watched Drew and Faith serving coffee and cake. Sarah was there too now, Ingrid taking photographs of the Vicar behind the café counter, two of Duckton-by-Dale's famous buns held up on plates in front of her. The American was certainly getting her money's worth.

'The stones never lie, that's good,' Jenny said and nodded. 'Here, top me up. I'm done with this exercise. Let's see if we can interest the group in a reading or two,' she said. 'Delia!' she shouted and nodded. 'Come on, we've got work to do.'

'I'll be over in a minute,' Delia said. She missed a step and huffed at the interruption.

Vera took Jenny's clammy hand and they walked across the field, the music booming over the speakers.

'Are we really getting married?' Jenny said, squeezing the warm hand.

Vera squeezed back, looked at the perspiring woman with affection that had secretly spanned more than thirty years. 'Yes, I believe we are.'

Jenny looked at Vera, the hot flush in full flow and smiled. 'What do you think about a Halloween wedding?' she said. 'I've always wanted to wear black at a wedding,' she added and chuckled.

Vera grinned. 'As long as there's black Lycra underneath,' she said.

'We'll need to speak to Faith,' Jenny said.

Vera nodded. 'And Harriet and Grace. Who do you want to give you away?'

Jenny pondered, looked from the Bake-Off tent where Harriet and Grace were to the dance floor and then studied Vera. 'I was thinking of asking Esther,' she said. 'Do you think Harriet would mind?'

Vera raised her eyebrows. 'You'll have to ask her. I'm sure she'll want to do the catering for us with Drew and the photos of course.'

'Reception in the pub?'

'I was thinking about the house.'

Jenny frowned.

'Hilda's never been seen in the pub,' Vera said and a coy smile appeared. 'I was hoping she might show up.' She shrugged apologetically.

Jenny smiled and looked lovingly into the soft gaze. 'She is family.'

Hilda was more family to Vera than her own mother had ever been. 'Yes, I guess she is.'

'That's settled then. What are you wearing?'

'I was thinking a black tux,' Vera said.

'Sexy,' Jenny said and gave Vera a look. 'Who's your best woman?'

Vera pondered. 'I would ask Nell, but she's got an expat reunion and will be away.' She sighed. 'I'll let her know.'

'Should we go with a different date?' Jenny said, with concern.

Vera shook her head. 'No. In truth, I feel closer to Grace,' she said and then smiled with a hint of sadness. She hadn't felt close to Nell until their intervention with Grace and since then she and Grace had spent more time together than she and her sister ever had.

Jenny nodded and squeezed Vera's arm reassuringly. 'We'll speak to Faith and the girls later,' Vera said.

'I love you so much, Ms Thistlethwaite,' Jenny said, and kissed Vera on the cheek.

*

'What do you think?' Grace said to the assembled judges, Mary Berry, Drew and Harriet.

'I have no idea,' Mary Berry said. 'I'm not a foodie, but I do like the nut brittle.'

Grace laughed.

'The nut brittle is good,' Drew said and Harriet nodded.

'So, nut brittle is one finalist,' Grace said.

Everyone agreed.

'The chocolate marshmallows in coconut?' Drew said.

'I'm not sure.' Harriet said. 'They would have been better with a dark-chocolate coating; they're too sweet and lack balance.'

'I love sweet,' Mary Berry said. 'Sweeter the better.'

She really wasn't a good judge!

Drew nodded. 'A bit, yes,' she said, agreeing with Harriet.

They tasted the salted caramel cheesecake and Drew grimaced. 'Good God!' she said.

'It looks better than it tastes! That's a definite no from me,' Harriet said.

'Pancakes?' Grace said, handing them out.

Harriet pondered as she chewed.

'Vanilla,' Drew said. 'Reminds me of the gin.'

Harriet laughed. 'That's it. It's Delia's herbs! The batter's a good texture too. Pancakes are a yes from me.'

'Agreed,' Drew said.

'So, we have two finalists,' Grace said. 'What about the boiled fruitcake?'

'Someone didn't realise boiled fruitcake still needs to be cooked in the oven,' Drew said and sniggered at the uncooked mixture. 'That's a no, from me! I'm not even tasting it.' She shuddered at the thought of the rough doughy texture.

'The breakfast bar? It's all raw; dried dates, crushed nuts, oats and cherries,' Grace said.

'That's a winner, from me,' Harriet said.

Mary Berry had an inane grin on her face. She was still polishing off the pancakes.

'Yep, me too.' Drew said.

'Good. So, it's between the burnt-caramel sweets topped with chocolate chips and ginger, and the egg-custard panna cotta looking thing, with raspberry sauce?' Grace glanced from Drew to Harriet and back again.

Mary Berry bit into the caramel sweet with a hearty crunch. 'Ouch!' she complained as the hard toffee cracked in her mouth. She spat out the sweet along with... She looked down. 'That broke my tooth!'

Harriet grimaced. 'Christ, they took the burnt seriously,' and she spat the sweet into a serviette.

Drew grinned. 'I'll skip that one then.' She dipped a spoon into the soggy custard of the last dish. 'This is too runny.' She sniffed, tasted. 'Smells of almond. God, that's grim,' she said and swallowed reluctantly.

'Marshmallows in chocolate and coconut then?' Grace said.

'Agreed,' Harriet said, sipping repeatedly at her water. 'That really was awful.' She was still trying to get over the burnt caramel dish.

Mary Berry was groaning and poking in her mouth.

Harriet glanced at her. 'I'm so sorry,' she said.

Mary stopped poking and looked at Harriet. 'It wasn't my tooth,' she said and smiled. She inspected the discarded sweet. 'That's a piece of tinfoil,' she said.

Drew sniggered.

Harriet breathed a sigh of relief. 'Thank heavens,' she said.

'Let's announce our finalists and get them baking,' Grace said. 'Well done, judges,' she added and kissed Harriet on the lips.

'I need to get back to the café,' Drew said, and her cheeks darkened as she looked across to Faith, who was talking to a very animated Sarah.

Harriet grinned with pride to discover that Luce had made the chocolate marshmallows in coconut and clapped with excitement as Grace announced her place as a finalist. Sheila Goldsworth looked very disappointed at the rejection of her burnt caramel sweets and Mary Berry, whose wig was perched precariously over her right eyebrow, was shaking her head at the announcement. Doris was being most supportive of Sheila and suggested they go and take part in the Zumbathon and grab a bite of lunch. Tilly had made the pancakes and looked both delighted and genuinely surprised at being selected. Annie was gazing at her with puppy-dog eyes and clapping furiously, then whistled through her fingers and whooped, causing Tilly to blush right down to her chest. The two other finalists, who were clearly from outside the village, smiled and congratulated each other with polite applause.

'We will take a half-hour break before the finals begin. Please remember that all the cakes will be sold off at the end of the day,' Grace announced.

'Oh, how quaint,' Sarah said. She had made her way from the café to the judging table and studied the dishes. She picked up a piece of burnt caramel and crunched. 'Oh, man, that is delicious,' she said in a loud voice.

Harriet looked at her and smiled. 'Please help yourself.'

'Thank you, so much,' Sarah said. 'You have such an awesome village. Ingrid, you just have to try this. It's to die for.'

Harriet couldn't argue with that!

'See, that American lady loves your caramel,' Doris said to Sheila as she started to step to Ellena's instructions.

Sheila smiled. 'I've always loved the Americans,' she said and started following the Zumba step-routine albeit half-a-pace behind the music.

*

'Hey, Vicar,' Drew said, with a seductive smile, gazing at the collar around Faith's neck.

Faith held her with a penetrating stare and her eyes darkened. 'Hey, Masterchef,' she said and grinned.

Drew smiled. 'Fancy a drink?'

'I could think of other things I fancy more,' Faith said, her gaze becoming more intense the longer she stared.

Drew cleared her throat, feeling the effect of Faith as it flowed through her in a warm tingling wave of desire. 'Vanilla?' Drew said.

'Any way you like it, baby,' Faith said, her gaze unwavering.

Drew felt heat sear her skin with the wave of excitement that zipped through her. And then she spotted Esther approaching and tried to shake off the desire. 'Hi mum,' she said, with a croak in her voice.

'I need a break from Zumba,' Esther said and smiled at Drew and then at Faith. 'Would you two like me to take over for a bit?'

Drew found it hard to swallow. Esther's timing was perfect. 'Half-hour?' she croaked.

'Take an hour,' Esther said and ushered Faith out from behind the counter.

Drew looked at her and smiled. 'Thanks, mum.'

'Go,' Esther said, waving them away. 'You're getting in the way of business.' She smiled affectionately.

Faith's gaze, less intense than it had been a moment earlier, still lingered on Drew and without speaking she set off for the road, Drew by her side.

'Where are they going?' Jenny said to Esther.

'Bed, I imagine,' Esther said, and then blushed.

Jenny grinned at her. 'Esther Pettigrew,' she said and mockingly covered her mouth with her hand, then laughed. 'Do you want a hand?'

Esther shook her head. 'It's quiet at the moment. I think everyone's more interested in the barbeque.' She nodding to the long queue and waved at Doug who was doing battle with the burgers and sausages. Neville seemed to be slowing the process down with his need to precisely measure and set out the cooking time for each. 'It's going to get busy when the runners descend,' she said.

'It will if Neville's left in control of it,' Jenny said and laughed. 'We can get Bryan to help them out.'

Vera approached with three gins in her hand. Handed one to Esther and one to Jenny. 'Have you asked her?' she said to Jenny.

'Asked me what?' Esther said. She sipped at the drink.

Vera raised her eyebrows and smiled.

'Vera and I are getting married and I was wondering if you'd give me away?' Jenny said excitedly.

Esther studied her with wide-eyes and then they glassed over and she blinked repeatedly, wiped at an errant tear. 'Oh, my goodness. Congratulations.' She looked to Vera with a broad, genuine smile and then back to Jenny. 'What about Harriet?'

'Harriet will help with catering and do the photographs. We're hoping for a Halloween wedding. We just need to check the date with Faith. It's only a small gathering of our friends and family. A low-key affair at the house.'

'And our ghost-hunter friends that weekend, of course,' Vera added.

Esther chuckled. 'That's your idea of small?' She stepped out from the counter and pulled Jenny into a hug. 'I'd be honoured,' she whispered. She let go of Jenny and went to Vera with open arms. 'I'm so happy for you both.'

'Come here, old fart,' Vera said and squeezed her friend tightly. When she let her go, she studied her with warmth. 'Lycra suits you,' she said and winked.

'Does this mean you'll hall?' Esther said.

Jenny and Vera frowned.

'Isn't that what happens?' Esther said.

Jenny continued to frown.

Vera started to smile. 'You mean U-haul?' she said and chuckled loudly.

'Yes, yes, that's it. I heard something on a documentary the other day. What does it mean?'

'Moving in together,' Vera said.

'Oh.' Esther said and seemed disappointed.

'We haven't decided where we'll live,' Vera said. 'I've got Hilda to think about.'

Jenny elbowed Vera in the ribs and chuckled. 'Anyone want a sausage?'

'Good god, no,' Vera said. 'That's Esther's territory.'

Esther frowned at Vera then the penny dropped and she blushed. Gosh!

*

Grace slumped onto the sofa and groaned. 'Your mum's getting married.' She looked at Harriet and smiled.

Archie made a huffing sound, turned full-circle in his bed and snuggled down again.

Harriet was grinning at Grace. 'I'm so happy for her. A Halloween wedding; what is she like, the bride in black?' She was shaking her head and chuckling.

'It will be fab,' Grace said and held out her hand.

Harriet took it, slid onto Grace's lap and lifted her chin, then placed a tender kiss to her lips. 'It was an incredible success today. The ghost party had a ball and Doug was beside himself that our team won the four-peaks race. He said he's never moving to Upper Duckton; too many winners here now.' Her chuckle subsided and she held Grace in an intense gaze, her fingers exploring Grace with tenderness. Softly tracing the tired eyes that caressed her with love, she kissed the supple lips that flipped her insides and caused parts of her to throb with longing.

Grace felt the tingling touch through her lips, reach into her core and ignite a fire there. 'The Bake-Off was fun.' She shifted Harriet in her lap, pulling her closer.

'Bless Luce, she did so well,' Harriet said, her smile reflecting how proud she was of her little sister for coming third.

'I'm glad Tilly won,' Grace said.

'That chocolate ganache really was to die for, as opposed to the burnt caramel which was to die from,' Harriet said.

'She's an asset to the pub,' Grace said.

'Yes. Seems to be getting on well with Annie, too.' Harriet pressed her thumb across Grace's lips.

'Annie will be good for the pub too. Great for publicity.'

Harriet caught Grace's attention and a smile formed slowly. 'And when did it all become about the pub?' she said teasingly and kissed Grace on the lips.

Grace kissed her back then grinned with a mischievous look in her eyes. 'Since I received the paperwork this morning to confirm the deeds are ready for transfer.'

Harriet squealed, excitedly. 'Really?'

Grace nodded. 'Yep, all done! The pub's officially...' she paused. 'Yours.'

'What?'

'Yep. I put the ownership in your name. It's now part of your business empire.' She grinned broadly. 'You'll need to sign the paperwork next week.'

Harriet's jaw dropped and she shook her head. Then, she took Grace's mouth with her own and kissed her with the full force of passion.

Grace moaned, pulled Harriet into her body and moaned again. When she eased out of the kiss, every part of her tingled and when she gazed into Harriet's dark eyes her heart ached. 'I love you so much,' she said and traced the shape of Harriet's face with a gentle touch. 'So much.'

'I love you, too, Grace Pinkerton,' Harriet said. She stood from Grace's lap, took Grace's hand, and pulled her to her feet.

'I was thinking,' Grace said as they headed towards the stairs.

'Uh-huh.'

'A driving lesson.'

Harriet turned to face Grace with a look of horror. 'No!'

Grace grinned. 'In the gin wagon.'

'No!'

'Tomorrow.'

'Never.'

Grace killed the objection with a tender kiss that grew in intensity and Harriet groaned. 'Just say maybe,' she whispered before nipping Harriet's earlobe.

Harriet moaned again, 'Maybe,' she whispered and Grace pulled her closer.

'I'll be gentle with you,' Grace said and raised her eyebrows as she smiled.

Harriet gazed with intensity. 'I hope not,' she said and led Grace up the stairs.

*

'We need a plan,' Vera said and sipped at her drink.

Jenny looked up from the bag of stones Delia had left on the table having taken one of the women for a private reading before they gathered for the final event of the evening. A few of the group had already started to mingle in the living room for the séance and were busy sampling the Vanilla gin, which seemed to be going down very well. 'I thought we're doing readings and a séance tonight?' she said, questioning the need for a plan.

'We are,' Vera said. 'I mean a plan to give love a helping hand,' she said and smiled conspiratorially.

'Oh!' Jenny said and sipped from her drink, pondering. 'I thought Tilly and Annie were getting on very well.'

Vera gazed at Jenny as if to say guess again. 'I'm not talking about a plan for Tilly.'

'Oh,' Jenny said and sat up. 'Who?'

'Sorry, that took a bit longer than expected,' Delia said as she approached and plonked the deck of cards on the table, interrupting the conversation.

Vera, eyes on Jenny, tilted her head towards Delia and grinned.

Jenny frowned.

Vera nodded towards Delia again and mouthed the word, Delia.

Jenny looked confused and then slowly her features shifted into a smile of comprehension. Really, she mouthed back.

'What are you two up to?' Delia said, staring from one woman to the next.

'Nothing,' Vera and Jenny said in unison.

'How did the reading go?' Vera said, quick to change to a topic Delia would be sure to get lost in.

'Good,' Delia said gazing suspiciously between Vera and Jenny.

Sarah was approaching and Vera looked towards her, breaking the trance between them.

'Delia, honey, would you mind? Could you do my reading? I think the timing is right,' Sarah said, full of considered thought.

Delia turned to the spirited American and smiled warmly. 'Of course, Sarah, please do take a seat.' Delia pointed to a chair and sat opposite Sarah. 'Close your eyes and focus on the situation and give me one word that represents it,' she said and her cheeks flushed.

Sarah sat with her eyes closed, the fine muscles around her them flickering and at that moment she revealed vulnerability. 'Love,' she said and kept her eyes shut tightly, pulling her top lip between her teeth, mulling over the situation in her mind's eye.

Delia continued to stare at Sarah, took in a deep breath and released it slowly, closed her eyes and held the cards, slipping into deep contemplation. Then she opened her eyes, stared at Sarah, and started to shuffle the pack.

Vera studied Delia and then Sarah and smiled at Jenny. 'She's good,' she said.

Jenny gazed at Delia. 'Yes, she is.'

Vera studied Jenny watching Delia and smiled with affection, and then Jenny noticed Vera and smiled.

'She seems to have a connection with our American friend,' Jenny said.

Vera gasped in mock horror. 'Jenny Haversham, you were reading my mind. We've merged.' She laughed.

Jenny chuckled and elbowed Vera affectionately. 'Do you seriously think Delia would?' Her gaydar may be bad, but not that off-mark, surely?

Vera pondered. 'I don't know.' She smiled at the two women studying the cards on the table in an animated fashion.

'Sarah wanted a place on the Halloween weekend, but we're fully booked,' Jenny said.

Vera nodded. 'They do get on well, and it's nice for Delia to know someone who's into in the psychic stuff as much as she is. We can invite Sarah to our wedding, I don't mind. The more the merrier,' she said and looked quizzically at Jenny.

Jenny pondered. 'She did see the real Hilda,' she said.

Vera frowned. 'That's true!'

22.

'Good evening, everyone,' Doris said. 'Thank you all so much for coming.'

Well that was a first! 'Thank you for inviting us,' Doug quipped and chuckled to himself.

All eyes were on Doris. The key question on the villager's minds was, how much did we make? The events of the previous weekend had been very well attended and there was a sweepstake going on the total raised.

'There are two items on the agenda this evening, but I hope we won't take long,' Doris announced.

'Get on with it, woman,' Doug mumbled and Esther shushed him. He slouched in his seat, looked at his watch. Surely no more than an hour and a half, please!

'The first is to say that the fundraising has raised eight thousand, seven hundred and forty-two pounds and fourteen pence.' She looked up and smiled at the nodding heads around the room.

'That's fantastic,' Harriet said and squeezed Grace's leg under the table.

Doug looked disappointed. 'Just short of the total,' he said.

'Everyone has done a brilliant job,' Doris said and gave Doug a stern look.

'Hand over your pound, everyone,' Bryan said with a guffaw. He had made the closest bid in the sweepstake by a long way.

Doug mumbled and crossed his arms.

'It is, indeed, a fantastic effort by all concerned,' Doris declared.

'I've minuted that, Mrs Akeman,' Sheila said with a smile.

'And, I'd like to thank you all. It wouldn't have come together without the dedication of everyone present in this room today,' Doris said.

'Bloody hell,' Doug mumbled. 'Has she been on the Vanilla?' he whispered.

Esther elbowed him in the ribs.

'I think our permanent Vicar has something to add,' Doris said with emphasis on the word permanent and looked at Faith with a broad smile.

Everyone looked at Faith.

Drew's cheeks lit up and she tingled through to her toes as she locked eyes briefly with Faith.

Faith cleared her throat and smiled. 'I'd just like to say that the Church will make up the difference to get to the ten-thousand-pound total for the project.'

Doug was the first to cheer and start the applause. Vera and Jenny followed with a whoop and a cheer and Harriet and Grace clapped and nodded at Faith.

Drew's cheeks darkened.

Faith quieted the room with a guiding hand.

'Thank you, Vicar,' Esther said and smiled.

'I'll speak to the contractors and we'll agree on a start date,' Grace said.

'I can get the farmers involved with construction,' Kev said.

Grace nodded and gave him a thumbs up. 'And we'll see if Annie will do some publicity for the opening,' she said.

'I can speak to her,' Tilly said and her smile gave her away.

Esther elbowed Doug in the ribs at the point his mouth opened.

'What was that for, woman?' he said and slouched in his seat.

'Thanks, Tilly,' Grace said.

'Did you minute that, Sheila?'

'Tilly's going to sort out Annie,' Sheila said placing a full-stop on the paper.

Doug sniggered. 'Ain't that a fact,' he quipped and then shifted in a defensive response to Esther's incoming elbow.

'If we could move on, please,' Doris said and glared at Doug. The next item on the agenda is the Christmas Nativity Play. Any ideas?'

Oh God, here we go!

Faith put up her hand.

Doug nodded approvingly. The Vicar was certainly picking things up quickly!

'Yes, Vicar,' Doris said and smiled, glancing over the top of her spectacles.

'I was wondering if we might like to do something based on a Disney movie?'

The room silenced.

'What, you mean no Virgin Mary sleeping a manger with the carpenter,' Doug said and chuckled at his joke.

Grace couldn't stop herself from sniggering, and Harriet stifled a laugh.

Faith smiled. 'Disney is usually more attractive to the children.' She gave Doug a fond look. 'We can hold a small event at the church to celebrate the birth of Christ, independently.'

Vera was nodding. 'So, something like Snow White and the Seven Dwarfs?'

'What about 'Cinderella?' Delia said. 'I do love Cate Blanchett.'

Doug's eyes widened. 'Bloody hell, she got it right,' he said and grinned. 'Quiz night a week on Wednesday,' he said and pointed at Delia.

Delia's cheeks darkened.

'Yes, any one of those,' Faith said. 'There's Aladdin, Jack and the Beanstalk, Dick Whittington, Peter Pan, Puss In Boots, Sleeping Beauty, Beauty and the Beast?'

Grace sat up in her chair. This was sounding like an interesting event. 'Have you done one before?' she said to Faith.

'Yes. It usually goes down well in the community,' Faith said. 'We can get hold of a play-script to guide us, and I'm sure Doris and Sheila's directing and organising skills will be perfect.'

Doris grew in the chair and Sheila looked up from scribbling a note then flustered that she might miss something and gave her attention back to the pen.

'Bloody hell,' Doug muttered.

'Farmers will help with the staging,' Kev offered.

'How are your sewing skills, Vera,' Doug said and chuckled. Vera wasn't the needlework type.

'I'll sew the costumes,' Esther said and looked down her nose at her husband for not thinking of her in the first instance.

'Excellent, thank you, Esther,' Faith said and smiled warmly at her.

'Esther's the best seamstress around,' Vera said and winked at Esther, who blushed.

'Nothing with a bloody cow in it,' Doug said, shaking his head, still pondering their options. 'Bloody Jonny, Wilkinson, bloody Jones put a stink bomb in the udder of the last one. Had my head over that damn thing for two hours, hopping around the bloody stage.'

Grace burst out laughing and Faith was giving it her best effort not to chuckle.

'Serves you right for opting for the cow's arse, when you thought Tilly was going to be the front end.' Vera said and laughed.

Tilly sniggered.

Doug's cheeks darkened and Esther glared at him.

'Teach you not to bloody listen,' Esther said to him. 'Everyone else knew it was Terry not Tilly at the front. It was a condition of us using his costume. How else do you think his son got the stink bomb inside? They're all the same, those Jones's,' she said and chuckled.

Doug mumbled and fidgeted in his chair, avoiding eye contact with the red-head across the table who was still grinning at him.

Sheila jotted down a note.

Faith glanced down and her eyes widened. 'Not Tilly's udders, Sheila,' she whispered.

'Oh, thank you, Vicar,' Sheila said. She picked up the ruler and drew a straight line through the words.

'No sheep,' Grace said, reminded of the sheep racing health and safety issue from the summer fete.

'Cinderella has quite a small cast, that might be easier for us to manage,' Harriet said.

'Agreed,' Jenny piped up.

'Does anyone object to Cinderella?' Faith said and looked around the room.

'Delia, you'll make a great fairy-godmother,' Doug said and nodded with a smile.

'I think we should set up a sub-committee to deal with the planning,' Grace said.

Harriet nodded.

Drew didn't give a shit. Her eyes were firmly fixed on Faith, imagining her as the Prince to her Cinderella. She looked around the room to see everyone's hand in the air. 'Did I miss something?' she whispered to Harriet.

'Put your hand up if you want to be in the sub-committee?' Harriet said and Drew lifted her arm.

'Bloody hell,' Doug said. He moved to pull his arm down, thought better of it and raised it higher.

'That will be interesting,' Grace whispered to Harriet.

'We can sort out sub, sub-groups,' Harriet said and smiled.

'Good, that's agreed,' Doris said.

'Sorry, what was agreed?' Sheila said. She looked flustered having had her hand in the air and had missed taking an important note.

'Cinderella and everyone's in the sub-group. We can discuss the details at the first sub-group meeting. I suggest we schedule that for the week after next, on account of the fact that we have a very special wedding planned for next Saturday,' Doris said. She smiled down the table at Vera and Jenny, a whoop and cheer went up around the room. 'Which brings me to the matter of any other business. I would like to congratulate Vera and Jenny on behalf of us all, and, I know it's a week early, but we'd like to present you with a small gift.' She stood, walked to the other end of the room and handed Jenny an envelope.

'Oh, my goodness,' Jenny said, and Vera blushed. 'Thank you, so much.' She pulled open the envelope and took out the embossed note inside.

Vera looked over Jenny's shoulder and read the details, her mouth opening as she registered the generous gift.

'A cruise around the Mediterranean,' Jenny said and covered her mouth with her hand. As she looked around the room at the smiling faces, tears streamed down her cheeks and when she turned to Vera, she too was wiping damp eyes. 'I've always wanted to go on a cruise.'

'I don't know what to say,' Vera said.

'Well, there's a first,' Doug quipped and laughed.

'We thought you might like to take it as a honeymoon trip,' Doris said, 'We can't have you away for the planning of Christmas though.' She grinned and went back to her seat.

Doug cleared his throat. He lifted the gavel from the middle of the table and stood, all eyes in the room on him. He approached Faith and held it out to her. 'I think this is rightfully in your control, now.'

Faith blushed and looked lost for words. She took the gavel and turned to the group, her eyes locking onto Drew. 'It's an honour to serve this community,' she said. 'You are amazing people. Thank you.'

Drew tilted her head and gazed at Faith as she admired the polished wooden implement. She wouldn't have to use it, that was a given. Faith had this village in the palm of her hands, figuratively speaking. Drew imagined Faith in the palm of her hand literally and found it difficult to swallow.

'Well, thank you Doug. What a perfect way to end the meeting, unless there is any other business?'

Doug prayed.

'Vanilla time,' Esther announced.

'Bravo, Esther,' Vera said and eased up from the seat. 'Come on,' she said to Esther, 'We need to talk about my wedding outfit.'

Esther chuckled. She walked with Vera and Jenny to the Crooked Billet, followed closely by the rest of the group.

23.

'How do I look?'

'Very sexy.'

'No, seriously, is this hanging evenly?'

'You look stunning. Even better without the dog collar.'

Faith gave Drew a look, rebalanced the robe around her neck and shifted the collar under her chin.

'You look nervous,' Drew said. It was cute.

'It's an important wedding.'

'Have you officiated a gay wedding before?'

'Yes,' Faith said. 'But not one where the brides feel like family.'

Drew studied Faith with affection; the slight tension that shaped her jaw, the narrowing of her eyes as she processed the ceremony, the worried expression that exposed her beauty. 'You will be the only one wearing white you know,' Drew said, and chuckled.

'I'm expected to wear white,' Faith said and raised an eyebrow.

'Unlike the bride, in this case, eh?' Drew said and watched Faith take in a deep breath and release it slowly.

'Grace has the rings?' Faith said.

'Yes.' Drew moved towards Faith and met her lips with a tender kiss that lingered. 'You look hot.'

'I need to get to the church,' Faith said.

Drew nodded. 'I need to get the buffet over to the house.'

Faith nodded. 'I'll see you there.'

'Yes.' Drew had an overwhelming urge to pull Faith into her arms and hold her, take her to bed, make love to her. She cleared her throat. 'Break a leg,' she said, and in an act of restraint kissed Faith on the cheek.

Faith's smile was distracted. She walked to the door and then turned back to look at Drew. 'Thank you,' she said in a whispered voice.

Drew shrugged and frowned.

'For being you,' Faith added.

Drew smiled. 'I love you,' she said and then a wave of heat filled her cheeks.

When Faith smiled, it was clear there was only one thing on her mind. 'I love you too,' she said and closed the door behind her.

Drew walked back to the café with a spring in her step. 'Morning, mum,' she said approaching the counter. 'How's it going?'

'Quiet,' Esther said. 'Doris and Sheila have just left. Everyone's getting ready for the wedding. Delia and Sarah took the ghost hunters up to the lake earlier, just to wear them out I think.'

'Good,' Drew said, intimating to Esther to get going.

Esther flustered with clearing up the counter that didn't need any clearing.

'Go!' Drew said and smiled. 'You'll be fabulous.'

Esther moved around the counter and Drew gave her a hug.

Esther looked at her daughter with a concerned gaze. 'I got them a toaster,' she said. 'Is that okay? It's a Russell Hobbs Retro in red, four slices.'

Drew stifled the laugh that grabbed her throat in a vice-grip and held her mum with a compassionate gaze.

'I read something about giving a toaster as a gift. Isn't it specific for lesbians?' Esther said.

Drew couldn't prevent the grin from spreading across her face, the water that dampened her eyes. She didn't have the heart to explain to her mother that the toaster myth was outdated, let alone what it was alleged to signify. She was sure

Vera and Jenny would see that Esther was trying. 'I'm sure they'll love it,' she said.

'Right, I'd better go and get ready,' she said.

'Thanks, mum,' Drew said.

Esther frowned.

'I love you,' Drew said and kissed Esther on the cheek.

Esther stopped short of dismissing the display of affection and looked at Drew. 'I love you, Drew. I always will.'

Drew nodded. 'I know.'

Drew watched Esther walk away from the café. Happiness settled in a warm feeling that expanded in her chest and as she continued to stare, the camper van pulled up outside the café. Was that Harriet driving?

Grace and Harriet climbed out of the wagon and entered the café. Harriet's smile grew as she approached the counter.

'You were driving?' Drew said, with a surprised look.

'Yes,' Harriet said, her cheeks rosy and shining.

'Can we get a coffee?' Grace said. 'We can take the food across in the van.'

'I'll drive it back up the road,' Harriet said.

Drew's eyes widened. It had taken hours to prepare the buffet, the last thing she needed was for the food to be upended by a learner driver.

'She's doing fine,' Grace said, wrapped an arm around Harriet's waist and placed a kiss on her cheek.

'I'll make coffee,' Harriet said.

'I'll start loading,' Grace said and headed into the kitchen.

'When did you start learning to drive?' Drew asked, feeling that she had missed something.

Harriet beamed a grin. 'Today,' she said and filled the coffee filter. 'Grace says I'm a natural.'

'Right,' Drew had a vision of flying buns come to her and she smiled. 'How did the ghost hunt go last night?'

'No sightings, but they're all very excited about having a Halloween wedding reception in the schedule later and Vera's optimistic Hilda will show up for it.'

'Well, Jenny certainly won't be available. She'll be otherwise occupied,' Drew said and laughed.

Harriet grinned. 'They're hatching another plan,' she said.

'Oh God, no!'

'Yes!'

'Tilly?'

'No, Delia!'

'Oh, my good God,' Drew blurted. 'You're not serious?'

Harriet nodded. She was still chuckling as she heated the milk, at a vision of Delia with the tall American who had been delighted to get a place on the ghost hunt weekend and then beyond ecstatic to receive a personal invitation to the wedding ceremony, and, it seemed, was now heavily involved in organising the activities with Delia. Vera and Esther seemed to be going all out to make this latest love match work.

*

Drew hadn't been able to take her eyes off Faith throughout the ceremony. Esther had done a great job of giving Jenny away, and Grace had been the perfect best woman to Vera who had for the first time in Drew's experience looked nervous and out of her comfort zone. Harriet, her best friend, had sat by her side, her attention shifting from a lustful gaze at Grace in her black tux, to admiring Jenny all in black. Apparently, Jenny had selected the dress because it was called a Ghost Iris Satin dress, which she had considered a done deal, given it was

Halloween and the middle name of the person she was marrying.

Faith was something else though. There had been no sign of the earlier nerves as the ceremony started and Faith had conducted the service with elegance and compassion that had touched everyone in the church. Even Doug had wiped a tear from his eye as he studied Esther at his side and then glanced with a loving smile from Faith to Drew.

As the ceremony ended and the brides turned to walk down the aisle, Drew became aware of Faith's gaze on her, burning through her, stealing the breath from her. She felt warmth flood her in waves and couldn't bring herself to look away, the intense fire taking up residence in her core. And Faith continuing to stare.

And then the American woman's voice came to her. She was approaching Faith with arms outstretched, pulling her into a firm embrace and congratulating her on the beautiful service. Drew observed as Faith took the woman in her stride, smiled and listened with genuine interest, expressed gratitude and wished her an enjoyable weekend. Hang on, was that, Delia taking the photographs of Sarah with Faith? Drew sniggered. How the hell had Vera and Jenny managed that little trick?

And then Faith was walking towards her and her heart was pounding. Her mouth was dry and all that came to her was the dark green of Faith's gaze. The eyes that had captured her the moment they had met. Only now, she knew without hesitation what that look meant. She felt it deeper and with greater intensity and struggled to form words as a result.

'I think we need to go outside for photos,' Faith said and smiled.

Drew looked around the emptying church. 'Oh, yes,' she said, her cheeks flushed. She looked at Faith, held her in a longing gaze. 'You were amazing.'

Faith blushed. 'Thanks.'

Drew stood staring at Faith and then cleared her throat. She became aware of the empty church. 'We'd better go,' she said in a whisper.

Faith nodded. She held out her hand and Drew took it and they walked out of the church together, joined the milling crowd, followed Harriet's instructions as to where to stand and smiled for the camera.

'Are you thinking what I'm thinking?' Drew whispered to Faith after Harriet had finished taking the group photos.

'I'll be taking more photos at the house,' Harriet announced.

'Here honey,' Sarah said and took the camera. 'You need some shots of the bride's daughter, surely,' she said and ushered Harriet to join the group.

Faith looked at Drew and her eyes smiled. 'I have no idea what you're thinking,' she said, her voice hoarse, her body pressed close to Drew for the photo shoot.

'Want me to show you?' Drew whispered, narrowing her eyes, her lips with a slight quiver that held Faith's attention.

'I want to get changed for the buffet,' Faith said.

'I'll help de-robe you,' Drew said with a tilt of her head, eyes searching the length of the ceremonial dress, teeth pulling on her lip, her mind on the body beneath the clothing, and then, swiftly, she dragged Faith around the side of the church and into the cottage.

*

Drew walked to Duckton House with a glow in her cheeks and a beaming smile on her face. The light was already drawing in and the air cold through the flimsy costume. She noticed the addition of a new sign on Duckton House and smiled. *Hilda's Haunt* was carved into the face of a piece of driftwood that hung from a metal chain above the front door.

Rows of carved pumpkins spanned both sides of the front of the house, tea light candles flickering inside their empty shells. She could hear the hum of chatter, music and laughter coming from the side of the house. She followed the path around and entered the garden through the gate. Flo bounded across the lawn at her sporting a red cravat and what looked like a waiter's black jacket designed for dogs, a ball clamped between her teeth. She dropped it at Drew's feet and sat staring at her intently. Drew ruffled the scruff of the dog's neck, 'Hello Flo; you're well behaved tonight,' and Flo let out a deep bark, jumped to all four paws and barked again. 'Okay,' she said. She balanced the tray on one hand, leaned down, and as she went to pick up the ball Flo dived for it. The dog barged Drew off the ball, throwing her off balance and launching the buns into the air, and she landed in a heap on the ground, the buns littering the lawn around her.

'Nice buns!' Faith said and started to chuckle.

She was standing in the doorway leading to the hunting room and kitchen and from the ground looked even more alluring than she had earlier when she had left her in bed. 'Jesus Christ!' Drew said, appraising the scattered buns.

'It's too late for His help,' Faith said and stepped into the garden.

Flo dived at a bun and ran off with it, then Archie appeared from the depths of the garden aptly dressed in a pair of devil-horns and a red jacket, yapped at Drew, snapped at a bun, and ran after Flo with a wagging tail. Winnie staggered over to a bun, sniffed at it, and staggered off then peed on the grass. Drew studied the stars and stripes pattern on the tutu-skirt around the dog's waist, the pom-poms tied around her head that looked like ears, and chuckled.

Faith held out a hand and pulled Drew to her feet. She didn't let go as Drew stood. She pulled her into a deep lingering kiss. 'I missed you,' she said and held Drew's gaze with dark-green piercing eyes.

Drew gasped at the grazing of sharp teeth on her lip and groaned at the warmth of Faith's chest pressed against her, the familiar perfume. 'You make one fucking hot vampire,' she moaned into Faith's ear.

'You are one scary zombie,' Faith whispered and eased back to admire the long black dress. 'Loving the cross, by the way.' She studied the large wooden crucifix around Drew's neck, picked it up and dragged Drew towards her. 'Very sexy.'

Drew felt the fiery lips stinging her skin again, the vampire teeth teasing her neck. She moaned loudly.

'Ghostbusters!'

The word chorused in song at the kitchen door, thrusting Faith and Drew out of the moment.

Drew looked at her mother, Jenny and Vera sporting their Ghostbuster outfits and pointing weapons at them and started laughing. Vera and Jenny looked happy together and her mother seemed to be enjoying herself as she turned back into the kitchen and headed into the house dancing and singing.

'You two look good,' Vera said. 'I didn't recognise you,' she said to Faith, eyeing her up and down. 'You make a fucking hot vampire.' Jenny poked her wife in the ribs with the weapon and Vera chuckled.

Drew flushed and started collecting the buns from the ground.

'Come in, join the party,' Jenny said. She grabbed Vera by the arm and pottered through the kitchen. They were singing again before they reached the foyer.

Drew and Faith wandered into the foyer hand in hand, dodging milling groups of strangers all chattering merrily about their readings and speculating over whether Hilda Spencer, Agnes Avery, or both, might appear later.

'Wow! You two look stunning,' Sarah said as she approached them. 'Delia, honey, get me a photo with these two, will you?' She squeezed between Drew and Faith and grinned for the camera, the all-white nun's costume, white teeth and white painted face providing perfect contrast with the red and black attire of the two women either side of her. Delia, in her wicked Devil costume, tucked a whip into the skirt that sat high above her knee, pointed the camera and clicked. 'Let me get one of you three,' Sarah said and swapped places with Delia. 'Come on, honey, Sarah said. She linked arms with Delia, and moved into the living room.

Drew listened to Delia and Sarah as they disappeared into the room bustling with more people.

'Ooh, let's get a photo with Mr Bones and the Dead Senorita,' Sarah said.

'I did love Bewitched,' Delia said.

'I think you mean Day of the Dead, honey,' Sarah said.

Drew chuckled. 'They seem to be getting on well,' she said to Faith and then realised Faith had been watching her watching them.

Faith smiled and the burning sensation that shot through her caused her breath to hitch.

'Hey,' Grace said as she approached. Drew stared at the long blades protruding from the cuffs of her black outfit and the wild-hair styled wig. And then Harriet appeared in a female version of the attire, black lace blouse, a very short, tight-fitting skirt and black boots that stopped just short of the top of her thigh.

'You two look great,' Drew said.

'You want a drink?' Grace said. She sipped at the deep red liquid in her glass that left a mark on her lip.

Drew grimaced.

'Don't be deceived. It tastes great,' she said. 'Delia's added a little something special to it tonight.' She smiled and wrapped an arm around Harriet's waist. 'Come on, Mrs Scissorhands,' she said. 'Delia promised me a reading.' They walked into the living room, which was buzzing with guests, many faces unrecognisable because of costume masks.

Drew knew the man who approached by his physique alone. 'Hi dad.'

'How did you guess?' Doug said, from beneath his black headless Ghost costume.

Drew tilted her head and smiled. 'You've got your black Lycra pants on underneath,' she said, pointing to his lower legs.

'Ahh, they've got a nice feel to them around the...'

'Great!' Drew said, not wanting to hear around what the pants felt good on him.

'What a beautiful, service, Vicar; well done,' Doug said addressing Faith. He was slurring his words and swaying. 'Have you seen my wife?'

'She was chasing ghosts last time I saw her,' Drew said.

'She's not bloody chasing me,' Doug said, sounding most put out.

Drew chuckled. 'The night is still young.' She took Faith's hand and tugged her closer.

Doug mumbled as he staggered back into the living room.

Drew watched Delia giving a reading to Grace who sat holding hands with Harriet. Grace seemed more interested in staring at her girlfriend than anything that Delia might have to say. Sarah was sat next to Delia and looked very animated over the cards. Delia was smiling excitedly at the American, and then both sipped at the blood-red drinks in unison and held each other's gaze as they talked about and agreed on the meaning of the symbols.

Drew smiled as Kelly and Jarid approached. 'How's it going?' she said.

Kelly huffed out a deep breath and clasped her hands around her swollen belly. 'This fallen angel has truly fallen,' she said to Drew and then turned to look at Jarid and said, 'Remind me never to do this again.'

'Oh, sweetheart, you're the best pregnant fallen angel here tonight,' Jarid said with a loving shine in his eyes and then glanced across at Doris and Sheila who had come dressed in the similar outfits and smiled cheekily.

Drew and Faith chuckled.

'You two look amazing,' Jarid said. 'Loving the vampire look,' he said to Faith.

Kelly nudged his attention back to her. 'Come on Voodoo King, take me home. Have a good evening,' she said to Drew and Faith and smiled wearily.

A man approached in a butcher's apron covered in blood, carrying a hook and chain around his neck and wearing a pig's head mask. He held out two glasses of punch.

Drew grimaced, took the drinks and handed one to Faith. 'Thanks' she said. That is grim!

Bryan lifted the mask and smiled. 'Ha! Didn't recognise me,' he said and guffawed.

'That's grim,' Faith said, echoing Drew's thoughts, and winced.

'Yes,' Bryan said. 'Real blood you know.' He pointed at the stained apron with pride.

'Enough!' Drew said and raised her palm to him with a broad smile. 'It's official. You win the grimmest costume competition.'

Bryan guffawed again. 'Don't tell Doug that,' he said and headed back to the drinks table, where Tilly stood talking to Annie, both dressed in white bridal bones costumes.

Drew smiled and then became aware of Faith watching her, the blood-red drink wet on her lips. Fuck! 'Don't do that!' she moaned into Faith's ear.

Faith took another sip of the drink, allowing it to wet her lips, and exposed the sharp incisors. 'What?' she said jokingly.

Faith's gaze slipped through Drew's defences, reached in and held her with tenderness.

'You're doing strange things to me,' Drew whispered.

'Like what?' Faith whispered back.

Drew hesitated, held Faith's unwavering gaze, her heart racing. 'Stealing my heart.'

The red liquid trickled menacingly from the side of Faith's lips as a tiny smile formed. And then her eyes became dark, focused and she closed the space between them. She leaned towards Drew and caused her to jolt when her mouth moved to the side of Drew's cheek.

Drew felt her insides flip with the breath at her ear, Faith's smooth, soft skin against hers and when the words, 'I'm in love with you, Drew,' came to her, she felt their effect in every cell in her body. And when Faith moved away and gazed into her watery eyes, she claimed the bloody-red lips with unbridled desire, a lingering kiss that deepened unashamedly in the centre of the busy room.

A thunderous crack brought Drew out of the kiss and she looked around the empty room. Everyone had made their way outside the house to watch the firework display.

Faith looked through the window, the crackling, fizzing sound, accompanying the multi-colour light display. 'Shall we go and watch?'

Drew read something else in her gaze. 'I'd rather go home,' she said and when Faith smiled, Drew recognised the quality of it from the first time she had set eyes on Faith in the café.

Faith took Drew's hand, led her out the front door and up the lane to the main road. They turned up the slope to the church and looked back at the loud crack that lit up the darkness and Faith tucked Drew into her shoulder. 'It's been a beautiful day.'

And then they both spotted the figure in a purple raincoat heading along the main road towards Duckton House. Drew turned to Faith and smiled. 'Did you see her?' she said.

'Hilda?'

'Yes.'

Faith nodded, smiled and held Drew's gaze. 'Vera and Jenny will be delighted.'

Drew nodded in agreement. 'Best guest they could wish for.'

Faith traced Drew's jaw and ran a thumb across her lips. 'Come to bed with me,' she said and bared her teeth with a wild looking grin.

'You are one fucking irresistible vampire,' Drew said and felt her insides melt and then tingle from the inside out.

Faith smiled. She had felt it too.

About Emma Nichols

Emma Nichols lives in Buckinghamshire with her partner and two children. She served for 12 years in the British Army, studied Psychology, and published several non-fiction books under another name, before dipping her toes into the world of lesbian fiction.

You can contact Emma through her website and social media:

www.emmanicholsauthor.com
www.facebook.com/EmmaNicholsAuthor
www.twitter.com/ENichols_Author

And do please leave a review if you enjoyed this book. Reviews really help independent authors to promote their work. Thank you.

Other Books by Emma Nichols

Visit **getbook.at/TheVincentiSeries** to discover The Vincenti Series: Finding You, Remember Us and The Hangover.

Visit **getbook.at/ForbiddenBook** to start reading **Forbidden**

Visit **getbook.at/Ariana** to delve into the bestselling summer lesbian romance Ariana.

Visit **viewbook.at/Madeleine** to be transported to post-WW2 France and a timeless lesbian romance.

Thanks for reading and supporting!

Printed in Poland
by Amazon Fulfillment
Poland Sp. z o o. Wrocław